HOW TO DATE A DOUCHEBAG SERIES BOOK FIVE

HOW TO DATE A DOUCHEBAG

THE LYING HOURS

#DOUCHEBAG

SARA NEY

I just want someone who will randomly bring me tacos and squeeze my junk. That's it. Why can't there be an app for that?

Abe

The first sentence is always the toughest. The opener. The beginning…

I stare hard at my cell phone, at the image of a girl smiling. Swipe my finger up her first photograph to scroll, viewing another of her with her head thrown back, laughing, sunlight catching her hair. Blonde, *of course*. Blue eyes. Slim. Tan in the middle of winter.

Nice, round tits—probably fake.

She matched with my roommate Jack Bartlett this morning on our campus's LoveU App and wants to chat, and now it's my turn to make a move. Well, technically, she's waiting for JB to make the move, not me.

See, JB's girlfriend broke up with him a few months ago, and ever since, he's been on a downward spiral of pent-up sexual frustration and emotional neediness that is seriously starting to get on my fucking nerves. He's going through women like frat guys go through beer, like women go through tampons during their period.

One. After. The. Other.

So fucked up, but not unusual for dudes our age.

I glance down again at what's written in her profile.

Shelby, 19, likes peanut butter, movies, and the color blue. She's also looking for something long-term, which I don't think Jack wants, but I swipe right to accept her invitation to chat anyway. He can't pump and dump them *all*, can he? One of these chicks is bound to stick, and this one looks like she might be a keeper.

There's only one way to find out.

I shoot her a brief message.

Me*: Name three things you can't stand listening to in a quiet room. Go.*

I set the phone next to the weight bench and recline until I'm lying flat on my back, three hundred and ten pounds of steel balanced on the bar above me. My spotter is missing, and I crane my head to see where the fuck he's at. I can't lift this weight off the rack until someone is here to make sure I don't break my neck.

And die.

Before Ben Carpenter can hustle his bony ass back to my bench to help me, my phone pings with the familiar LoveU notification chime.

Damn, our girl Shelby is quick on the draw.

Shelby*: Um, haha. I'd have to say...listening to potato chip bags. Haha. And snoring? Um. The wind is really loud outside my window and that's super annoying. Haha.*

Okay, so our girl Shelby definitely overuses the word "*um*" and typed "*haha*" a few too many times, but it's not like JB is going to give a shit. He'll be too busy staring at her tits and trying to fuck her.

I wonder if this is how Shelby will speak in person, and I'd bet money that it is. She also hasn't mastered the etiquette of making conversation; everyone knows at the end of your damn response you're supposed to ask a question to keep the flow of conversation going.

Jesus.

Instead, Shelby leaves me hanging. I'm going to have to pull another question out of my ass as I continue pretending to be my roommate.

Me: *I hate the sound of potato chip bags, too. And I don't snore. Ha. Ha.*

At least I've never heard JB snoring from the other room. Maybe he does. Who the hell knows.

I'm tempted to tell her I hate the sound of farting but resist the urge.

It's too soon, and the goal here is to be romantic, not gross.

Shelby: *That's good, haha.*

This chick seriously needs to cool it with the *haha* before she drives me nuts. It's only been two chats back and forth and she's used that word—I scroll up and count— four times.

Christ almighty.

Normally I'm not this big of an asshole. In fact, I'm the least douchey of all my friends, but this morning, I'm not in the mood for any of this. I'm not in the mood to be JB's lackey, not in the mood for Ben Carpenter to be fucking around instead of spotting me like he's supposed to, not in the mood to be in the gym so damn early in the morning.

Logging into my roommate's LoveU account and lying to girls in an attempt to win them over because JB doesn't have the confidence to do it himself *isn't* my idea of a good time. Plus, it makes no sense, considering JB is ridiculously attractive when he's not acting like a dick. Women usually fall all over themselves when he's around. I have no idea what he needs a dating app for. He can get laid any time he wants.

I don't do so bad with girls myself, but I'm not the one looking for a fuck buddy; JB is.

I'm more of a long-term relationship guy.

Before I can reply to Shelby's last message, Ben appears, sweaty and dripping wet.

"Where the fuck have you been, dude?"

"Sorry man, I overheated and had to dunk my head."

Well, shit. That's not cool. "Maybe you should get someone else to spot me and sit this one out then." The last thing I need is some rookie passing out while I'm lifting all this weight.

He scratches at his head, water dripping from the short, black spikes of hair. "You sure?"

The dude is a mess.

"Yeah. Send JB over."

My roommate is doing squats on the far side of the weight room, watching himself in the mirror as he bends his knees, a bar behind his neck holding over three hundred pounds of weight. I can hear him grunting out his count from here.

Fifty-four.

Fifty-five.

Fifty-six...

"He's almost done, Carpenter. Grab him when he hits

5

seventy-five, would ya? He'll be glad for the break."

My phone chimes again, and I glance down at the screen. Groan out loud, perspiration dripping down the valley between my pecs.

It's two more LoveU notifications.

Good news, JB! You've matched with Tiffany C and Kristy M. Swipe right to begin a convo!

I curse.

Then I swipe right on both of them.

2

#DOUCHEBAG

Instead of texting me to come over,
she just sends me a batman
symbol. SOS, send sex. Coolest
chick ever.

Abe

"I don't know what you're doing setting me up with these airheads, man. You have to start screening them a little better."

I swivel in my desk chair when JB appears in my doorway, lingering at the threshold, large frame leaning against the jamb.

"Or. You can start doing this yourself."

He scoffs, running a hand along his jawline. "You're so much better at it than I am."

"It's basically texting. I think you can handle it." I stare him down, tapping a pencil against the surface of my desk. "Haven't any of them noticed you can't remember jack shit about what they've told you?"

"No. They're too busy twirling their hair." He laughs. "This one tonight though—she was pretty hot."

Kristy M.

I remember her.

Brunette. Local. Loves kitties, glitter, and her sorority sisters. Oh, and she would, like, *die* for a decent sushi restaurant in town.

"If she was so hot, what was the problem?"

"I wanted my dick sucked, not to listen to her talk about her two fucking cats all night."

This makes me laugh. "But you like a little pussy."

"Not the same kind of pussy Kristy likes." He smirks, still lingering at the door. "Too hairy." JB sticks out his tongue and licks the air.

"Here's a thought, maybe you should stop going out with girls you think are hot. Maybe—and call me crazy for suggesting this—you should try having something in common with them?"

"But I'm not the one talking to them. You are." He sounds confused, bless his clueless soul.

"Right, well." I toss my pencil on the desk, swiveling around until I'm presenting him with my broad back and shrug. "I thought you wanted a girlfriend, not an easy lay."

"I want both."

"Then stop trying to screw every warm body you take on a date." I still won't look at him.

"They're not dates. We meet for drinks."

"That's what you're calling it? Meeting for drinks?" What a crock of shit. "Semantics."

"What's the big deal?" I hear him shuffle his feet as I pop open my laptop, powering it up. "If I have to abort the mission, I don't want the commitment of having to eat an entire meal for another half an hour, especially if the chick is a stage five clinger—fuck that would be painful."

I'll give him this one—that actually makes sense. But still.

"I get that, but you should still be the one talking to these girls, not me. It's fucked up on so many levels."

"You're better at English than I am, dude. Plus, you're better with girls."

9

"How the hell am I better with girls?" I haven't been on a date in over a year, which means I haven't had sex in over a year, which means I haven't seen an actual pair of tits in a year.

My dating life is fucking pathetic.

"Dude, I read what you said to that Tiffany chick—it was brilliant. That shit about everything happening for a reason and beauty being on the inside? Genius."

"Yes. I'm a genius all right." I mean, I kind of am. I've been on the dean's list for the past three years. My current grade point average is three point nine. Not too bad for someone who barely has time to wipe his own ass, let alone study. "So when are you going on your date with Shelby?"

JB rubs the spot behind his neck that's always cramping, working out the knot while he considers my question. "I don't know. She's been pretty annoying."

Yeah, she has been.

"She told me she wasn't looking for a pen pal, whatever the fuck that means."

I saw that but haven't replied to it yet. "It means she doesn't want to keep talking. She wants to actually meet you so she can figure out if she's wasting her time or not."

"I don't know, man. Do I really want to sit through a date with someone who uses the words *um* and *haha* eight thousand fucking times in one day?"

Nope.

"That's up to you, man."

I wouldn't date her, but I'm not JB, and it's not my

LoveU account. I might be the puppet master pulling the strings, but he's the one dancing up on stage.

Jesus, I'm crap when it comes to analogies.

As if he can hear my thoughts straying, my roommate lets a long, loud sigh drag from his giant body. "Cut her loose, would ya? Let's start looking for quality, not quantity."

Well *this* is certainly a new development. JB getting serious about dating someone? Color me surprised. "Any special requirements?"

He gives it some thought. Inhales and stands up straight. "Probably a girl I could take home to my mom if I wanted to, but who also wants to fuck a lot."

Right. Cannot forget that.

"She's out there waiting for you, champ." I laugh, shooting him a look over my shoulder. "Somewhere on this campus is some buttoned-up cutie just waiting to be boned by the great Jack Bartlett."

"Goddamn I hope so."

Poor kid can't even tell when someone is being sarcastic anymore. Clearly his brain has been addled from the strain of his face being pressed against the wrestling mat one too many times.

JB is a decent wrestler. Good, but not great.

He used to be until Tasha broke up with him; since then, his pins have taken a nosedive and he's shit about practicing.

His grades have definitely gone downhill. One could even say they *suck*. Long story short: Jack should be less focused on finding a replacemend for Tasha, and more focused on wrestling and school. At the rate he's going, it's going to take him another year to meet the university's requirements to graduate with a degree.

If he wants to climb up my ass and beg for favors, he should be begging me to tutor him, not find him a girlfriend.

Whatever.

It's not my place to judge, and I'll do whatever it takes to get him back on track. Back to winning, back to a better GPA, back to being involved. If that means sitting on a dating app and pretending to be him a few hours a week, so be it. I want my friends to be the best they can possibly freaking be.

What he does in his free time is none of my damn business, as long as he pays his share of the rent on time and stays out of my shit—but I can't help feeling somewhat responsible for him since he's my roommate and teammate. That's just the kind of guy I am.

His parents give him a hard time for all the fucking around he's been doing lately—and they don't know the half of what their son's been up to.

I don't mind having the bastard around, so I'm willing to help keep it that way.

"I think you should go in for a concussion test on Monday," I joke.

"Nah. I just had one a few months ago." He picks lint off his hoodie and flicks it onto my carpet. "I should be good."

Dang. See what I mean? The kid cannot tell when

someone is being sarcastic.

I clear my throat and end the conversation. "All right, if that's all you needed…" My sentence trails off when I hold up the textbook that's been lying open on my desk next to my laptop. The spread on my desk makes it look like I'm about to do some serious cramming, but the truth is, school comes pretty naturally. I'll only be at it for an hour to review some notes, tops. "To summarize: quality girl, not quantity. Down to fuck." My brows go up. "I don't think I'm missing anything."

"Nope, that's perfect. I'll log in later and swipe on whoever."

Whoever.

And there's the problem.

"Yeah, thanks for the extra hand."

He shoots me a pair of finger guns, pushing off from the doorjamb. "No problem."

Then he's gone, pulling my door closed behind him, the steps of his big feet echoing down the hall.

I stare out my window, out into the dark, at the house next door, every window in the two-story glowing. The bathroom sits directly across from mine, its interior obscured by two billowing white drapes hanging there. They're sheer, just opaque enough that I'm unable to see through them—not that I've tried.

It's a houseful of girls, none of whom I've ever spoken to.

The few times I've stepped outside at the same time as them (they always seem to travel in clumps), I've imme-

13

diately put my feet to the pavement, head down to avoid them and dodge direct eye contact.

Pretty. Outgoing, most of them. Friendly, if their waves and polite greetings are enough to go by. Tons of makeup and loud laughing. Their place always has the music blasting, and I'm almost positive one or two of them are football cheerleaders. One is a dancer. Another few are in a sorority.

Why do I avoid them? They're not my type; they're Jack's—*not* that I discriminate based on extracurricular activities. That would make me an asshole, and I'm not one of those, either.

I like to think I have a good head on my shoulders, not one in the clouds.

The shadow of a figure appears in front of the bathroom window, her outline a silhouette behind the curtain. My fingers pause over the textbook page I've been reading and, with a guilty stare, I study the shape of her body. I can tell she's removing a shirt, dragging it up over her head slowly as if she knows I'm sitting here watching. She dips, probably removing her bottoms and *Christ, I feel like such a fucking creeper.*

I swear I'm not doing it on purpose. The bathroom window is *right fucking there* in front of me, front and center, and this is the first time I've ever really noticed anyone in that room taking their clothes off. Honest to God, I barely pay attention.

Ashamed, my eyes cast downward, trained on my textbook, mind spinning. Sex on the brain.

Do not touch your dick while you're watching, Abe. Do

not touch your fucking dick.

I don't touch my dick.

I'll wait and do it later when I'm in bed, when the cloudy image of a nameless, faceless girl with giant boobs removing her clothes is erased from my brain by the biology literature in front of me.

Line after line, word after word filters through my mind, not one bit of it being retained.

I cannot concentrate.

Zero focus.

My broad chest heaves, frustrated, and I run a hand through my thick, dark hair.

My eyes stray to the cell phone I have flipped upside down so it doesn't distract me from studying, and I snatch it up, thumb gliding over the smooth surface.

I hesitate a few moments before deciding which app to open. Check my Snapchat and add to my story, send a short video to my younger brother, another to my younger sister.

My thumb lingers on that damn dating app, and as much as I protest and pretend to hate the freaking thing, parts of me resent the fact that Jack has the balls to use it. Well, not himself, but at least he's putting himself out there by going on dates.

I'm hiding behind his persona, pretending to be him for fuck's sake, too damn busy and scared to date someone myself.

No loss there. So few of the girls on LoveU have caught *my* interest. Most of them come off as way too fake, and don't get me started on all the cutesy animal filters most of them use. How the hell is a dude supposed to know what a girl looks like when she has a CGI dog tongue hanging out of her mouth?

So fucking weird.

Let's not forget to mention the fake eyelashes. Spray tans. Fake tits and push-up bras. Drawn-on eyebrows.

Jesus, I'd be afraid to run my fingers through my date's long hair—what if I accidentally pulled a clump of it out?

I'm looking for someone real.

Just haven't found her yet.

Not even after scrolling through hundreds of profiles.

I tap on the app, pretending to be bored by the entire process. The truth is that I am interested in finding a girlfriend myself.

But I sure as shit am not going to find her on some stupid app.

Having a vajaja doesn't stop me
from knowing my balls are
bigger than his.

Skylar

"**H**onestly. Where have all the nice guys gone?" I grab a few fries from my tray, dip them in mayonnaise—then ketchup—popping all four of them into my mouth at the same time, gesturing around my table of friends. "Where. Where'd they go?"

My friends stare back, all of them either in a relationship or happily single.

I'm neither.

I like to complain about my single status because I've been actively searching for love—in all the wrong places, apparently.

Bethany smirks. "You know what they say—all the good ones are either gay or taken."

"Or in the library, so forget that—those guys are never going to hit on you, and you're never going to meet a future doctor because you never go to the library." *Thanks Hannah.*

"You know where the building with books is, don't you? At the end of campus next to the science department…?" Bethany teases with a nudge.

I chuckle. "Ha ha, very funny."

It's funny because it's true, but I'm not about to admit that out loud. I haven't been in the university's library since my sophomore year—and *that* was because I had to sign in for a special project. I don't even know where the study rooms are on campus, which might explain my less than stellar grade point average…

Whatever.

"Right." My best friend Hannah dangles a carrot from her fingertips and points it in my direction. "And if they're studying to become doctors and engineers, they're not going to the bars on the weekend. Girl, they're busy gettin' that degree! Which…" Her brows go up, the unfinished sentence dangling in the air like her uneaten carrot.

…which is what you should be doing.

She doesn't say the words, but I've heard them from Hannah a dozen times. It's almost like she's in cahoots with my mother, being the mother-hen type herself. She loves doling out advice, Hannah with near perfect grades.

Perfect hair. Perfect boobs.

And she's almost always right.

I ignore her implication. "I love you, Hannah, but now isn't the time to bring up my shitty grades. Midterms haven't been released, so let me enjoy my ignorant bliss. Right this second I want to talk about my love life—or lack thereof."

Her shoulders shrug. "I'm just sayin'."

She's always *just sayin'*.

Hannah rolls her pretty brown eyes and bites down on the end of her carrot, chewing thoughtfully. "You're constantly complaining like you have no options."

"Oh. And what are those?"

"You can let one of us set you up on a blind date."

"We tried that once, remember? Cliff's fraternity brother? Didn't talk the entire time then called me for a second date incessantly? That guy?"

"I asked you to forget about that."

"Can't. He ordered chicken tenders for dinner." What guy does that?

"I said I was sorry."

I harumph and catch Bethany's eye roll.

"What about the university's new dating app?"

"Uhhh," I groan. "How about *not*."

Nope. I'm not doing a dating app. The only guys online are desperate or want an easy hook-up, and I'm not looking for either of those things.

I want a long-term relationship. Something *real*. I'm not going to find that swiping my finger on stupid profiles.

"Why are you so quick to shoot it down? Jessica met her boyfriend on LoveU."

Our friend Jessica nods. "You love Aaron."

We all do.

I really like her boyfriend. Aaron is awesome, even though he's not remotely my type. And therein lies the problem; I'm beginning to think my type doesn't exist in the real world. He only lives on paper and in my imagination, neither of which are convenient.

So what is my type? Believe me, I've given this matter hour upon hour of consideration, mostly after my friends tell me I'm being too picky. Or too judgy.

My type is tall. Not crazy, *Big Foot* tall, but at least six feet—minimum—would be amazing. An Adonis. Some-one who will make me feel petite and small, and feminine. Dark hair—*God I love dark hair*—and I wouldn't mind if some of it was on his chest, either. No facial hair—*that's* gross, and makes me think of my father, who has a beard and always has food stuck in it.

My boyfriend will be strong. Thoughtful. The kind of guy who thinks before he speaks, so when he does it means something.

Handsome, but not pretty. He needn't be perfect, or in great shape. Lord knows I'm certainly not.

Nice hands. *Big* hands.

Maybe he likes to read in his free time, like I do? That would be nice.

A dimple would make me melt, but it's hardly required.

I prop my chin in my hands and lean on the table when I'm done zoning out, suddenly realizing all three of my friends are staring at me.

"What?"

"Are you even listening?" Bethany gives me a nudge under the table with the toe of her boot.

"Uh, no. Sorry."

"I was asking what you have against the dating app. It's just for fun. You wouldn't actually have to meet any of these guys in person, but what's the harm in looking?"

"Focus, Sky. You're the one who said you wanted to put yourself out there. Well, this would be you putting yourself out there."

"We'll help you."

I laugh and pop another fry into my mouth. "No thanks. If I'm going to do this, I'm doing it without the three of you."

Hannah's smirk is smug. "So you're going to do it?"

Shit. They just trapped me into it. Damn them.

"I'll think about it."

"It's freeeee," Jessica sing-songs, knowing I'm a cheapskate who pinches every penny. I get an allowance from my parents occasionally but try not to spend it on booze, parties, or frivolities.

Like dating apps.

So many of them cost money.

"I said I would think about it—don't push."

"Yeah yeah, you're gonna do it. Stop denying it." Jessica digs in her backpack for a notebook and pen. "Can we at least help you write the bio?"

"Could you not?" Lord knows what it would say. "And I haven't even created a profile yet, so cool your jets."

She stuffs her notebook back into her bag. "Fine. Promise us you'll at least let us see it before you post it."

We'll see.

BlueAsTheSky, 21.

I stare at the fake name I created, not wild about using my real one, and smile. I like it. It's playful and gives a little hint about who the real me is.

If I actually start chatting with a guy, he can learn my

name. Until then, he's stuck only knowing the nickname.

Let's see, what else can I tell people about myself... what else, what else...

I stare at my tiny phone screen, at the three photos I uploaded. None of them are full face shots; my face is half cut off in every single one. God forbid some dude recognizes me on campus and tries to hit on me in real life.

Or announces to everyone that he's seen me on LoveU.

I would *die.*

I run through a bio that goes something like this:

My friends said I need to put myself out there, so here I am, putting myself out there. Hey there. I'm only outgoing once I get to know someone. Slender. Love going to the movies, esp. chick flicks. You are: tall and funny. Not sarcastic funny, but the haha kind of funny. I can't promise to laugh at you, but you can try to amuse me.

Shit. That's not good—I sound kind of bitchy. Plus, I'm almost out of characters and need to shorten it up.

It takes me another half an hour to get it the way I want it, another few minutes to edit and finalize the photos, and no time at all to press publish.

I am live on LoveU.

My stomach does a somersault, butterflies balancing on the uneven bars, wings fluttering in the breeze.

I want to vomit.

The first ten guys who swipe on my profile aren't keepers; I delete them immediately without reading their information. Okay, I'll admit it, I'm judging them based on appearances.

So I want to be sexually attracted to my partner—sue me! I want to take one look at him and *know*. Or at least kind of know. I want to feel the butterflies dance when I meet him for the first time, and I won't want to meet him at all if my girl parts don't tingle at least a little when I see his profile picture.

Is that so wrong?

My phone pings with a notification from LoveU with another match. He sends me a message almost immediately, and I groan, already sensing this isn't going to be a match. Knew it the second I swiped on him but curious enough to give him a chance.

Luke: *Sup*

Me*: Not much, what are you up to?*

Luke: *Nothing*

I wait and wait for more words from Luke, but none come. Rack my brain for something new and original to say. I mean, if he doesn't want to talk, why did he message me?

I stare, wondering if Luke is familiar with the standard flow of a conversation, how it's his turn to ask a question to keep the chat going. Swiping my thumb over his photo, I open his profile and scan it. Pretty basic, not much detail, nothing really to go on, and apparently, he has no desire to talk. Name, age, and one line: *Don't bore me.*

I delete Luke and find six more connections when I swipe myself back to the home page. Drag my finger over a kid named Eric, 21. He's a finance major with a hand-some face and dimples. His first photograph is a selfie from the gym; he's wearing a ball cap, leaning into the camera. Half-smile. Stubble.

I know he's online because the tiny green dot is lit up next to his name, so I'm not at all shocked when he sends me a quick note. Rather, I'm pleased to not have to make the first move.

I hate the feeling that I'm chatting a guy up.

Eric: *You feeling blue?*

Me: *Haha, no. I'm doing homework. What are you up to?*

Eric: *Not homework! I'm sitting on a weight bench at the gym.*

Me: *You mention the gym in your bio—do you live there?*

Eric: *I could probably bench press you.*

Assuming I wanted him to.

Which I don't.

Me: *Where do you hang out when you're not working out?*

Eric: *The bar, my house, the frat house. What about you?*

Me: *I like the movies, hanging out at home, and spend-ing time with my friends.*

Eric: *What about parties?*

Me*: Meh, depends on my friends. We like going out in groups, it's more fun.*

Eric*: Are any of your friends hot?*

Um. Okay. Bye, Eric. He and I aren't ever going to be a thing. Who the hell asks a question like that? What an idiot.

I delete Eric. Sigh before grabbing the remote, flipping through the channels to find my favorite show. Toss the controller on the far side of the bed—far enough that I don't land on it, but still within reach—and flop down on the bed, phone in my hand, head propped on a pillow.

I manage to occupy myself with bad reality television for more than two hours.

Check my phone to see the little yellow and black icon lit up.

Skeptical—because after ten more wildly mismatched matches, this app seems to be a bust—I swipe it open to unlock my new potential partner.

Hmm.

Okay. This one doesn't seem so terrible.

I give his small photograph a good, hard look. Actually cock my head to the side as I study it.

Not bad. Not bad at all…

He's easy on the eyes, and my gaze lingers on his first photo. Drifts down to his name and lands on his profile.

JB, 22

Hopeless romantic looking for long-term; where have all the nice girls gone? Fit, tall, college athlete. ISO: some-

one to take home to Mom. Long conversations, dates to the park, movies, and dinner. You: fit, girl next door, likes to laugh and smile.

Well, well, well—hello JB.

He sure is a looker, and as a bonus, he's actually filled out a biography, which is more than most guys have done.

I get excited.

Not going to lie—this one has potential. And wow, he's pretty darn cute—so attractive I feel that familiar flutter deep in my belly. Shoulders give a tiny shudder as I bite down on my bottom lip with a grin.

JB wants to chat.

My index finger hovers over his profile—over that green dot he wants me to press down on so we can talk—and a sound carries up my throat.

"Guh!" I squeak out as I tap, sealing my fate. Connecting with JB, opening the door to opportunity.

It takes no time at all before he's replying, sending me a cool, *Hey Blue. Quick—tell me what you ate for breakfast.*

That's an easy one.

Me: *As soon as I wake up, I'm starving. This morning I made myself an omelet [Please note: the pan is still sitting on the stove]*

I think for a second then shoot him back another message: *Quick—what's your strangest habit?*

I don't think *I* have one. But, in the spirit of the conversation, I pull something out of my ass, knowing it's inevitably going to come up in this conversation.

It takes JB much longer to reply than it took me, and I impatiently wonder what's taking him so long.

JB: *I'd have to say my strangest habit is…I put ketch-up on everything? Is that weird?*

Me: *Not at all, try again. Get really weird.*

JB: *All right, but you can't repeat this to anyone and you can't make fun of me for it.*

Me: *Go. Your secret is safe with me—I don't even know you.*

JB: *Here goes nothing then—I have a troll doll in my gym bag and rub it for good luck.*

I can hardly not laugh at that. Seriously. I've heard athletes are superstitious, but don't they usually just wear the same socks to practice and jump up and down five times in the same spot? Maybe utter the same curse word before walking onto the field? Slap their bro on the ass?

I have no clue—but a troll doll?

Me: *What color is its hair?*

JB: *Yellow.*

Me: *School colors?*

JB: *Exactly.*

Me: *That makes sense I guess. I don't have any strange habits—not like that one. Sometimes when I'm pissed at my mom, I step on cracks in the sidewalk ;) But that's not a habit, that's just me being spiteful. **angel emoji***

JB: *LOLOLOL*

Me: *I would never tell her that of course. She'd be so mad, considering she's always complaining about her bad back.*

JB: *LOLOLOL*

He's laughing at me again, which I take as a good sign. I wouldn't say I'm stand-up comedian funny, but I do like to think I have a great sense of humor, and I'd like my boyfriend to appreciate it.

And laugh at me.

With me.

JB: *Favorite filter to use on your photos?*

Me: *NO FILTER. I especially cannot stand the dog ear/tongue filter. WHY DO GIRLS USE THAT?*

JB: *No idea. I've been on enough dates to know that the girl showing up looks nothing like her puppy alter ego…*

Me: *That bad, eh?*

JB: *I mean…for the most part, people don't look how you expect them to look based on their pictures.*

Me: *Sounds like you have plenty of experience.*

JB: *I'm not a serial dater or anything, but after two or three dates show up and they're barely recognizable, it tends to get…*

Me: *Old?*

JB: *Yeah, kind of.*

He fires off another quick message: What about you?

Me*: I haven't been on any dates yet, but I expect that most guys will look like themselves since most guys don't use filters*

Me*: And can I just say—guys should NOT be taking selfies in the first place. It's so weird!*

JB*: Really? Girls think it's weird when dudes take selfies?*

Me*: I have no idea what other girls think, but I personally think it looks bizarre. A poll definitely needs to be taken about this topic.*

JB*: Noted. I will take your word for it and will never take a selfie.*

Me*: The women of the world thank you.*

JB*: At your service **takes a deep bow***

Me*: Are you always a gentleman?*

JB*: Yes? No. LOL*

Me*: Lol only when you're trying?*

JB*: If I'm being honest, I have to work at it. I probably spend way too much time with guys. Full disclosure: it's something my ex-girlfriend used to complain about.*

Ugh, an ex-girlfriend. And he's already bringing her up? Red flag.

I tread lightly, not really wanting to talk about it yet feeling the need to acknowledge it.

Me*: How long were you together?*

JB*: Let me think for a second. Um. Just over a year?*

He's not sure? Typical guy.

Me*: When did you break up?*

Jesus, why am I asking? It's not like I really care. Still. The time frame between relationships can say a lot about a person. It will tell me if he's a relationship jumper, AKA always needs to be in one. It'll also tell me if he's looking for a rebound, even though he says he's looking for something long-term.

JB*: It's been about three months.*

Hmm.

Questionable, but not terrible. I guess time will tell. Then, because I cannot help myself, I venture to ask,

Me*: Who broke up with who?*

A few minutes go by before JB's conversation bubbles pop up on my screen.

JB*: She broke up with me.*

Ouch. At least he's honest. For once, I resist the urge to ask the question niggling in my brain: *Do you know why she broke up with you?*

Tempting—so, so tempting.

Me*: Ah, I see.*

JB: *Yeah.*

Although I really don't see, because I may never know why she dumped him after a little over a year. Did he cheat

31

on her? Did she cheat on him? Was he a jerk? Was she too selfish? Did they fight all the time?

I'm sure he'd give me a million excuses as to the reason why, so I don't bother asking. There are two sides to every story, and if he and I keep talking, I can ask him to give me his side in person.

I must be taking too long to message him again because my phone dings and it's him, asking, *Hey Sky, you still there?*

Me: *I'm here. Sorry.*

JB: *What have you been up to tonight?*

Me: *I was hanging out with friends. They're the ones who convinced me to sign up for this dumb app. No offense.*

JB: *None taken. It is kind of dumb.*

Me: *Really? You think so?*

JB: *Mostly yes. I haven't had any luck. You would be surprised how many girls just want to hook up.*

Me: *And you don't?*

His pause is long enough for me to know he's debating about his reply, long enough for me to know he doesn't want to offend me by being honest.

JB: *I didn't say that LOL*

Yeah, that's what I thought.

JB: *I'm just being honest.*

Me: *It's the best policy!*

JB: *But judging you solely on your pictures, you don't look like the kind of girl who is into hook-ups.*

Me: *What else can you tell about me judging solely on my pictures?*

JB: *Well, let me think for a second. Let me go STARE.*

It takes him an entire minute. I guess he's really thinking it through.

JB: *Okay. I bet you like going out with your friends, but you don't like being bothered by guys. You're there with them, not to get picked up. You hate cheesy pick-up lines.*

Me: *Go on…*

JB: *You get just okay grades because you're too social, but…you don't really care. Do you?*

Wait—is he spying on me? How would he know a thing like that?

Me: *You can tell all that just from looking at my pictures?*

JB: *Those observations weren't insults; they were compliments.*

Me: *Stop. Can we please quickly acknowledge your proper use of a semicolon in your last message?*

JB: *Good thing or a bad thing?*

Me: *If I'm being honest, I'm a sucker for good grammar. What are you a sucker for?*

JB: *Now that's a loaded question if I've ever heard one...*

Me: ***eye roll***

JB: *I don't know—I don't think I've taken the time to figure it out yet. It seems like all I do is go to practice, eat, sleep, and study.*

Me: *Same, minus the practice part. What is it you're practicing for?*

JB: *Don't stalk me or anything, but I'm on the wrestling team.*

Me: *Here?*

JB: *Yes, here, LOL—where else would I be?*

Me: *I haven't met any wrestlers on this campus yet. Football players, yes. Wrestlers, no.*

JB: *Jock chasers love it, the rest of them hate it. It's not easy dating an athlete.*

JB: *It's probably not easy being on a date with one, either.*

Me: *Why wouldn't it be easy being on a date with one??*

JB: *If someone recognizes us, they want to talk, and suddenly we're being interrupted, which ruins the mood. Trust me.*

Me: *You have lots of experience with that?*

JB: *Enough to know it sucks.*

34

Me*: I have NO experience with that, so…I'm a nobody, haha.*

JB*: Oh god, don't say HAHA.*

Me*: Why? Pet peeve of yours?*

JB*: Sort of. There was this girl on here—the app, I mean—and she used it four times within two messages. It was so obnoxious, I thought for sure that was how she was going to talk in person.*

Me*: So she annoyed you but you went out with her.*

There's another pause in our conversation.

JB: *Yes.*

Me*: Ahhh. So, you're not really all that discriminating. Good to know. I can let myself go and you'd give me a free pass as long as you thought you might score some action. Is that it?*

JB*: Haha, very funny.*

Me*: But am I kind of right? Be honest: you have nothing to lose. There is always the next swipe if I don't like your answer and you don't like mine, LOL*

Hell, he's probably having three other conversations right now at the same time he's speaking to me.

JB*: I like how you switched it up and went with LOL instead of HAHA. Very smooth… But to answer your question, no, I'm not here to score some action. Action is NICE but not the point of all this.*

Me*: So you ARE looking for something serious?*

JB: *If it's out there, yes. But I'm not going to force it either. Don't you agree?*

Me: *Yes. But I'm also not going to make out or have sex with some guy I've chatted with for a few hours and met for a drink then never have him contact me again. No thanks, not into it.*

JB: *So what you're saying is: you have standards.*

Me: *Some, LOL*

JB: *I have a few, but most of them are questionable, LOL*

I can't tell if he's being serious or not, but it makes me laugh anyway, to the point where I'm giggling out loud with a hand covering my mouth.

Me: *I'm not even going to ask what those questionable standards are. I'm too scared. I actually don't get out much.*

JB: *Somehow I doubt that.*

Me: *Are you basing that on my pictures again?*

JB: *Yes. You're way too cute to be sitting home.*

Me: *Cute. See, that right there is the problem. At the risk of getting too personal on a dating app, I'll tell you a little TMI: I've always been cute—never hot, or whatever. Girl-next-door cute. For some reason, that's always bothered me.*

JB: *Trust me, hot is overrated. And did I say cute? I meant pretty.*

Me: *Please don't think I'm whining or whatever. I'm not insecure, but sometimes that word just makes me* *cringe.*

JB: *That's another thing that drives me crazy about being an athlete. Girls think they have to meet some unrealistic criteria if they're dating one. Like they have to be Miss America or something. And instead of acting normal, we get all these fake airheads pretending to give a shit about us when in reality it's only to project an image they think we want.*

Me: *So you're saying that's not what athletes want? Hot girlfriends?*

JB: *I mean...fine. Some of them do.*

Me: *But you're not one of them?*

JB: *I'd rather have someone who gave a shit about me at the end of the day, because this wrestling thing isn't turning into a career. I'll probably work in some bullshit office in a suit and tie after I graduate, God willing I'm able to actually get a fucking job.*

JB: *Shit. Pardon my French.*

His apology makes me laugh, because obviously he could have deleted the curse word before he sent the message.

Me: *What's your major?*

JB: *Business.*

How cliché.

JB: *What's yours?*

Me: *Business with an emphasis on advertising/marketing. I've known that's what I want to do since I was in middle school. Before that, I wanted to be an archaeologist, but then I realized you have to be good at math and science, and I suck at both. No dinosaur carbon dating for me **crying emoji***

Me: *Is yours just general business, or do you have something specific you want to do?*

JB: *My plan is to work for my dad.*

He doesn't expand on that, so I prod him.

Me: *Doing what exactly?*

JB: *Financial planning and investments.*

Me: *So what you're saying is, you're good at math, and probably science too.*

JB: *I get by okay, LOL. I'm not a tutor or anything.*

Me: *But you could be?*

JB: *Incidentally, my roommate is actually a math tutor.*

Me: *Is he a wrestler, too?*

Abe

I wonder how much to tell her about me. I mean, I'm supposed to be pretending to be JB, not giving her the dirt on myself. I've never done that before, given personal details that weren't about my roommate.

And now I am.

What is it about this girl that has me breaking my own rules?

Rule 1: Don't get personal. This is not your account.

Rule 2: *Do not* get personal. This is not your account.

Rule 3: Start the conversation, but don't get invested.

Rule 4: These girls come and go like yesterday's practice routine. Don't get attached to any of them. They are not for you.

Rule 5: See all of the above. Repeat.

Once JB takes this Blue Sky girl out on a date, he'll never speak to her again, so what good would it do me to continue having this in-depth conversation with her? She's only going to get dumped after he realizes she's not going to sleep with him.

No. She's going to want to get to know him first, and he'll never put in the time required for a girl like her.

She's a keeper; I can already tell.

My heart pounds in my chest when I stare down at her last message, the yellow conversation bubble mocking me.

Suddenly I feel like a fucking idiot, speaking about myself in the third person, although she has no idea that's what's happening here, no idea I'm pretending to be someone else.

BlueAsTheSky: *There you go again with the good grammar. Swoon! Both commas in the proper place? You're on a roll here, JB. Keep it up.*

Me: *You sure you're not an English major?*

BlueAsTheSky: *No! I love to read, but I'm not a writer. Not by a long shot. I'm definitely the creative type, but I can never remember if it's I before E except after C...*

Me: *Sounds about right.*

BlueAsTheSky: *But I still have to say it when I'm spelling words! I SAY IT OUT LOUD, JB, not in my head. LOL I'm so ridiculous.*

Me: *Do you use your fingers to do math?*

BlueAsTheSky: *Only when I'm multiplying by 9.*

Me: *Huh? That makes no sense.*

BlueAsTheSky: *Let me see if I can explain this so it makes sense (I had an old tutor teach me this trick in—no lie—fourth grade): whenever you need to multiply by nine, you count on your fingers the number you're multiplying by. So, say it's nine times seven. Take your seventh finger and fold it down. You now have six fingers on the left side of the seventh, 3 on the right. The answer is 63.*

BlueAsTheSky: *That is seriously the only way I can multiply by nine. I suck SOOOO bad. Don't judge me now that I've told you my secret, and NEVER bring it up again.*

I stare down at my fingers and mentally calculate nine times five—then fold down the fifth finger on my left hand. Four fingers remain on that hand, five on the other. Forty-five.

Me: *Holy shit, you're right.*

BlueAsTheSky: *Yeah, I guess you could count it as a stupid party trick, but it only works for nines. Which totally* *screwed me during math exams since I'm horrible at all multiplication and not just nines. Sigh.*

BlueAsTheSky: *My teachers were probably so confused about why I was killing it with that number but failing the rest. I'm so awkward sometimes. Actually, I'm awkward all the time.*

If she's anything like this in person, there is no doubt in my mind that I would find her fucking delightful.

Me: *Bullshit, you are not.*

BlueAsTheSky: *Okay, I'm not. I actually talk a lot and am quite personable, LOL*

Me: *Random question.*

BlueAsTheSky: *Fire away*

Me: *Is your name Blue, or...something else? I can't figure out what BlueAsTheSky means. Are your eyes blue, or did you just randomly make it up?*

BlueAsTheSky: *It's not randomly made up. I mean, it is, but it has to do with my name.*

Me: *Which you have no intention of telling me?*

BlueAsTheSky: *No, not yet. Sorry, I'm still a little gun-shy.*

Me: *That's okay. I totally get it.*

BlueAsTheSky: *Besides, it's not like JB is your actual name, so technically I don't know yours either.*

Yeah, and she never will, because my initials will never be JB because I am not Jack Bartlett and never will be.

Me: *JB is obviously my initials.*

BlueAsTheSky: *Obviously, lol*

Me: *I'm not nearly as creative as you.*

BlueAsTheSky: *You couldn't get any less creative with your profile name if you tried. Which you clearly did not. LOL*

Me: *I'm not usually a fan of sarcasm, but I find yours irresistible.*

JB hates being mocked or teased in any way. He's kind of a sensitive prick, actually. A titty baby, as an old member of the team used to call Jack when he was a freshman.

Zeke Daniels has long since departed, but some of the shit he said stuck with me.

Like my roommate being a complete sissy when it comes to taking direction or being the subject of a joke. So much so that I feel the need to point this out to Blue, even though we haven't gotten to the part where I'm setting her up on a date with Jack.

She should know he gets butthurt easily.

BlueAsTheSky: *You don't like being teased, or you don't like sarcasm?*

Me: *At the risk of sounding like a sissy, I hate being the butt of jokes.*

BlueAsTheSky: *Noted. It's a good thing I'm not a sarcastic asshole.*

Me: *There are some real assholes on the wrestling team I've had to deal with, so...*

I hit send before I can think twice about it, knowing that if JB goes back through the conversation after he logs in later, he's probably going to be pissed I told her that.

Oh well.

It's out there and I can't take it back.

A small part of me gets a cheap thrill at dishing out that particular bit of information, knowing it was a shitty thing to tell her.

BlueAsTheSky: *I respect that; thanks for telling me.*

I roll my eyes toward the ceiling, not looking forward to the argument I'll have with my roommate about it later.

I'm making him sound like a pussy.

And in all honesty, since Tasha broke up with him, he's been acting like one. He kind of was one before, but for the past three months, it's been worse.

He fucking hates being picked on, and you know how dudes are—constantly giving each other shit, especially in the gym and practice room. It's almost like we have nothing better to do than screw around when we're supposed to be focused.

Dick jokes.

Lowbrow insults.

Mocking someone's intelligence is always a favorite go-to.

We're all pretty offensive, and at the same time, we're like one big happy dysfunctional family. It's really fucked up in a weird way that only makes sense if you're part of it.

Anyway.

Jack is a titty baby and he's going to hate that I told Blue.

I change the subject.

Me: *So there is no chance you'll tell me your name?*

BlueAsTheSky: *Not tonight. Sorry big guy.*

I am a big guy.

Much bigger than JB, not that she would have any way of knowing that. All she sees are his photographs; she'll never see mine, and why I'm even thinking about it is beyond me.

I wonder what she would think of me.

Me as me.

Abe.

Me: *You said you like tall guys, right?*

JB says he's six foot, but that's a total lie. He's five ten on a good day; I have several inches on him, measuring in at six two.

BlueAsTheSky: *I do. I really do.*

Then you're going to be disappointed when you meet me in person, I start to type.

Delete.

Me: *I'm your guy then.*

BlueAsTheSky: *I'll have to take your word for it.*

You're not going to show up for our date and be standing eye to eye with me, are you? Because I love wearing heels, haha.

I flip back to her profile to see if she makes any mention of how tall she is.

Nothing.

Me*: How tall did you say you were?*

BlueAsTheSky*: I didn't. I'm five seven.*

Oh shit, that's pretty tall for a female. Only three inches shorter than JB if you're doing the math.

That's not going to end well.

I wonder if I should say something but decide against it. No reason to put the cart before the horse, and who knows—

maybe she won't even notice, or care.

I laugh at the thought, knowing that when a girl has her mind made up about something—especially what they consider their "type" to be—there isn't much room to change their mind.

Especially not when the entire relationship is built on a lie.

Five foot eight.

That's pretty fucking sexy, and my mind quickly wanders, wondering about her legs. How long they are, if they're smooth. If she ever wears skirts or favors jeans.

I wonder how closely she resembles the pictures in her profile. One thing is for certain, she's not using any filters. Still, you never really know until you're face to face with a person.

I have no right to be having these thoughts. When I lift my eyes and stare out my bedroom window, the bathroom across the way is dark, the white curtain flapping a little with the breeze since the girls living there have cracked the window open a bit.

BlueAsTheSky: *You still there, JB?*

I drop my eyes back down to the phone in my hand.

Me: *I'm here. Sorry, I was just…*

I hit send even though I didn't finish my sentence.

Me: *Staring out the window, LOL*

BlueAsTheSky: *Fair enough. I just flopped down on my bed. I give up on studying. I'm never going to ace this midterm no matter what I do.*

Me: *What class?*

BlueAsTheSky: *Microeconomics. It's not my finest work. I feel like I end up reading the same paragraph over and over and I'm not retaining any of the information!*

My pre-med, biology class heavy schedule isn't going to help Blue with an economics class, so I bite my tongue and don't reply…though, as JB, I should *technically* know some of that shit since *technically*, as JB, I would have taken it, too.

Everything on my desk is in perfect order. Straight. Tidy. Organized.

Like me.

The fact that I'm wrapped up in this shit is a paradox

when you consider that, among my friends and teammates, I'm the trustworthy and reliable one.

The do-gooder.

The nice guy.

The person everyone goes to when they have a problem

or need a ride home at the ass crack of dawn or help with homework.

The one they call when they need to be bailed out after one too many beers has them pissing on the side of a building and hauled into custody for public urination.

I'm the guy they always call.

I'm the guy they go to when they want something fixed, like their car.

Or their love life.

When I was a sophomore last year, one of the guys nicknamed me The Grandfather and the name stuck. I even have a rocking chair in the corner of my room, one they bought me as a gag gift for my birthday back in October. One of the guys found a ratty old afghan and it's folded into a square, draped over the back.

Ironically, I sit in the fucking thing every so often.

I stand, kicking back my desk chair to pace the room, thumbs hovering over the keypad of my cell.

Me*: Any plans this weekend?*

No time like the present to be setting her up for a date with Jack. The sooner I can get them together, the sooner I can stop chatting with her. I've never gone on this long making small talk with anyone on the app.

BlueAsTheSky: *Yeah, I have tickets to see a comedian in the city. I'm driving in with a few friends and we're gonna spend the night.*

BlueAsTheSky: *What about you?*

Me: *I have a wrestling meet on Friday afternoon, but I'm free the rest of the weekend.*

At least, I am—I have no idea what JB is doing, but I assume he'd be down for a quick date if Blue was available. They never last very long, anyway.

Personally, I'll be lying on my bed as usual, a biology textbook open and a movie playing on my laptop.

Exciting shit, I tell ya.

BlueAsTheSky: *Guess you're stuck chatting with me until we decide if we want to meet, eh?*

Me: *Guess so.*

No sooner do I hit send on the message than my bedroom door blows open, Jack Bartlett standing in my doorway, towel wrapped around his waist, hair dripping wet.

"Dude. You still fuckin' around in here? Are you coming for tacos or what?"

It's Tuesday and I'm starving, and the local Mexican restaurant has dollar tacos from four to five.

"Yeah, I'm just finishing something up."

His eyes trail to the cell phone in my hand. "You talking to someone in here, Grandpa?"

"Yes."

"For me?"

The *yes* gets pushed through my lips reluctantly.

"She decent?" JB tightens the knot in his terrycloth towel and enters the room. Holds out his palm. "Give. Let me see."

I give.

JB scans the bio then the conversation, his mouth doing a weird lilt every so often as his thumb scrolls.

"Why the hell did you tell her I hate being teased?"

"Because you hate being teased." In any way, shape, or form. Because you're a pussy.

"You don't tell girls that shit."

"Then tell her shit about yourself *yourself.*"

He ignores me and keeps talking.

"Dude, why are you discussing this garbage? Discuss something else—like music and what her favorite colors are and that other bullshit girls care about. Puppies and shit."

Colors and music? Puppies and shit? No wonder the guy can't keep his girlfriends around.

He has no idea what girls want—not that I'm a freaking expert, but I do know enough to know Blue couldn't care less what my favorite color is. She wants to know if he's a decent guy. Caring. If he's going to be her rock, or split when times are tough.

JB tosses the phone on my bed; it lands with a thump. "Whatever. When can she meet me?"

He didn't read that far. Typical. "Not this weekend."

"What about during the week? I wanna get this over with."

Get this over with.

Nice.

"This one could be a game-changer, so don't be an asshole."

"She looks boring."

"No she doesn't. You're just not used to girls who are wearing clothes."

"That's probably true." His fingers fiddle with the waist of his towel. "Hurry up and get your shit together—I wanna leave here in ten minutes."

"You're the one standing in the middle of my room dripping wet from a shower."

"Yeah, but it takes me three seconds to get ready. None of this"—he trails his fingers up and down his torso—"requires any work to look good."

"Fuck off, Bartlett."

"Fuck yourself, Grandpa."

My eyes roll toward the ceiling. "Am I driving?"

"Duh."

Typical.

4

#DOUCHEBAG

Last night I was so drunk, I
thought his shirt said YALE. This
morning it definitely said Old
Navy.

Skylar

Days pass before I hear from JB again. Which is confusing the crap out of me. I thought we were having a great conversation.

One minute we were talking about our plans for the weekend, and the next...

Nothing.

Dead silence.

No explanation—nothing.

This. This right here is why I want nothing to do with dating. Guys pulling shit like this. No respect for the person on the other side, waiting patiently.

Waiting for *something*.

Give me anything.

Say good morning. Tell me you're busy. Tell me you'll get back to me in a few days, but don't just stop talking to me.

Frustrated and confused, I put my cell on silent and flip it over on the table I'm using as a desk; I don't want to see the stupid notification if the dumb jerk finally decides to message me.

Deep breath, Skylar.

Focus on yourself and your studying and the fun you had this weekend with your friends.

We laughed our asses off at the comedian over the weekend, and Hannah's parents were awesome enough to put us up in a hotel so we didn't have to drive all the way back to campus so late at night.

"Don't think about that great guy who turned out to be kind of an ass. He even admitted he wasn't going to turn down the chance to get laid—that's probably what he was doing this weekend while you were drinking virgin daiquiris and giggling in your cat pajamas."

Great. Now I'm talking to myself.

Yes, out loud.

Me, in my cat pajamas.

I glance down at the white, two-piece set with its orange tabby cat printed top and matching bottoms.

I don't even own a cat, let alone a tabby, yet here I sit dressed as one—a joke from my friends, who tease that I'm going to wind up a bitter, old cat lady if I don't put myself out there.

"Meow."

Oh my god, stop before you completely lose your damn mind.

Nearby, my phone vibrates and I roll my eyes at it, playing the game I love to play with myself before I grab it: the Who Is Messaging Me game.

Jessica.

No—she went home for the weekend and isn't driving back until tomorrow.

Hannah? Yeah, it's got to be her. She ran to the grocery store and is probably asking if I need anything.

I do kind of wants chips and salsa. Or popcorn. Because I'm only going to pretend to study for twenty more minutes before ransacking the kitchen and vegging out in front of the TV. I'll text her and put in my requests.

My phone vibrates again.

And it's not Hannah.

It's the LoveU app, and there is only one person I've been talking to, though more than thirty guys have swiped to match with me.

One guy. One conversation.

JB.

Ugh. It's been days.

Am I just an asshole with high expectations, or should he have messaged me at least once?

Although I did tell him I was going to be gone this weekend.

On the other hand, who cares? He can still shoot me a note if we were having a good time talking and he still wants to chat? Right?

I want to be mad, but he's just so good-looking. And insightful, and quick with the comebacks.

Reluctantly, I tap open the conversation.

JB: *Hey stranger. How was your weekend? Does your throat hurt from laughing last night?*

Aww, he remembered I went to see a comedian! Oh my god, he is so sweet for asking.

Me: *It was so fun—we had a blast. I'm exhausted, though. I was about to wrap up "studying" and eat my* *feelings on the couch.*

JB: *Sounds like my kind of Sunday.*

Me: *You're allowed to eat your feelings?*

JB: *Well, no. I mean—I can eat as many lean proteins and vegetables as I want...*

Me: *Why does that sound kind of gross?*

JB: *Lean protein sounds gross?*

Me: *It doesn't sound like chips and salsa, that's all I'm saying.*

JB: *So, no to chicken and hardboiled eggs.*

Me: *Maybe to chicken. No to hardboiled eggs.*

JB: *Noted.*

JB: *What are you binging on Netflix right meow?*

Me: *Everything. I think I've been through them all, and now I don't know what to do with myself. Which is why I subscribed to Hulu.*

JB: *It sounds like you have a procrastination problem.*

Me: *It's genetic. My sister has the same affliction. She's a solid C+ student like I am. We're basically winning at colleging.*

JB: *Is she at Iowa, too?*

Me: *No, she goes to small private university in Missouri. Our parents are so proud of their mediocre students. Every semester they send us newspaper clippings of the* *dean's list.*

JB: *Why?*

Me: *Because we're never on it. It's my dad's idea of a sick joke, although my brother more than made up for it. He's the only one who ever got good grades without even trying.*

JB: *Do you get along with him?*

Me: *Yes, mostly. He's...a riot. But he's a pain in the ass, always up in our business.*

JB: *How?*

Me: *He lives in Iowa too—I'm actually from Indiana—and every once in a while he'll "pop in" unexpectedly to check up on me. It's so annoying.*

JB: *That sounds kind of cool.*

Me: *You haven't met my brother.*

JB: *How old is he?*

Me: *Twenty-four. He thinks he's thirty, and he thinks his shit doesn't stink because he started his own company with his dumb friends. Now he knows everything about everything.*

Me: *What about you—any brothers or sisters?*

JB: *Me? Um, no.*

Me: *Dang, you're lucky.*

Me: *I would trade my brother for a few dollar bills and* *a package of Tim Tams.*

Okay, I really have to stop making stupid jokes at my brother's expense. He might be a total, grade-A pain in my ass, but he's a pretty decent guy, and he only butts into my life because he loves me.

I'm kind of impossible not to love and adore.

My siblings would throw up in their mouths if they heard me saying that, and then they'd both laugh in my face.

I smirk at my bedroom full of no one.

JB*: So, I guess I should have asked you this last week— and sorry I didn't message you over the weekend but I figured you were out of town, and I had that wrestling meet and I was just so fucking tired.*

JB*: I know it's not the weekend, but do you wanna grab a drink or something this week? Like Wednesday?*

Me: *Wednesday?*

My stomach actually gurgles—*gurgles* for God's sake!—from nerves, a sensation way worse than any butterflies.

A date.

An actual date.

Ugh, I think I might be sick.

I want to say yes, but I'm chickenshit, no good at this dating business.

Just say no, my stomach thunders

Say yes, you idiot! my heart pounds.

Hesitate a little longer, my brain mocks.

JB*: Or…not? A different day maybe?*

Me*: No. Wednesday works. What did you have in mind?*

JB*: Maybe just drinks. Keep it simple? That way…you know…*

Me*: If there's no chemistry, we both have an easy out?*

JB*: LOL exactly.*

But we're going to have amazing chemistry, I just know it. I can feel it—look at how easy it is for us to talk. We haven't had a single lull in the conversation, if you don't count this weekend when he ghosted me.

I take a deep breath and go out on a limb.

Me*: We're not going to want an easy out. We won't need it **wink***

JB*: You don't think so?*

Me*: No. I think we're going to have fun. Don't you?*

JB doesn't respond right away, and my stomach does another gurgle, this one filled with insecurity. *Did I say something wrong? Was that too forward?*

Did I come on too strong with the optimism? Shit, I really need to learn to be more pessimistic.

Some people hate positive people. Maybe he's one of them, and if he is, we're not a good match.

Finally, he messages me.

JB: *What's your drink of choice?*

I have to give this one some serious thought, because I hate the taste of alcohol, and the first and last time I got drunk was my twenty-first birthday.

Me: *Honestly? Iced tea? LOL*

Me: *What about you?*

JB: *Beer*

Oh.

That one words leaves me oddly disappointed. For some reason I thought he'd say he wasn't a big drinker either, but guess I was wrong.

My phone pings again.

JB: *I like beer, but because of the carbs, I usually drink vodka.*

Oh, great—the hard stuff. *Even better.*

Nothing would thrill me more than a boyfriend who probably outweighs me by a hundred pounds getting drunk at a bar on hard liquor and forcing me to figure out how to get his sloppy ass home.

No thanks.

Still. I'm putting the cart before the horse here; we haven't gone out on a date, let alone gone out drinking.

But my grandfather was an alcoholic before he died, and it really affected my mother, who passed down her aversion of alcohol to me.

It's just…one of those things.

One of *my* things.

I can't help the fact that alcohol is a deal breaker for me, and that one word—VODKA—glowing like a headlight on my cell phone, has the hairs on the back of my neck tingling, and not in a good way.

I feel like a buzzkill when I'm the only one drinking an iced tea, or water, or something else that's not alcoholic, though I know no one is actually judging me for it.

It's a fact: drunk people absolutely *do not give a shit* if you're drunk or not, as long as they are. They're too busy being drunk to care.

Peer pressure (for the record) has never been my thing. When it comes to hard limits, I won't let anyone force me into crossing them.

I'm stubborn like that.

My teeth rake across my bottom lip as I deliberate what to say to JB that isn't snarky, or judgmental, or short. After all, he's in college and over the age of twenty-one, so what business is it of mine if he imbibes? I just want to know if he's one of those guys who parties too hard or someone who knows his limits.

JB: *I don't go out very often, in case you're wondering. We're really not allowed to.*

I let out the pent-up air I was holding in my lungs, a little sigh of relief passing through my lips.

Seriously, is this guy a mind reader?

Me: *I'm too busy being lazy to go out very often. My friends and I like hoofing it to the city to hang out—my roommate's dad is an entertainment lawyer, so he gets tickets for us a lot. It's pretty awesome.*

JB: *That does sound awesome. Way more awesome than going out downtown, which now sounds incredibly lame.*

Me: *It's nice because I'm not a big partier, and it takes a lot of the pressure off. I mean, I go to parties SOMEtimes, but it's rare.*

JB: *We all have our thing. Yours isn't parties. Mine isn't hanging out at home. I like to be busy.*

Me: *Must be easy considering you practice all the time, and have meets and stuff?*

JB: *Yeah, there isn't much downtime.*

Me: *But doesn't it get old?*

He doesn't respond right away, which surprises me. It's almost like he's taking his time and thinking about his answer.

JB: *Yes. It gets old.*

Me: *I'm sensing some hesitation…*

He hesitates again, the tiny conversation bubbles appearing then disappearing. Appearing.

JB: *It's not easy to admit that despite having this quote-unquote great life, in reality, it's kind of fucking dull. No one wants to admit that to someone they're trying to impress.*

He's trying to impress me?

My heart does a clichéd little leap.

Me: *I think my life is pretty basic, if I'm keeping things* *real. And at the risk of sounding...off-putting? I'm pretty boring, LOLOL*

Me*: How is that for an endorsement? It just screams DATE ME! DATE ME! doesn't it?*

JB*: No more off-putting than me saying I like beer and vodka!!! LOLOL*

Me*: I mean...you do, right?*

JB*: Not THAT much! LOL*

Me*: Okay, well, I binged three different shows this week. Which—now that I'm thinking about it, could be why my grades are sub-par.*

JB*: I ate twelve tacos for dinner last week.*

Me*: In one week?*

JB*: No. For dinner one night.*

Me*: WHAT??? WHO EATS 12 TACOS*

JB: *Me?*

Me*: What kind were they?*

JB*: Uh, steak. You know, the shredded beef. I skip the cheese and load up on lettuce and tomato.*

Me*: Ahhh, to make the taco healthier. Good plan **wink***

JB*: Are you being sarcastic?*

Me*: Yes? Not on purpose?*

Me*: I had pizza for dinner if that makes you feel better, and I'm waiting for my roomie to come home with chips and salsa to wash it all down with. She's taking forever.*

Me*: The sooner she gets back, the sooner I can go sit on the couch and OMG you probably think that's all I do— watch TV. IT'S NOT. I swear I do other things. LOL*

JB*: Do you jog or run or anything like that?*

Me*: Actually, yes. I run—mostly walk—a few times a week. I have to or I'll never fit into my leggings, haha.*

JB*: Maybe we could run together sometime.*

Me*: I don't know if I'd be able to keep up. I'm a light jogger. Mostly I stare at birds and dodge anyone on roller blades.*

Me*: And stop to pet dogs.*

JB*: Oh god.*

Me*: What? Not a dog person?*

JB*: I am, I just…you stop to pet every dog?*

Me*: Yeah? You don't?!*

JB*: Uh, NO. It would take forever to run a mile!*

Me*: **grumbles under breath** I know, tell me about it…*

Me*: They like the bacon I keep in my pockets!*

JB*: You are killing me.*

Me*: I'm kidding about the bacon BTW*

JB: *I figured, but you never know…*

Me: *LOL that's true.*

I hear the front door of our apartment open and close then the deadbolt being slid into place.

Hannah is back with the snacks.

My mouth waters.

Me: *Um. My roommate is back, I'm going to go say hey.*

JB: *And eat?*

Me: *Yes, and eat, LOL*

JB: *Cool.*

JB: *So…Wednesday?*

Me: *Sure. Shoot me the details?*

JB: *Do you want me to text them to you?*

What? No way! I like talking to this guy, but he could still end up being a creep in real life.

Me: *No, here is fine. Does 7 work for you?*

JB: *Works for me.*

Me: *Great.*

JB: *Do you have a place in mind, or…*

Me: *No, you choose. I'm pretty easygoing since it's just drinks.*

JB: *Do you know where McGuillicudy's is?*

He wants to meet me at an Irish burger bar? One with sticky floors and crappy food? Maybe that was a typo and he wants to meet somewhere else.

Me*: That bar on Main?*

JB*: That's the one. 7 on Wednesday?*

Me*: Uh. Sure.*

JB*: Sweet.*

"Skylar, you still here?" Hannah's knuckles rap on my bedroom door, her knee slowly pushing it open. "Oh good, you're not in here diddling yourself. I'd hate to walk in on that."

I roll my eyes and set my cell phone down. "When have I ever done that?"

"You should. Not that I want to see it, I'm just saying—you should."

"Why are we discussing this?"

My roommate shrugs, a brown paper bag propped on one hip. "I brought you treats."

"You gonna hang out with me? Friends don't let friends snack alone."

"Yeah, I bought myself ice cream, so…"

"What kind?"

"Cookies and cream."

Gross. That's my least favorite and she knows it. "Did you buy that so I wouldn't eat it?"

"Yes." She laughs.

"You bitch!"

Hannah laughs again, adjusting the weight of the bag. "I'm changing into pajamas. Couch in five."

"Good, because I have something to tell you," I say cryptically, wiggling my eyebrows.

I almost never have news to share, and her perfectly manicured brows go up, interested.

"Is that so?"

"Yup. Now go away so I can change, too."

"I'm going, I'm going…" The door closes behind her and I make short work of removing my jeans and sweater, swapping the outfit out for pajama pants and a baggy Iowa sweatshirt.

Sex appeal has never been my thing; there's no telling if I'll ever master the art.

Unlike Hannah, who's sitting in the living room, already lounging in a matching, pretty pink satin top and bottom combo, hair in an adorably messy top knot and looking perfect.

I drag my eyes down my body begrudgingly, the plaid flannel bottoms I stole from my brother dragging across the carpet. Which, by the way, he totally bitched about once he realized I'd taken them.

Pfft, like he doesn't have ten more pairs. That's all the dude wears to bed, isn't it?

I plop my unsexy self down next to my goddess of a roommate and nudge her with my knee, popping a chip into my mouth from the open bag she's holding out in front of me like a feed bag. A bowl of cookies and cream ice cream is propped in her other hand. Like I'm going to eat it. As if.

I pop another chip into my mouth.

One or two crumbs fall from my mouth before I get any words out. "So, as I was saying—I have a life update."

Hannah rubs our shoulders together. "It's about time! Is this about a guy? Did you do the thing?"

"The LoveU app? Yeah, I did the thing I said I wasn't going to do."

"Andddd…?"

"And there's this guy—"

Hannah immediately interrupts. "Already? Let me see him."

My hand goes up, hoping she'll cool her jets. "Can you just be patient?

"You're going to show him to me, right? I need to see right meow."

I haven't even gotten six words of the story out. "As I was saying, we've been talking for a few days. He's a junior here and he's on the wres—"

"He goes to school here? Did you recognize him right away?" Hannah has ice cream in her mouth, and I can see it melted on her tongue, white and slimy. It's grossing me out.

"Oh my god, stop interrupting!" She is seriously so obnoxious. Didn't her mother teach her *any* manners?

"I can't help how excited I am." Now she's bouncing on the couch cushions like a little kid. "Sorry not sorry."

I grimace. "No one says *sorry not sorry* out loud.

That's a hashtag."

Hannah also overuses the acronyms LOL and OMG when speaking, along with the term low-key, which drives me insane.

"I can say it out loud if I want to, bossy pants. Stop trying to distract me by scolding. Finish what you were going to say before I interrupted."

That makes me giggle, despite irritation.

She is pretty stinkin' adorable.

I settle in, repositioning myself so I'm sitting cross-legged, bag of chips in my lap and salsa strategically positioned within reach. If I'm going to tell her all the details, I must be comfortable.

I start from the beginning. Again.

"So even though I said I would never do it, I downloaded the stupid dating app. I made up some bullshit profile bio because I didn't know what to say, added a few basic pictures—"

"You didn't crop me out of any, did you?"

I shrug, guilty.

"Number one rule of online dating: do not use cropped photos."

What? I've never heard of that rule.

"Why?" I pop a chip and chew, seriously wanting to know the answer.

"Because. A guy might think you're cropping out an old boyfriend or something."

"Then he's an idiot."

"Who?"

"Any guy whose brain goes to that place." I add an eye roll to emphasize just how lame this fictional person is. "Anyway, as I was saying…"

Hannah gives her hand a flippant wave, her ice cream spoon airily wafting about. "Please proceed."

"At first I had a ton of guys swiping on me. My inbox had, like, thirty guys in it. Not a single one was decent."

"I can imagine." Hannah shudders, shoveling dessert into her face.

"But then…" I pause dramatically. "Then JB swiped on me."

"BJ?" My friend wrinkles her pert little nose.

"No. *JB*."

"B J stands for blowjob."

Jesus. Could she not? "That's not at all what his name is."

"But that's probably what I'm going to call him."

"Please don't."

"Too late. He'll forever be known as Blowjob."

"Why are you like this?"

"Don't date someone with the initials BJ and I won't make jokes about it."

"We haven't been out on a date, and that's not the order of his initials." At this point, there is nothing I can do. My friend is a beast, and I know she's going to run with this information as far as she can. Not only that, there is no doubt in my mind she's going to tell Jessica and Bethany, and they're going to start calling the poor guy Blowjob, too.

Eff my life.

"He seems really fun. And smart—so smart."

"What's his major?"

"Business."

Hannah groans. "So generic. That could be anything."

"My major is business, you asshole."

For the record, so is hers.

"Duh, I didn't say it wasn't. I just said it was generic."

Fine. She wins that round. "He's also an athlete."

"Which sport?"

"Wrestling."

She considers this, tilting her head to the side in thought. "I wonder if his ears are all jacked up."

"Why would his ears be all jacked up?"

"They wear those head things that squish their ears, that's why. You would think their moms put them on when they're born—that's how funky their ears look. No way can those ear guards jack their shit up that much after only a few years of wearing them. I bet it's from *not* wearing them that makes their ears all funkadelic."

The way her brain works…

She scares me sometimes.

"I saw a few of his pictures, but I didn't notice if his ears were wonky or not."

"Bet they are."

"Guess we'll see," I intone cryptically.

"So you're going out with him?"

"Yes."

"What!" she shouts. "When?"

"Wednesday."

That nose of hers wrinkles again. "Wednesday? Why not Friday? Why not Saturday?"

"I don't know, Hannah. He said Wednesday! And I didn't have anything going on, so I said yes—why are you being hysterical about it?"

"Dating rule number two: guys who want to see you during the week are trying to keep their weekend wide open for something better. Everyone knows that."

"Would you stop saying that?"

"It's a fact."

"Where are you getting these 'facts'?"

"When it comes to dating, I'm like Yoda—I just know stuff." Her shoulders bob up and down in a shrug. "And now you know for next time. No more midweek dates. You are a weekend date kind of girl."

My lips twitch.

"Right. I'll keep that in mind." I shoot her a look that says *I won't be keeping that in mind, but thanks anyway for the advice.* "Am I allowed to continue talking?"

"Yeah, tell me more. What does he look like?"

I want to show her pictures, but I also don't need her going online and stalking him before I've had the chance to do it myself.

So I just tell her, "He's gorgeous."

Really gorgeous, as a matter of fact. Handsome in a rugged kind of way, if his photos aren't lying.

"Be more specific." Hannah pronounces the word specific like *pacific*, which drives me cuckoo. But I won't get into that right now.

"Dark blond hair—"

She interrupts with a drawn-out, "*Hmmm…*"

"Now what?"

A diminutive shrug. "It's just that I've never met a dude with blond hair I thought was attractive."

"JB is an attractive blond."

"Blowjob is an attractive blond, you mean?" She chuckles like the troll she is. "I'll have to take your word for it since you're obviously not going to show me his pictures."

"If I show you his picture, you're going to stalk him on every social media site you can find him on."

"True, but it's not like I can't find him without your help. You've already told me his name and given me his hair color, *and* you told me he wrestles. It will take me three seconds to find him."

"Well wait until you're alone in your bedroom, would ya?"

"Fine. I'll wait to stalk him."

"And don't give me shit about it, because I haven't gone out with him and the date could totally suck, and I'll never hear the end of it." There's still time for him to cancel on me, too.

"The date isn't going to suck."

"How do you know?"

"Because you're glowing, and you never glow."

Am I glowing? "Gee, thanks."

"I can't lie to you, Sky. You only glow when you're wearing tons of blush, which is a look we try to avoid. Ruddy doesn't look good on anyone, least of all you."

"Gee. *Thanks*."

"My point is, you practically skipped out of your bedroom, so that must mean something, yeah?"

She's right.

She knows I spend most of my time daydreaming about my future, one where I have it all. A partner and a career and—maybe someday—a child or two?

Daydreaming is food for the soul, my grandmother used to tell me. Don't be stingy with your dreams, Skylar. Close your eyes and imagine…

Closing my eyes and imagining myself somewhere else has never been the problem for me; keeping my feet planted firmly on the ground has. Staying focused instead of getting distracted has.

When I was younger, on family road trips, I'd sit in the back seat of my parents' car and lean my head against the window. Close my eyes and think. Write stories in my head, plot out romances—if I were to write one. I would never read—I'd get too carsick for that—so instead, I daydreamed the days away while my dad drove. Hours and hours I would sit, thinking—never sleeping.

Daydreaming.

Writing in journals. Notebooks.

Notes and phrases and stories. A diary of sorts, fiction woven between the pages and in the words.

It's probably not a good thing, because...well, here we are.

Mediocre grades.

Mediocre love life.

Hopeless romantic in a world where guys don't call anymore. They'd rather slide into your inbox. Or send you a picture of their *dick*.

To be fair, I've never been on the receiving end of a dick pic, which in itself is rather insulting.

Am I not dick pic worthy?

How rude. At least send me one so I can act disgusted, tell all my friends, and then delete it.

Dick pic FOMO, Bethany once called it.

"I am pretty excited."

"Where are you going for this Wednesday date of yours?"

God, I don't even want to tell her. She's going to judge JB for his choice, and then she's going to judge me for agreeing to it.

"I don't want to say," I admit.

Her brows go up and her mouth falls open. "Why?"

"You're going to get judgy."

"Oh honey, I'm judging you anyway. Because I'm your friend and that's what friends do."

I laugh, pointing out the obvious. "Actually, that's the opposite of what friends do."

"You know what I mean."

I do. Hannah is the least judgmental person I know, and one of the sweetest. If I asked her to come along on this date, she would. If I asked her to hide in the bushes wearing camouflage, she would do it.

If I asked her never to utter another syllable about this date again—well, she'd never do that, so it would be pointless to ask.

"He wants to meet at McGuillicudy's."

"McGuillicudy's?" She asks like she heard me incorrectly, her inflection indicating disbelief. "The *bar.*"

"Yeah."

"The burger joint right next to campus, where they have wild parties and dye the beer green, where some guy went down on Tamara Stewart in the hall by the bathrooms freshman year?"

Tamara was in Hannah's sorority before she transferred schools. "The very same."

"McGuillicudy's. The bar."

"Is there an echo in here?"

"You can't be serious. Does this guy have any class?"

Apparently not. "You said you weren't going to judge me."

"No I didn't—I said I *was* going to, and I am. Because he's taking you to a dive bar."

"In his defense—"

Hannah flops her ice cream spoon in my direction, almost bopping me on the nose with the end of it. "No. You

75

and I both know that's a shitty place to take a first date."

"Maybe so," I admit reluctantly. "But we both also know the whole thing could end up going south, and why go to a decent place and waste time if we hate each other?"

"You get two points for making a semi-decent point. However!" Her spoon rises. "How. Ever. There are way better places than an Irish pub. Literally any other place, Skylar." My roommate takes a lick of her spoon. "So he either plans to ditch you halfway through the date, has friends planning on crashing the date, or he's just a fuck-ing idiot—which one do you think it is?"

"I don't think he's an idiot. I think he's a guy."

"Let's not be blaming his lack of dating aptitude on his gender. He's probably been on forty LoveU dates, and he's taken them all to that stupid bar."

"JB isn't like that."

"You don't even know him."

"I'm getting to know him! I'm trying! You're the one who made me download the freaking app, Hannah!"

"I'm not the one who told you to agree to McGuil-licudy's! The place is a cheap knockoff of the liquor brand! And not even a decent one! The owner asked Jessica on a date once—do you know how old that dude is? Forty-three! He's ancient! God, gag me."

Could she be any more dramatic? "Forty-three is not ancient."

"Puh-leaze. My dad is in his forties, Skylar."

"Your dad is fifty-one, Hannah. I was there for his birthday."

Her bubble bursts. "Oh."

"In any case, I feel like I would know if JB was a slime ball. I would have picked up on the vibe. We've been chatting for almost an entire week—don't you think I would have picked up on it by now?"

"Probably. But still—McGuillicudy's? That place is so awful." She makes her body shiver. "I was going to say we should talk about what you're going to wear on your date, but it's…in a seedy bar. Technically you could wear that."

Hannah points at my pajama bottoms with the tip of her spoon.

"All right, stop being so dramatic—the place isn't that bad."

"No. But you could legit wear that on your date and no one would bat an eye."

She makes a very valid point. "Maybe just jeans then, and a flirty top?"

"Ratty t-shirt? I don't want you to ruin anything—do you know how many airborne STDs are probably floating through the air in that place? *Allll* the herpes, yo, straight to your vajajay."

My roommate is certifiable.

I can't even argue with her—she'll only keep going on and on, because if there is one thing she loves to do, it's shock people.

I pretend she's not talking. "What about that blue shirt that's cut a little lower? It's not too revealing, kind of perfect?"

She ponders my suggestion. "Yeah, that's cute…what

about wearing something red? You look so good in that color, and you can do red lips."

"You don't think red lips are a bit much for a dive bar?"

Hannah nods. "Good point." Thinks a few seconds. "What about a black turtleneck? That sends the message that you're not willing to fool around on the first date."

"Ah, a modern-day chastity belt?"

"Exactly!"

"No." I laugh. "What the hell is wrong with you?" I dig into the chip bag, making a ton of noise in the process while I root around for one or two—the sound drives Hannah nutso—then shove three tortilla chips in my mouth at the same time. Bite down and chew. Swallow. "Okay, how about a black camisole and jean jacket?"

"Yes, yes, I love that. Just enough skin without being revealing, and the denim makes it casual enough that it doesn't look like you're trying too hard. Yes. Perfect."

I nod. "It is quite perfect."

"Plus"—Hannah eyes me slyly—"if things get heated, you can slide the jacket off and—"

"Stop. Just…don't even say it."

She rattles the bottom of her ice cream bowl with the metal spoon in her hand, the hollow, empty sound making her frown and tip the bowl sideways.

"Empty. Empty like my heart."

"Oh my god, shut up." I laugh, tossing a chip in her direction. She snatches it up and pops it in her mouth even though it just landed on the couch.

"The date is going to be fine. If anything, it will be a

good practice run. Right?"

Right. It's going to be fine.

What's the worst thing that could happen? He turns out to be a mass murderer? The Craigslist Killer?

"He's going to fall madly in love with you." Hannah leans toward me, wrapping her free arm around my shoulders. "He's gonna love you like I love you, only he's going to want to sex you, too." Long pause. "Not that I don't want to sex you sometimes."

"Shut up, Hannah!"

She shrugs. "What can I say? You're adorable."

Adorable.

Great.

#DOUCHEBAG

If you ask what I did this
weekend, don't get pissed when I
say I "masturbated." You knew I
was single.

Abe

"You're not seriously going to meet her at that bar," I deadpan to Jack, who's studying for the first time this semester—that I've seen, anyway. When I walked into his bedroom after Blue confirmed their date, I found him with an *actual* textbook open and a highlighter in his hand.

I almost fainted from shock.

Blew my fucking mind.

He looks up from his book, a pair of actual, authentic reading glasses perched on his nose. "What's wrong with McGuillicudy's? I take all my dates there. No one has had a problem with it yet."

I know he takes all his dates there. That's why this feels so…wrong. A girl like Blue doesn't deserve to be treated like all his other dates. She's classier; I know this without even meeting her.

I've spoken to her long enough to know the idea doesn't thrill her. It took her several minutes to respond and confirm the date to begin with.

"These women aren't going to tell you they hate it to your face." I pause, thinking. "Ethan Ransick finger-bangs someone in the hallway by the bathrooms almost every weekend, and the last football victory party was there. One of the linebackers got wasted and tore the kitchen door off."

"Dude, why do you sound so surprised? I have literally

taken at least twelve girls there."

"Twenty-one, but who's counting."

"Sounds like you are." He sounds aggravated.

"Only because I'm the one setting all this shit up. Change it up a little for God's sake. You're becoming way too predictable."

JB stretches his neck, ignoring my barb. "Why should I change shit up when you're doing such a great job being me? Keep up the good work, buddy."

"Fuck you, Bartlett."

He pulls the glasses off his face and lays them on his open book, finally giving me his attention. "What the hell is your problem, Davis?"

BlueAsTheSky is my problem; she's one of the good ones and dipshit here is going to fucking ruin it by being... *himself.*

My lips seal shut, pulled into a straight line as I fold my arms across my chest. "Maybe it's time to get serious. You say you want a girlfriend and you're over Tasha, but you're not actually trying."

"How the hell would you know?"

"Statistics."

"Huh?"

I cross my ankles and lean against the doorjamb. "You bag seventy-five percent of your dates, and odds are you're going to bag this one. This chick is...she's—"

"This chick is *what*?"

A keeper.

Funny. Smart.

Clever. Pretty.

Someone you'd take home to your family.

"Nothing. I just don't… Let's just say I have a good feeling about this one."

"Yeah?" JB's brows rise, interested. "What kind of feeling?"

"She—"

"Makes your dick tingle?" He's smirking at himself, one side of his mouth turned up, kind of like the Joker in Batman. It's creepy as hell.

"Shut the fuck up, Bartlett. Be serious for a second."

JB rolls to his back, laughing at the ceiling. "I am being serious, Grandpa. Jesus, act your age for a change." My roommate laughs again. "I made a rhyme."

God he's an idiot.

"Is that what this is about? This chick gives you a woody?"

"No, you asshole. She doesn't get me hard."

I'm lying, obviously.

I'm lying because if he finds out I've been fantasizing about taking Blue out myself, the most likely scenario here is that JB would try to pick a fight—because he's a whiny bitch like that—and do his best to hand me my ass. Or tell everyone on the wrestling team I'm poaching girls from his dating pool.

Which is ridiculous.

Me finding one of these girls remotely interesting was

bound to happen eventually, and it happens to be Blue.

Him calling me out about it makes my left eye twitch.

JB opens his mouth to talk. "Of course she doesn't get you hard—I've seen her *and* her cardigan sweaters. No one wants to fuck a girl wearing a cardigan, Grandpa—except maybe you."

He says the word cardigan as if it's something distasteful, says it like Blue has a contagious disease. Like syphilis.

Or gonorrhea.

"She's funny." My argument is weak. Funny is good, but to a guy like JB, hot is better. Sexy is better. Sexually adventurous?

Even better.

"Funny," he repeats, unimpressed. Bored with the conversation. "Next you'll be telling me she has a great personality. Honestly, Gramps, all I give a shit about right now—this very second—is how great her tits are."

"Have you looked back at our conversations? Your date is tonight—you should know what we talked about so you don't sound like a moron."

He's going to sound like he developed amnesia overnight.

"Stop talking to these girls so damn much. Your job is to swipe and get the date, not swipe and get to know them. You're acting like a female, getting all personal. Knock that shit off so I can keep up with what's going on. It's my account, not yours, fucker."

I get it. I crossed the line.

I crossed it and I regret it.

So damn much.

Skylar

He's late.

JB is officially—I look down at the purple watch circling my wrist—twenty-five minutes late.

Not a great first impression, but I'll give him five more minutes before bailing.

No message to let me know he's running late. Nothing.

In the time we've been talking, he just hasn't struck me as the kind of guy who would stand a girl up for a first date. Quite the opposite, in fact.

If he can't chat, he lets me know. He says good morning and good night, and has been…consistent. Reliable in his communication? Reliability is a trait I value and am looking for.

So the fact that he's almost half an hour late disappoints me.

One strike against him.

I fiddle with my purse strap, self-consciously tugging on the brown leather, and debate grabbing us a booth to sit in—if he ever shows up.

It's busy in here for a Wednesday night, but in a college town, that's to be expected—Wasted Wednesday and all that jazz. Students play pool in the back room, beers perched on the ledges surrounding them.

The music is almost deafening; a song I don't recognize is blasting out of the speakers located in each corner of the main bar, my ears already ringing. Close to bleeding actually, ha.

The place smells like grease, spilled beer, and bad decisions, and I know as soon as I walk in the door tonight after this date is over, I'll beeline for the shower.

Guaranteed.

Twenty-six minutes late.

Twenty-seven.

Is this a joke to him? Is that what this is about?

I'm reaching across the booth where I've dropped my things, grabbing for my jacket and rising, when the heavy glass door at the front swings open.

JB fills the doorway, his entire frame boxed out as his dark eyes scan the bar (I know they're dark because I've studied his photographs no less than dozens of times). He's not that tall or imposing, but his arms are positioned away from his body, hanging at his sides—shoulders back, chin up.

Arrogant.

Hmm.

I clutch the coat in my hands, fingers tightening on the black polyester fabric, nails digging into the puff.

JB struts forward, automatically recognizing me as his target, a slow smile spreading across his features.

He's handsome. No—he's *hot*.

Not as tall as I thought he'd be, and a little...sharper. For some reason I thought he'd be more...approachable?

This guy feels like he's trying to intimidate me rather than reassure me, and I know instantly that he's not going to apologize for keeping me waiting almost half an hour.

I also know he isn't taking this date seriously.

How?

It's cold, but he's not wearing a jacket—just an Iowa wrestling hoodie with the yellow school logo splashed across the front and the number eight in the corner.

Who wears a hoodie on a first date, even if it is just drinks?

A healthy dose of disappointment begins creeping up my chest, along with the dull ache of embarrassment that I'm standing here in a cami, jeans, and heeled boots when he showed up in clothes he probably wore to the gym.

"Hey," is the first word out of his mouth. "You BlueAsTheSky?"

A reminder that I haven't yet told him my name. *Or have I?*

Ugh.

"Hi. It's Skylar." I put my hand out to shake his, and instead of taking it, he slides into the booth, hands skimming the tabletop.

Okay then.

"You want to sit up at the bar, or will this work?" JB asks, grabbing at one of the menus wedged in between the salt and pepper shakers, beside the condiments.

"Um, this is fine." Sit at the bar? I don't think so, pal.

Despite his first impression, I'm still naïvely hopeful that JB will pull his head out of his ass and be the guy

I've been chatting with on the app. So. I'm going to plop myself down across from him, order a drink, and pray for a miracle.

Mirroring his actions, I grab a menu and let my eyes roam the selections, not quite sure if I should go out on a limb and order alcohol.

"You getting anything, babe?" He doesn't look up at me, and for whatever reason, his use of an endearment rubs me the wrong way. I might not date much, but I do know guys often use pet names when they can't remember someone's actual name.

"It's Skylar."

He finally lowers the menu, lifting his face to look directly at me. Smiles. "I know."

"What does the J stand for?"

The menu lowers again. "Jack."

Rises.

"Jack. I like that." There happens to be a straw on the table, so I take it and start rolling it between my fingers to stop myself from fiddling with my shirt. Or the small hole slowly growing on the thigh of my jeans.

I've stuck my finger in it four times already, and I know this little factoid because I counted.

"Thanks."

His short answers are killing me softly. Frustrated, I blow out a puff of air, my brown hair floating away from my face.

"Um..."

JB sets the menu down. "I'm getting a draft beer. How

'bout you? Wine or something girly?"

Wine? In *this* place? It probably comes in a cardboard box.

"Undecided." It's clear to me that this conversation—or lack thereof—isn't going to improve the longer we sit here. JB and I have no chemistry; if we did, I would have felt it already.

Instantly.

"What about something fruity—don't all chicks dig those fruity drinks?" He laughs, eyes sparkling, as if he's just told a joke and expects me to laugh. "Sex on the Beach?"

It takes me several seconds to respond, and I seriously wish I could see the expression on my own face.

"I'll take a pass on a fruity drink, but thank you for the suggestion."

The guy winks. "No problem, babe."

"It's Skylar."

"Right." He shoots me another winning smile—one he probably considers a *wicked grin*—then licks his lips. "Tell me about your cat, Skylar."

"My cat?"

"Yeah, didn't you say you have a cat? I love animals, too."

"I don't have a cat."

"Oh, that's right—you're a dog person. Tell me about your dog."

What the hell is he talking about?

"I don't have one of those either. I said on the rare occasions I go running, I always stop to pet dogs. I never said I had one."

The menu in front of me that's been lying on the table gets pushed aside.

I clearly won't be needing it since I won't be staying.

JB is an asshole who clearly has no idea who I am.

Which means:

1. He's obviously talking to so many girls at the moment he can't keep any of them straight.
2. He's out for numbers, not something meaningful.
3. I am not the girl for him, and probably not even his type.

"Sorry, it's been a long day," he muses.

"Oh? How so?"

And he tells me. Every. Single. Detail about his day. How he had to wake up at the "ass crack of dawn and jog three fucking miles in the damn dark" then locked himself out of his house and had to go to class with no books while wearing a sweaty t-shirt and track pants.

"Jesus Christ, I was so hungry by the time I made it home this afternoon—after practice, of course. Totally brutal today." He shoots me a pointed look. "We have qualifiers for the WIAA championship coming up, so...yeah."

I have no idea what that's supposed to mean, but judging by his tone and his raised brow, JB is expecting me to be impressed.

I'm not.

I'm irritated.

He keeps talking, droning on above the music scream-ing out of the subwoofers, never once taking a breath so I can interject, ask a question, or participate in the conversa-tion.

"You know, I don't know what I'll do when I graduate, but I have clear goals. I'm getting a business degree but I think I'll end up working for my dad. Why not, right? I can make six figures straight out of college doing nothing but pushing pencils, and my dad knows a guy at this huge network so I can always try broadcasting. Nepotism at its finest, right? But who gives a shit if I don't have to work at getting a gig. Am I right or am I right?"

It sounds like a speech he has memorized and has giv-en dozens of times.

Gross.

"Only a fool would pass up an opportunity like that," is the only thing I can think to say.

Other phrases that come to mind that I don't have the lady balls to say: Where is the real JB and what have you done with him? and You are a freaking idiot and Why are you still talking?

Better yet, why am I still sitting here listening?

I'm the moron, not him.

What I should do is haul my ass up out of this booth, put on my damn jacket, and walk out.

So that's what I do.

I press my palms against the wooden table, the pads of my fingers landing in something unidentifiable and sticky, and push myself up to stand.

"Know what, Jack, I really think I need to get going."

He flips his phone over and checks the time. "Already? It's been like ten minutes."

I check the time on my phone.

Eight.

It's been eight excruciating minutes.

"It might have been longer if you'd shown up on time." I can't help mentioning it since he never did.

"Are you seriously pissed because I was late?"

"No. I don't even know you—and in hindsight, you actually did me a favor."

"That doesn't make sense."

I slide one arm into my puffy coat sleeve and then the other, bending to zip it. "If you'd been on time, I probably would have sat here longer trying to find something we might have in common when it's clear that there's nothing, which would have wasted more of my time."

"So? It's not like you had better shit to do tonight."

I pause. "That was a really rude thing to say."

"Hey, look—I'm just hungry. I know you like food, so let's order something. Don't you love tacos?"

No. I don't even like tacos.

"I don't think I'll be staying. Sorry."

"Really? You're going to leave?"

"Yeah, JB, I really am going to leave."

"How can I change your mind? Want to go back to my

place?"

That gives me pause. "And do what?"

The nerve of this guy!

"We can have drinks there."

"Oh, is that what you call sex? *Having drinks?*" I use air-quotes around the last two words and roll my eyes, pulling my gloves from my pockets. "Thanks but no thanks."

"Don't stand there and tell me you're not thirsty."

Thirsty.

There's a word no man on this earth has ever called me before.

Definition of thirsty: eager to get something, desperate, desperate for attention.

I ignore the hard knot forming in my stomach and the urge to lean over and smack the stupid smile off his dumb mouth. I ignore the desire to begin verbally sparring with him, knowing he will win, knowing I don't have the stomach to be snarky and it would fly over his head like a helium-filled balloon anyway.

"Have a great night, Jack."

Not.

I hope his night is shitty. And that he can't get hard later when he's jerking off because he came here to get laid but didn't.

Asshole.

Abe

"Hey asshole. That co-ed you set me up with tonight was the definition of frigid bitch."

My roommate lets the door slam behind him, kicking his shoes off against the wall, and I let my eyes roam over his outfit.

"Did you just come from the gym?" Why the fuck is he dressed like that?

"No, dude, I came from McGuillicudy's."

"From your date?"

His brows crease. "Yes."

"That's what you wore?"

"Ask me one more stupid question," he says, showing me his back as he strolls into the kitchen and yanks the fridge open.

"Jack, tell me that is not what you wore to meet Blue."

"Who?"

Jesus.

"The girl you had a date with tonight."

"She said her name was Skylar." He sounds affronted, like she lied about her name when, in fact, we hadn't even known what it was. "Why did you call her Blue?"

Skylar.

Now the moniker BlueAsTheSky makes so much sense. I roll this new information about her around in my head.

Skylar, Skylar, Skylar…

Damn. I can't stop saying it in my mind.

"Her name is Skylar?"

"That's what she said it was—was she full of shit?"

I ignore his question. "And that's what you wore on your date with her?"

"It wasn't a date—so what if this is what I wore?" JB looks down at his hoodie, stuffing his hands in his pockets. "I went straight from the gym."

"You look like you don't give a shit."

JB shrugs, stretching his shoulders and rolling the knots in his back. I hear it pop. "Because I don't. I'm not there to make conversation."

"Then what the hell is it you're doing?"

"You know I eventually want a girlfriend, but sometimes all I want is to get laid, bro."

"Which one was it tonight?" He knew this girl was the serious type; he said it himself—he'd seen her cardigans and knew she wasn't the kind of girl you nail and bail.

"A blowjob wouldn't have killed her, but she was obviously not the type."

"What makes you say that?"

He looks disgusted. "She was dressed up. Everyone knows that place is a shit-hole."

"And yet you keep taking girls there. Class it up, dude."

"Like I can afford to?"

Here's the thing: he totally can afford to. JB gets a stipend from the university for being an athlete *and* an allowance from his parents.

I think he rat-holes it, though we've never actually discussed it.

I don't get why he's being so cheap.

He was never like this when he was dating Tasha. I remember when they first met, he tripped all over himself, trying to impress her with home-cooked meals and expensive dates. When she dumped him, he actually sulked around the house for a good three weeks, all pissy and moody.

Then one day, it's like he woke up and had suddenly snapped out of his funk. "The best way to get over someone is to get under someone else," he told me one morning in the kitchen while shoveling cereal into his face from a giant mixing bowl and using a soup ladle as a spoon.

I stare at him now, blankly. "You know what, I don't think I can do this for you anymore. Clean up your own messes and find your own fucking dates—I'm done."

Jack stares, confused. "Why?"

Why?

"Because I do everything but wipe your ass, JB. I help with your homework, I find you chicks to date, I clean up after you around this place. You don't even know where the trash cans are."

"Yes I do—aren't they on the side of the house?"

"No, they're on the side of the garage by the alley. Jesus, Jack—grow up."

"Whoa, whoa, whoa." He reappears from behind the refrigerator door, shoving a hunk of pineapple into his gullet. "You can't tell me to grow up because I don't know where the fucking trash cans are, dude."

I realize then that no matter what I say, it's not going to sink in with him.

"Take some responsibility. That's all I'm saying."

"Honestly, what is your fucking problem right now?" He continues to eat, swiping a bagel off the counter and jamming that in his hole, too. "All I did was be myself tonight. I don't get what the issue is."

He's right.

All he did was be himself, and I need to chill out.

This is my business, but it's none of my business, which makes the whole situation kind of fucked up.

"You're right. You're just doing you."

Still, he cocks his head to the side as he chews, studying me. "You want me to message her and apologize or something? She seemed pretty pissed when she stormed off."

"She stormed off?"

He tears a chunk off the bagel with his teeth. "Yeah, in a huff or whatever."

Crap.

That's not good.

"I doubt you'll be able to come back from her storming off in a huff."

"Do I really want to? She wasn't into it, and neither was I."

"Probably a lost cause."

97

"Yeah," he agrees, using his forefinger to stuff in the last bite of bagel.

But, ten minutes later, when I close the door to my room and sink down onto my desk chair, I can't stop the guilty, nagging feeling inhabiting the pit of my damn stomach like a slowly spreading plague. I swivel, facing the bed, then rock back and forth, unsure.

Disconcerted.

This is none of my business.

Leave it be, Abe. No good will come of this.

It's a shame I don't listen to my own advice, fingers already opening LoveU and tapping on Blue's profile. I compose a message before I can think twice and change my mind.

Cause apparently JB isn't the only idiot in this house.

Me: *Hey. Have you blocked me yet?*

The little bubble at the top of the app appears then disappears. Then reappears again—which means she's typing.

Stops.

Types.

Then,

BlueAsTheSky: *I thought about it but haven't yet.*

BlueAsTheSky: *Obviously.*

Me: *Are you open to apologies?*

BlueAsTheSky: *I guess that depends; what are you apologizing for?*

Me: *Being an ass.*

BlueAsTheSky: *I'm listening...*

BlueAsTheSky: *But I have to be honest—I really didn't feel like we were a good match, and I'm not going to say I want to remain friends, because that's not why I'm doing this.*

Me: *I get that. And I'm sorry.*

BlueAsTheSky: *For what exactly? Say again and say it in my good ear.*

Okay. This is a good sign; she hasn't blocked me yet, and she's still talking to me—I mean, Jack—which means she was pissed but isn't a completely lost cause.

Me: *For being a complete asshole.*

BlueAsTheSky: *Not COMPLETELY...I'm sure there are worse guys out there than you. LOL*

Me: *I don't know what my problem was. All I can honestly say is I don't normally act like that.*

BlueAsTheSky: *What do you normally act like, then? Because I'm going to be totally honest—that seemed like status quo behavior.*

BlueAsTheSky: *I'm not looking to be a notch on anyone's bedpost.*

I can't resist saying, I don't have bedposts.

BlueAsTheSky: *Too soon for jokes, bro.*

Me: *Did you just call me bro?*

BlueAsTheSky: *LOL it felt like the right moment.*

Me: *Indeed it did.*

Me: *Anyway. I'm glad you didn't block me, because I feel like a dick about the way I acted tonight. I came from practice and was distracted, and that's shitty but it's the truth.*

BlueAsTheSky: *It's fine.*

I have a strange feeling if we were having an actual conversation about this, in person, she'd be saying *It's fine* in a way that means it's not fine at all—the way girls say it when they're setting a trap and want to argue.

Bet her lips would be pursed. Chin tilted up.

I wonder what Skylar looks like in person, since I've only ever stared at the few photos she uploaded in the app. We haven't sent selfies—I couldn't even if I wanted to, since I'm pretending to be Jack.

BlueAsTheSky: *No harm done. But I don't think I want to see you again—sorry.*

Me: *I was that bad?*

BlueAsTheSky: *Yes, you were that bad.*

What the hell did JB do on this date?

BlueAsTheSky: *So, if there is nothing else you need...*

She's trying to give me the brushoff, but I'm not ready to let her go yet.

Me: *There is no way I can make it up to you?*

BlueAsTheSky: *I don't think so.*

Me: *What if...*

I pause, not sure how to end the sentence.

BlueAsTheSky: *What if...?*

Me: *What if we go out again, and I let you pick the place?*

BlueAsTheSky: *I don't know, JB... I think we both need to move on. It was fun talking to you, but in person we have nothing in common.*

She's right; *they* have nothing in common and never will. Because Skylar is sweet and funny, and Jack is a complete douchebag with fucked-up priorities who isn't ready to settle down with anyone, and certainly not someone like Blue.

What he wants right now is the physical gratification—not an emotional connection—that he isn't getting in the weight room or in the middle of the wrestling mat.

Blue wants more, and she'll never find it with my roommate.

So why won't I let this go?

Give it a rest, Abe.

BlueAsTheSky: *You know I'm right about this. It's not like you were into me, either.*

She couldn't be more right, but I'm not going to insult her by agreeing.

BlueAsTheSky: *There are better girls out there for you than me, someone who's okay with a one-night stand and isn't going to get her feelings hurt when you don't mes-*

sage her the next day.

All very true.

Me*: Maybe that's not what I need right now.*

God, what the hell am I saying.

Jack is going to kill me when he sees this.

BlueAsTheSky*: Are you saying this because you hate the fact that I walked away from you? And not the other way around?*

Me*: No, that's not it at all.*

BlueAsTheSky*: Then what is it? Because tonight you didn't seem to care that I left before even ordering a drink.*

Shit. She hadn't even ordered *anything*?

How long was the date, fifteen minutes?

Me*: I have a lot of pride, but not THAT much pride. I know when I've screwed up.*

I do. Me, Abe.

I'm suddenly speaking for myself, not for my room-mate, who almost always screws up but makes no apologies for his behavior.

Me? I can't live like that. I'm always atoning for my sins and mistakes—though few and far between they may be.

I try not to be a dick.

BlueAsTheSky: *Hmm.*

Me*: Is that a good hmm or a bad hmmm?*

BlueAsTheSky: *I'm thinking about it.*

Hope springs up inside my chest, but I tamp it down—because even if she agrees to go out with me again, it's going to be with Jack.

Unless...

Me: *Do you have any single friends?*

BlueAsTheSky: *Yes...*

BlueAsTheSky: *Why?*

Me: *We could double date. I have a single roommate. Remember, he's a tutor?*

There's a long pause before she responds, but that bubble continues to appear, disappear, and reappear.

BlueAsTheSky: *Oh? Tell me more about this roommate of yours—do you have much in common?*

Me: *If you're trying to find out if he's a douchebag, the answer is no. He's a pretty decent guy.*

BlueAsTheSky: *How so?*

Me: *The guys on the team call him Grandpa because he's so responsible.*

BlueAsTheSky: *Why is he single?*

I hate this question, as if being single is as bad as having a contagious disease. And far be it from me to point out that she is single, too, and not once have I asked why.

I wasn't interested before.

But I am now.

Me: *He studies a lot when he's not practicing.*

BlueAsTheSky: *Practicing what?*

Me: *He's a wrestler, too.*

BlueAsTheSky: *Hmmm?*

What the hell does that mean?

Me: *But he's quiet, doesn't go out much.*

BlueAsTheSky: *Kind of like a hermit? What's wrong with him?*

Me: *Noting is wrong with him; he's just not into partying and casual dating.*

BlueAsTheSky: *I see.*

BlueAsTheSky: *Will he talk, or is he gonna just sit there?*

Me: *He'll talk, LOL—he's not a mute.*

BlueAsTheSky: *Well I DON'T KNOW—you said he doesn't go out much so I assumed he doesn't like peopling.*

Me: *What the hell is peopling?*

BlueAsTheSky: *You know, going out in public. Seeing people. Some people hate people LOL*

BlueAsTheSky: *What's his name?*

Me: *Are you going to look him up?*

BlueAsTheSky: *Probably. I have to—I have to know who I'm setting my friend up with.*

Me: *Which friend?*

BlueAsTheSky: *My roommate is single. Her name is Hannah.*

Me: *My roommate's name is Abe.*

BlueAsTheSky: *Abe _____ (fill in blank) If I'm going to properly stalk him, I'll need his full name. Please and thank you.*

Me: *Abe Davis*

Silence.

Absolute silence, and I—

BlueAsTheSky: *Gosh. Abe Davis is kind of super cute. No offense.*

Another sensation forms in my gut; instead of guilt, this one feels more like a sucker punch of stone, cold irony to the stomach. She thinks Abe Davis is cute, doesn't really care for JB.

Me: *Why would I be offended?*

BlueAsTheSky: *Because I just called your roommate cute.*

Me: *Correction—you called him Super Cute.*

BlueAsTheSky: *He's not a superhero—you can lay off making it a proper noun.*

Me: *I have to though.*

BlueAsTheSky: *LOL*

105

Me: *So does that mean you're willing to double date?*

BlueAsTheSky: *Um. Sure. I think she'd be cool with that, and it'll be nice to have two other people there so you'll be on your best behavior...*

Me: *Very funny.*

BlueAsTheSky: *It's the truth. I wasn't impressed with you—AT. ALL.*

Me: *You don't hold back, do you?*

BlueAsTheSky: *I see no reason to.*

Me: *Obviously not.*

My roommate was being such a bitch I changed all my passwords on her. Now that's a 21st Century slap in the face, ladies & gentleman.

Skylar

"**I**s that what you're wearing?"

Hannah is already pestering me from her bedroom door, and I ignore her.

She fills the silence. "The correct answer is no. No, you cannot wear that on this date."

"But—"

"Ah ah ah!" Hannah tsks. "I don't care if he wore pajamas on your first date. You are not wearing those gross leggings. Put on jeans and have a little dignity. Show him what he's missing by acting like douche dribble."

What the fuuuu...

"I *can't* believe you just said that."

She gives her hair a toss. "Do you like it? Douche dribble."

"Oh, I heard you the first time."

"Heard it in the cafeteria yesterday when I was grabbing a salad between classes."

"It's godawful."

"It's *creative*."

She sounds so put out that I laugh, giving her a once-over. She's not taking this date seriously either, judging by her barely made-up face and the straight hair she refuses to take time to curl.

We both decided earlier this date with JB is probably

going to be a waste of time—once a douchebag, always a douchebag.

"Throw those jeans on and let's get this show on the road," Miss Bossy Pants tells me, pointing at the bed, where the dark denim is neatly folded and waiting to be put on.

"I wasn't actually going to wear leggings, just so you know."

"Bullshit." Hannah laughs. "Don't lie."

"Fine. I was planning on wearing the leggings." But with a cute shirt—so it's not like I planned on looking like a slob.

Sheesh.

"If you don't hurry, we're going to be late."

I give her a blank stare. "The plan was to purposely get there late, remember."

"Yeah, but—"

"I know being late is going to make you twitchy, but we're trying to prove a point here."

My best friend *hates* being late; promptness is a virtue written deep in the Book of Hannah. I've told her a million times she should probably reevaluate our friendship and find someone who isn't perpetually tardy for the party every time her foot steps out the door like I am.

"What was the point we're trying to make? Remind me."

I sigh. I've gone over this with her a million times. "JB was late for our first date and didn't apologize when he walked in."

He might have sent his apologies via app message, but that wasn't until hours later.

"If by some miracle this date goes better and I see him again, I don't want to set a precedent that he can take me for granted. I have to prove a point."

Hannah sighs. "Fair enough."

"So you're going to have to chillax."

"Roger that. Chillaxing." My roommate pauses. "Who is this guy I'm going out with again?"

I grab a jacket from my closet and shut the door. "JB's roommate—his name is Abe."

Once I had a name, I did what any decent friend and roommate would do: I stalked Abe online to make sure he wasn't a creeper. Honestly, I'm already a bit jealous because Abraham Davis looks like a great guy—if one can tell that from a few pictures on the internet. Tons of wrestling photos of him on the mats. Many wins.

His eyes.

Something about those eyes of his made me sigh as I stared at his wrestling headshot; they're deep and brown and *kind*.

Abe is honest and kind. Don't ask me how I know; I just *do*.

Thick black hair that looks freshly cut.

Skin the color of light bronze.

He's beautiful.

If I'm being truthful, I'm more attracted to him than I am to JB, but that fact hardly matters because he is not who my date is with.

I shake my head, trying to get Abe's image out of my mind, superficially focusing on my outfit instead. Toss on my jacket and pull on my boots, knowing it won't do me any good to dwell on the wrong handsome face, the one that has been consuming my thoughts since I googled him.

It's going to be a long night.

Low and behold, JB is on time.

The guys are inside the restaurant when we walk in, Hannah giving her stride a bit of sashay. Hips swinging dramatically as she cases the joint, eyes roaming the entire restaurant.

It's an actual restaurant.

Not a bar. Not a grill. Not a combination of the two.

You can't get pitas here, or wraps, or soup and sand-wiches—it's a nice, sit-down establishment. One I hadn't heard of before but that JB randomly pulled out of his ass as a suggestion.

I'm suitably impressed, and so is Hannah.

She lets out a low whistle when the hostess tells us our dates are waiting for us at the bar near the lobby.

"Nice place. He must really be dying to get into your granny panties."

I nudge her in the ribcage. "Shut up. I'm not wearing granny panties."

"Liar." She laughs.

Yeah, she's right—I totally am. "They're your underwear, so I wouldn't laugh so hard if I were you."

"Shit. You're right."

The fact that we share underwear to begin with, let alone our comfortable, cotton panties would gross most people out. But after doing laundry and not knowing whose underwear was whose—because we shop together, too—we both gave up and now just grab whichever pair from the dryer.

"Pull down your shirt." Hannah tugs at my collar, and I slap her hand away.

"Knock it off!"

"Show a little boob."

"I have no boobs." The shirt I threw on is black, cotton, and off the shoulder. Nothing too sexy, just a bit flirty, it's a glorified t-shirt. "If I pull down my shirt, it will be down to my belly button—there is nowhere to go but down."

"Exactly."

"Don't be such a tramp." I give her the side-eye, glancing over her pretty, light pink sweater and jeans. Cute and conservative, funny considering she kept trying to sex me up before we left the apartment.

Hypocrite.

Then again, she's not really in this to find a boyfriend.

"Chin up, tits out." One last reminder from her and I paste on a smile, heading toward JB and his roommate, Abe.

Wow.

Abe Davis in photographs is nothing like Abe Davis in person.

Tall. Broad.

Dark.

Friendly.

His eyes are smiling—his mouth, too—and that smile is directed at me. Not Hannah.

Not the cute hostess behind us with the menus. Not the pretty little waitress throwing both guys a teasing glance as she saunters past us. I watch as she gives them both a once-over before passing and glancing over her shoulder.

"Skylar." JB's hands are shoved in his pockets, and he's dressed himself up a bit. Not much, but it's a vast improvement over the hoodie and track pants he wore on our first date. This time it's a black half-zip, embroidered Iowa logo on the chest, dark jeans. Freshly washed hair—it's still damp—and black tennis shoes.

Abe, on the other hand…

With a black leather jacket draped over his forearm, he's wearing a navy blue polo shirt tucked into jeans with a belt and dress shoes.

I stare.

I stare, and I can't help myself, because his eyes are incredible and they're looking right at me, and I'm looking back and—

Stop it, Skylar. You are not here for him.

You are here with JB.

JB.

The guy barely knows what to do with himself, not at all at ease, clearly finding himself in unfamiliar territory.

113

"Hey guys." I peel my eyes off of Abe Davis and force myself to smile at JB. "You're on time."

"Why wouldn't we be?" JB laughs. "They have our table ready if we want to sit down. I'm fucking famished."

Next to him, Abe loudly coughs into the palm of his hand.

"Sorry. I mean—I'm hungry."

"Should we do introductions first?" I suggest. "Guys, this is my roommate, Hannah. Hannah, this is JB, and… Abe, is it?"

Abe transfers his jacket from one arm to the other, offering Hannah his free hand, pumping it once. "Good to meet you."

She shifts her weight from one foot to the other, not impressed. "Hi."

"Should we sit? It will be easier to talk at the table," Abe politely suggests.

We sit. We order drinks. We get menus.

An awkward silence ensues, and I rack my brain for a topic of conversation—but Abe beats me to it.

Words are coming out of his mouth, but I'm barely listening, fixated on his straight white teeth, the small cleft in his chin.

"…right, Jack?" He nudges his roommate into action.

"Right."

"Who's Jack? You?" Hannah asks.

I like that name, even though I don't necessarily care for him. We've been here less than ten minutes and already

I know this whole second date is for naught; I'm not going to fall in love with or date JB.

"I'm sorry, can you repeat that?" I ask, feeling like a complete idiot.

"I was saying that being part of a team is great, but at some point, that can't be all there is. And JB agreed with me." His dark eyes bore into me as he explains himself, long lashes blinking every so often, tiny indent at the corner of his mouth pressing into his skin.

Kind of want to press my finger there.

Abe blinks at me.

I blink back.

He seriously needs to stop watching me like this; it's making me nervous, sweaty, and excited. It's making me feel things I have no right to feel for someone I've only just met, someone who is not my date.

Butterflies. Flutters.

Feels.

"You know what?" Hannah stands abruptly. "I think I want something from the bar. All the drinks." She moves around the table, bumping JB—he's seated at the end of it—with her hip. "Come give me a hand."

Come give me a hand? What the heck is she doing?

It takes JB a few seconds to rise; he's confused and clueless—until Hannah grabs a fistful of his shirt and tugs. "Move it or lose it. I need a hand, and you look strong."

Above their heads, she rolls her eyes then pointedly glances down at the back of Abe's head. Wiggles her well-manicured eyebrows before leading my date to the bar. My

115

gaze trails along after them.

What the...

We're alone.

I'm alone, in a room full of people, with Abe.

Okay. No big deal.

I can handle this; I'm an adult!

"Is it just me, or was that weird?" I blurt out, trying to sound nonchalant.

"Is your roommate a drunk? How many drinks does she plan on ordering?" Abe wonders out loud with a laugh. "Furthermore, why couldn't she have just ordered from the waitress when she came back?"

"Are you pre-law?"

He laughs, and it's magic. "No. Not even close."

I bite back a huge grin. "Well, I stopped trying to figure Hannah out years ago. She's been my best friend since we were little and I've been confused by her every single minute of every day since we met." I take a sip from my water, which is iced down and has a lemon it in. "What do you think of her?"

There's a long pause. "Honestly? I don't know yet. She hasn't said much."

She hasn't, which is so unlike her. "I don't know what her problem is—she's usually the chatty one."

"It's fine. This setup is kind of..."

I try to guess what he's thinking. "Not feeling it?"

"I didn't say that." Beneath the soft fabric of his shirt, I see the muscles of his shoulders contract, letting my eyes skim curiously down the front of him. Over the firm muscles of his pecs, nipples stiff.

He inadvertently flexes his arms, the thick biceps strong and—

Um.

No.

Skylar, *focus*.

But wow, those arms…

"So, are you on the LoveU app, too?"

His body goes still. "No."

"I didn't think so. I feel like I would have seen you."

"Oh yeah?" he teases. "Would you have swiped right?"

Yes.

No.

I don't know. I would have wanted to but probably would have been too scared. Or intimidated. Chickenshit, as my friends like to call me. Abe is terribly handsome, larger than life, and kind.

He seems like the kind of guy who could have any girl on campus if he set his mind to it; what would he want with a girl like me?

I might not be a great student, but I try hard-ish, sort of study (kind of), work hard, love my friends—but I am no brainiac or social butterfly. I don't do parties, I'm not in a sorority. I don't play a sport, not even intramurals. I don't wear tons of makeup, or have extensions, or fake eyelashes. My lips aren't plump and juicy, and nothing about me inspires sexual fantasies.

I'm just me. Regular me.

I was enough for JB to swipe on, the little voice inside my head interjects. Good-looking, athletic, not-too-bright Jack Bartlett.

He swiped on me, but he turned out to be some sort of fuck boy.

I don't know Abe Davis, but every instinct tells me he's nothing like his roommate—nothing at all.

"Would I have swiped on you?" I play with my straw. "The better question here is would you have swiped on *me*—that's what I want to know, since you asked." I push out a laugh; it sounds forced, even to my own ears, and I wonder if he can hear it too.

The vulnerability. It's something I don't want to project.

"In a heartbeat." No hesitation, quick nod of the chin to go along with it.

Well then.

My face flushes bright pink, heating my neck as I wonder what that might mean—what would have happened if it had been Abe contacting me that night instead of Jack?

What date would this be? Number two? Three?

In a heartbeat.

In a heartbeat...

Those words do something to my heart and it swells, pleased. Three words. So simple. So damn *nice* to hear...

"Did you know last year JB raised the most amount of money for a campus fundraiser?"

"Um, no, I didn't. Which one was it?"

"The Lambdas host an auction every spring, and last year Jack had the highest bid. The cause is reading programs for at-risk youth."

I twirl my straw around my glass. "So what you're telling me is girls went wild for the guy and bid stupid crazy amounts of money so he'd take them out?"

"Yeah."

"What did they end up doing?"

He's silent a few seconds. "Car wash."

My head tilts to the side. "A car wash." My voice has no inflection. "That makes no sense."

"Er. A, um. Topless carwash."

"What the hell is *that*?" I quickly cover my mouth with the palm of my hand. "Sorry."

"JB washed a bunch of cars with no shirt on."

"While they gawked at him." Probably got him all soapy with buckets of water, too.

"There was probably some gawking, yes." He looks a little sheepish now.

"Well." I sound like a prude; I even feel my lips purse tightly. It's the face my grandmother makes when she's pissed at my mom. "Sounds like an elaborate ploy to get some guy you have the hots for to take his shirt off instead of just watching him in the gym like normal girls do when they're creeping. There are cheaper ways to go about it."

And I highly doubt JB auctioning himself off to a bunch of women was charitably motivated.

I can barely contain my eye roll.

Abe stares. "I hadn't thought of it that way."

That's because men and women think differently, hailing from completely different planets according to the author of *Men Are From Mars, Women Are From Venus*.

"He likes to draw."

"Who does?"

"Jack."

"I like to color—does that count?"

Abe laughs. "Like those adult coloring books for relaxation and shit?"

It really does sound nerdy.

Embarrassed, I giggle. "Hey pal, don't knock it. I've invested a lot of time and money in markers."

"No judging." He pauses. "Know what I do to relax that's weird? I have one of those slime containers and I sit and play with it at my desk when no one is looking."

"Stop it, you do not. What color is it?"

"Blue."

"Do you watch those 'oddly satisfying' videos online, too?"

Another laugh. "Sometimes. Do you?"

"Duh—doesn't everyone?"

"No!" He cackles. "No they do *not*. Because it's lame!"

"We are the furthest thing from lame, Abraham."

He goes still for the second time since we've been alone. "Good guess."

"Not really. I stalked you online before I agreed to this double date."

He's quiet again, tearing at a tiny, pink sugar packet. "Find out anything interesting about me?"

"Not really." I laugh. "Tons of wrestling stuff. Some pictures from high school."

"And you decided I wasn't a murderer."

"Statistically, I'm more likely to get murdered on a date than by a stranger in my own home." I'm stating facts, but it makes us both laugh. "So technically, you still have time to kill me. Or Hannah, I mean. Her. Not me."

Abe's white smile is blinding against his darker skin and my eyes linger on his mouth; mine curves too, mimicking his expression. Dopey, kind of.

Smitten.

God, he is so cute, his eyes the perfect shade of brown, and if he was my date, I'd reach out and run my palm along the clean cut of his hair. I wonder if it's as coarse as it looks, wonder what it would feel like beneath my fingertips.

Oh god, this is bad.

He breaks the spell. "Right. Hannah."

"Hannah."

He raises a brow. "*Jack.*"

Hannah and Jack: the reason we're sitting here now.

And speak of the devil…

"We're back!" Hannah sing-songs, carrying two glasses, setting one in front of me as she plops down, filling the empty chair across from me.

JB has a drink, too; it looks like a cocktail, amber colored and full of ice. He takes a swig, and I try to admire the column of his throat where his Adam's apple bobs when he swallows. It's a nice throat, clean shaven and thick. Athletic.

Meaty, one might say, if one were into that sort of thing.

Lord, listen to me, describing him like I've just popped out of a historical novel.

His lips are wet when he's done, and I do my best to imagine kissing his mouth. Full bottom lip, a bit pouty. Strong jawline. Masculine chin I imagine gets dark from beard stubble shortly after it's been shaved.

JB's hair is still wet and badly in need of a trim, but it works for him. He's an athlete and looks like one—a bit rough around the edges, scarred and bruised. Disheveled and unkempt.

Scruffy in a way most girls love these days, just not... me.

I don't love it. He is not my type.

When JB raises his glass for another chug of whatever he's drinking, I can't help notice Abe elbowing him in the gut.

JB sets the glass down.

Hmm. That's weird, right?

My head tilts to the side, thoughtful.

Vigilant.

"JB here used to be the captain of the wrestling team," Abe informs the table, like he's suddenly become the factotum of all things JB.

"*Used* to be?" Hannah snickers, and I want to smack her.

"When was that?" I ask, kicking her under the table to shut her up, hoping it's her shin my toe made contact with.

"Sophomore year for about five minutes," JB answers without expanding on the thought.

"And you're a junior?"

"Yeah."

Riveting.

"What about you, Abe?" Hannah gives her attention to him, batting her eyelashes. "What year are you?"

"Junior."

"Have you ever been the captain of the wrestling team?"

"No. I've never had the honor."

"What else do you do besides wrestle? Are you a party boy? Do you go out a lot?" Hannah asks the questions rapid-fire, sucking through the straw of her soda.

"I study a lot—I don't make time to go out. I haven't been to a party in months." He shoots a gaze in my direction. "I, uh, like to cook."

This interests my roommate, and she leans in. "Oh? What's your favorite?"

"Italian food."

"The nerd makes his own pasta." JB laughs, seizing the opportunity to chug down his liquor.

Hannah gives him her murder face. "It's not nerdy to

make your own noodles." She's biting her tongue; I know she wants to tack on an insult to the end of her sentence, but for once, she doesn't. "It's nice. More guys should have a life skill instead of just being *pretty*."

Jack's nostrils flare. "Did you just call me pretty?"

Hannah snorts. Then shrugs. "Get over yourself."

Oh Jesus.

"Are you always a salty bi—"

"Okay! Who wants to order an appetizer?" Abe practically shouts, craning his head for the waitress, who hasn't reappeared since taking our drink orders. We need drinks. And food. And a referee.

The restaurant is busy, but not crazy enough that she should be ignoring us.

Hannah glares across the table at my date, lip curled. "I've suddenly lost my appetite."

At this point, I notice a theme unfolding. Abe not only does most of the talking, he's the voice box for both of them; JB doesn't seem to have an original thought of his own. He's a yes man, agreeing with every word coming from his roommate's gorgeous mouth.

"Skylar babe." My roommate slides out of the booth and stands next to the table. "Care to join me in the ladies' room for a second?"

Did she just call me *babe*?

Still hungry, I look down at my plate, the warm, half-eaten food I've been too nervous to actually eat. "Not really?"

She rolls her eyes, giving me a tight-lipped smile. Grabs a handful of my shirt and tugs. "I need your help."

It's on the tip of my tongue to ask, *With what?* but I manage to zip my lips.

This is the fourth time Hannah has gotten up from the table since we've gotten here, once when she went to the bar and twice with JB to find music on the jukebox.

"Want to tell me why you're being such a troll?" I hiss as she goes in one stall, me into another. "Can you not behave for five seconds?"

Unzip my jeans. Squat above the toilet seat and start peeing.

"That guy is a douche. Why are we wasting our time here?" She huffs a loud, dramatic sigh. "Let's leave."

"We can't just walk out!"

I can hear her pants unzipping. "Why?"

"It's rude!" I practically shout, voice echoing, bouncing off the tile walls. "We don't have our purses!"

"Valid point."

"Jack being a dick isn't good enough reason to bail without saying goodbye." I hunt for the end of the toilet paper, dipping my head to peer under the dispenser. Find it and wipe. "You've called him a dickhead three times."

"Because he is a prickhead! I'm being generous."

"How kind of you," I mutter, pulling up my underwear and jeans as I stand, flushing the toilet with the tip of my shoe. Join Hannah by the sinks to wash my hands.

125

She's watching me through the mirror. "Want me to try to give you time with Abe? I'm willing to take one for the team and get that dick back to the bar if you want to be alone with Wrestler McHottie. Did you see his hands? My. God."

Yes, I did notice his hands. Large hands. Strong fingers...

"Why would you do that?"

Our reflections are an old western showdown. "Duh. He's into you. JB isn't."

"He isn't?"

"No. He is into *himself.*" She stops drying her hands to turn and stare at me blankly. "Did you hear any of what I just said?"

Douche. Dick.

Prickhead.

That's a new one; I should stop her before she creates new, more creative insults, but I'm curious to see where she'll go with this.

"Yes. You just said JB isn't into me."

Her head shakes. "No, Skylar. I'm talking about the part where I said Abe *is* into you—the critical part of the storyline. That boy is beautiful and hot, and you'd be an idiot not to go back out there and flirt with him."

"Have you forgotten? I am on a date with his roommate *right now!*" What the hell is wrong with her?

"So? I'll distract that sack of crap you're here with, and you get to know the one who can't stop staring at you."

"Don't you dare, Hannah—I will kill you."

"Please. I agreed to this little farce we're calling a *double date* as a favor. Now do *yourself* a favor—ditch the idiot for the guy who seems to really like you." She suddenly shifts gears, softening her approach. "Skylar, every time you open your mouth to talk, he smiles."

"Shut up, he does not." Does he?

"Wanna make a bet?"

Yes. "Pfft. *No!*"

Hannah leans against the counter, which has somehow become completely saturated with water. "I bet you, the next time you talk, the corners of Abe's mouth turn up like this." Her lips twitch slightly, curving into a miniscule grin. She taps the corner of her mouth with the tip of her finger to show me how he'll smile. "Just like this. You'll see what I mean—all you have to do is speak."

I roll my eyes. She's delirious.

"You're so clueless sometimes, Skylar. You could march back out there and announce to the boys that you have your period, and Abe would smile like an idiot. It couldn't be more obvious that he thinks you're cute, but he's not going to make a move—not with dipshit sitting there. Bro code and all that."

Would he? Would he have been into me if I'd met him first?

He would have swiped on me in a heartbeat...

Or had he just said that to be polite? He seems like the type that knows manners—when and what to say to avoid hurting someone's feelings.

"Take the bet, Sky. You'll see what I'm talkin' about."

127

I shoot her a dark scowl. "I'm not making any more bets with you."

This wouldn't be the first time; Hannah loves making bets. Harmless ones for the most part, to liven things up.

"Come on." She nudges me with an elbow then presses her hands together pleadingly. "Take a chance."

"All I've been doing lately is taking chances, thanks to you. I didn't want to download that stupid app in the first place, and now look at the mess I'm in!" I ball up the brown paper towel I used to dry my hands and toss it in the trash can. "I'm on a date with a guy who is nothing like he is online. It's as if he's not even the same person!"

Hannah ignores my ranting. "I bet you my car."

"Your car?!" Is she insane?

She rolls her eyes. "I *mean* you can drive it for a week. You can't have the damn thing—I'm not insane."

Oh.

Still. Her car is a sweet ride, while mine is a total piece of shit.

"You know you want to." She should start a career in sales; she knows how to relentlessly browbeat me into submission. I'm such a chump.

But I do really like her car…

"Fine." I say it like she's putting me out. "It's a bet."

Hannah literally rubs her hands together. "Oh, this is gonna be good…"

Dammit. She's right.

Every time I've opened my mouth to talk, Abe has smiled. Oh, he hides it well enough; I'll give him kudos for that, burying his mouth in the collar of his shirt or coughing so no one sees him.

No one but me.

And Hannah, the eagle eye out to prove a point.

But sure enough, there it is again, plastered to his face, making me blush and squirm in my seat, and resent the guy I'm here on a date with.

JB has done nothing to redeem himself in the time we've been sitting at this table, picking at the appetizers we finally ordered.

If anything, he's more arrogant and flippant with an audience than he was on our first date.

"Abe, tell me." Hannah touches Abe's forearm, purposely trailing a finger along the firm muscles. "Do you date much? You seem like a great catch, so where are you hiding yourself?"

Oh brother. She sounds like a forty-year-old woman out on the prowl.

I try not to groan out loud.

"Abe date?" JB laughs rudely.

"He's on one now, isn't he?" Hannah volleys back, removing her hand from her date's arm.

"Abe here is always the bridesmaid, never the bride." He claps a huge hand on his friend's shoulder, giving him a shake that's slightly aggressive for the circumstances. "Ain'tcha, buddy."

Abe's nostrils flare and he chooses that moment to lift his ice water and chug down a healthy swig, downing half the glass in a single swallow.

"Wow. You just keep racking up the douche points, don't you?"

JB's brows shoot clear up into his hairline, expression incredulous. "What the hell did I say now?"

Hannah leans back against the booth, crossing her arms over her pair of amazing boobs. She plucks an imaginary piece of lint off her gray sweater. "You think you're the only catch at this table? Please."

JB's grin is slow and lazy and directed at my roommate's cleavage. "Are you talking about yourself?"

"Um, no—I'm talking about Abe. I bet he could give you a run for your money if your head wasn't stuck up your own ass." Hannah straightens in her seat. "You're the kind of guy who cockblocks his friends, aren't you? Even if a girl was into Abe, you're the douchey friend who swoops in and steals her away to be a dick. Aren't you?"

I've lost count of how many times she's lobbed out the D word tonight.

"Okay." I toss my napkin on the table and rise, shoving my chair out in the process. "I think this has gone on long enough." I have to get my friend out of here before she grabs a butter knife and stabs my date with it. She's seething, nearly hissing like a feral cat.

She either hates JB or wants to bone him, and I can't figure out which one it is. Sexual tension rises off both of them like steam from a hot bath, and I have no interest in seeing how this little scene is going to play out.

We'll be booted from the restaurant first. Once Hannah latches onto an idea, she rolls with it, and right now, she's homing in on the idea of a verbal altercation with JB.

It's time to exit stage right.

Snatching my purse, I grab her by the back of the shirt, tugging her up. "We're going."

"But I was just getting started."

"I know. That's why we're leaving." I snag her purse, too, shooting Abe an apologetic look. "Sorry guys."

"Don't say *sorry guys*—don't apologize to that asshole." Hannah's chin tilts up. "She won't be seeing you again. We don't like you like that."

Oh my god.

I hold in my laugh—*barely*—and catch Abe's eyes. They're boring into me, intense. Dark. Troubled, too, his expression almost unreadable.

Why is he looking at me like that?

Is he mad we're ditching mid-date? I don't actually consider this ditching, though; it's more like an emergency evacuation.

Does he seriously expect me to sit here and let my best friend *destroy* his roommate with a sharp-witted tongue-lashing? Not going to happen.

"You don't like me like that?" JB, on the other hand, couldn't look more affronted. He's clearly shocked. "I don't like you either, babe."

Babe?

I snort, mouth open to retort.

Hannah beats me to it. "Skylar is too nice to say this to your face, so I'm going to say it for her: you're nothing like your conversations on the app. Before, you were charming and smart and funny. In person you're just... such...an...idiot."

Okay. That was a bit harsh. I never would have said that...

To his face.

But she isn't finished. "Maybe if you acted more like your app self, you'd stand a chance with her."

Can I get an amen?

"*Bye.*" Hannah's hands are planted on her hips.

JB laughs. "See ya."

"We're *going.*"

"Bye."

I literally have to grab her arm so we actually do some leaving instead of embarrassing ourselves further.

"You don't get to be the last one to say bye. We're the ones saying b—"

My roommate gets a shove toward the door. "Oh my god, shut up! Stop trying to get the last word in."

"But he—"

"I'm going to kill you. I really am." This couldn't have gone any more terribly unless an actual murder had taken place. Perhaps my hands wrapping around her neck to strangle her.

"Why are you yelling at me?" Hannah has the lady balls to ask as I shove her through the front door, the little hostess fascinated by the spectacle of us.

"I'm not yelling! This isn't yelling!" I yell once we're in the parking lot. "Get in the car! Get. In. The. Car!"

Hannah rawrs like a cat.

"I hate when you do that," I grumble, glaring at her over the roof of my piece-of-shit car, secretly hoping she bangs her forehead on the doorframe (as she so often does) as punishment for being obnoxious.

It doesn't happen.

She glides in unscathed, perfect hair still perfect. Lipstick completely intact. Skin dewy.

"Well," she says, buckling herself in. "I think that could have gone better."

I twist my torso, facing her, mouth falling open. "Are you for real right now? That was a train wreck."

She yawns. "I did you a favor."

"How?"

"He's definitely *never* going to want to see you again."

Neither is Abe.

JB: *Hey*

Me*: Uh. Hey?*

JB*: Don't be so surprised.*

Me*: You're seriously messaging me right now? I would have thought you'd have unmatched me for sure.*

JB: *Why?*

Me*: Are you insane? That date was a disaster.*

JB: *LOL*

Me*: My roommate's face is still blue from the outrage.*

JB*: What did she think of Abe?*

Me*: She didn't. She was too busy hating on you. Sorry, this isn't going to work. I assumed you realized that when I was dragging her out of the restaurant.*

Me*: Or are you one of those guys who likes psychopaths? Do you love being in dramatic relationships? Are you a glutton for punishment?*

JB*: No, no, and no.*

Me*: Then WHY ARE YOU MESSAGNING ME*

JB*: Wait—did you just call yourself a psychopath?*

Me*: No. But I could be.*

JB*: You're too nice to be nuts.*

Me*: The last guy who called me nuts disappeared. They haven't heard from him since.*

JB*: See? We can get along…*

Me*: …but not in person, apparently. We're destined to be pen pals, sorry dude.*

JB*: Ouch—you called me dude. That's friend zone shit right there.*

Me: *Even that's a stretch.*

JB: *So, while we're on the subject, what did YOU think of Abe?*

Me: *Your roommate? I wasn't thinking of him at all. Should I have been?*

JB: *No. Just wondering what you thought.*

Me: *Why. Did he say something?*

Me: *About me, specifically?*

JB: *Yeah, we talked about it.*

Me: *Oh?*

Me: *Be honest—he thinks we're a terrible match.*

JB: *It did come up, LOL*

Me: *Awesome…*

Me: *What else did he say?*

JB: *For someone who's not interested in my roommate, you sure seem interested in what he had to say about you.*

Me: *So you admit he said some things about me…*

JB: *A few things.*

Me: *Like?*

JB: *The usual.*

Me: *I swear to God, if you're going to continue dangling bait and then not telling me anything, I'm hanging* *up.*

JB: ***eye roll***

Me: *You know what I mean…*

JB: *How about we do this: you give me a detail about yourself, and I'll tell you one thing Abe said about you.*

Me: *Oddly, that sounds like extortion.*

JB: *#Semantics. Take it or leave it.*

Me: *OR we do this: for every detail you tell me about Abe, you also give me one thing he said about me after the double date from hell.*

JB: *You're calling it the double date from hell, too??!!!*

Me: *Haha, very funny…*

JB: *Why are you suddenly curious about Abe?*

Me: *You're the one who brought him up.*

JB: ***shrugs** Suit yourself…*

Me: *Just riddle me this: it's obvious I'm not your type, so why do you care to hear details? I'm not the kind of girl you're going to date, and I wouldn't go out with you again if I was being paid…*

Me: *…okay MAYBE if I was being paid. But it would have to be a lot of money.*

JB: *Since when is it a bad thing to want to know information about someone?*

Me: *It's not in most cases except this one, LOL. I don't* *like you. Like—at all.*

JB: *Did you like Abe?*

Me: *What would make you ask that?*

JB: *I'm curious.*

Me: *I'll admit I thought he was really nice.*

JB: *Nice?*

Me: *Yes, NICE. That's a great quality, last time I checked. You should try it sometime.*

JB: *Ouch.*

Me: *Truth serum. Sorry.*

JB: *So you thought he was nice. Anything else?*

Me: *You're being weird. I mean, I thought you were weird already, but now I'm questioning your sanity. Are you trying to hook me up with your roommate? I thought that went against bro code*

JB: *I'm not trying to set you up with him.*

JB: *Unless you WANT to be set up with him?*

Me: *I mean... **shrugs***

JB: *What does THAT mean?*

Me: *It means **shrugs***

JB: *Is that a yes or a no?*

Me: *What are you going to do with my answer?*

137

JB: *What do you mean?*

Me*: Are you going to run to Abe and tell him I want him to take me out??*

JB*: Not unless you want me to.*

Me*: Why? You don't even like me.*

JB*: No, I don't. But Abe does, and I'm not a total asshole.*

Me*: Abe likes me?*

JB*: You're not the worst.*

Me*: LOL gee thanks.*

JB*: So….?*

Me*: This whole situation is so weird, but okay. Yes. If Abe wants to go out, give him my number…*

Ignoring messages is only okay
when I do it.

Abe

Ihave her number.

We're going out.

"Bro. Let me see some of these chicks you've been dating."

I watch as JB taps open the LoveU app and holds his phone out to Cliff Phillips, a sophomore on the team.

"Oh, I know her—she's in my business communication class. She doesn't talk much."

"I don't need her to talk much." JB laughs as if he has some dirty secret about Skylar.

"She seems too nice for you."

"She's boring as fuck."

He doesn't mention any of the shit that went down this weekend on the double date from hell. The fact that he was late on his first date with Skylar. Got into a fight with her roommate. Drank straight liquor, before and after the girls walked out on us. Went home afterward, drunk dialed his ex-girlfriend until she blocked him, then passed out on the couch.

JB presses down on Skylar's profile picture with the intention to swipe and delete, the telltale red line illuminating the screen visible from my spot on the weight bench.

Are you sure you want to unmatch with BlueAsTheSky? The app verifies before the deed can be done and, transfixed, I watch as JB taps the red button, permanently erasing Skylar from his matches.

Done.

Gone for good.

I let out a breath and turn my back, guilt about going behind his back and secretly contacting her eating away at my conscience. But what the hell were my other options? I couldn't come out and ask the idiot for permission to talk to her with his account.

He'd have laughed in my face.

After sitting across from her at that table this past weekend, I haven't been able to get Skylar off my mind. Since I couldn't come out and *ask* for her phone number, messaging through LoveU was my only option.

So I did what I did. I got her phone number.

And now we're going out.

It's done and I have no regrets; I'll figure the rest out later.

"What about this one?" JB is showing Cliff a brunette with tits I can see from here. "She looks like a nice girl."

They laugh.

JB swipes right without reading her profile.

"Does this mean I'm officially relieved of my duty to find you women to hook up with?" Then I suggest, half joking, "Maybe you should delete the entire app and lay off for a while."

"That's not happening."

"Why? It's not like you're having any luck."

"I'm playing the numbers game."

Abe: I don't think she planned on giving me head in the shower.

Skylar: I basically slipped and fell to my knees—it seemed like a good idea while I was down there.

Skylar

Abe is incredible.

My entire body has been blushing the whole time we've been sitting here, and it's not because the heater in the restaurant is turned up too high.

Though it kind of is.

The butterflies in my stomach are out, dancing and rolling, causing me to place my hand there a time or two as Abe tells another story that makes me laugh.

"...and then I just sat there not sure what to say, because I didn't know the answer. So, finally, the kid sitting next to me whispers some bullshit, and I say it out loud, right—because everyone is staring at me. And you know how huge those lecture halls are."

I nod; the lecture halls are gigantic. "What happened?"

"It was the wrong answer. The professor goes, 'How did you come up with that?' and my freaking stomach just drops. I want to kill the kid sitting next to me, but it's not his fault. It's mine for not doing the studying."

I give him another enthusiastic nod; I'm on the edge of my seat.

"I don't know what to say, and I can't lie for shit. So, I look at my professor then I look at the kid next to me, and I say, 'He gave me the answer.'"

"You did not!" My eyes are nearly out of my skull.

"I promise you, I did."

"What did the professor say?"

"I doubt anyone has said that to him before—the guy looked as shocked to hear it as I was by me saying it. Then he just kept teaching and never called on me again after that."

"Ever?"

"Nope. Not for the rest of the semester."

"Dang…"

"Want to hear the best part?"

"Yes—what's the best part?"

"I was his TA the next semester, and he just wrote me a recommendation for a job this summer."

"Stop it!" I laugh. "What?"

"You can't make this shit up." Abe laughs, stabbing a piece of the chicken on his plate.

"That's a good story. I have nothing nearly as good, how sad is that?"

"Trust me, you should be glad you don't have any stories like that, it means you fly under the radar. I find you fascinating."

Well then…

That's one of the most romantic things any guy has ever said to me, and it's hardly the stuff romance novels are made of. At least—in the novels I read when I have free time.

Little does he know, I drink pumpkin spice lattes and wear ugly, furry boots when it gets cold, and have a big, black puffy coat, and get sun burn in the summer, and freckle up, and listen to the same 80s and 90s music my mother listens to.

Still.

I'm willing to believe he finds me fascinating.

Abe Davis could charm me out of my pants if I'm not careful. My virginal, denim pants.

I'm glad he texted me.

At first, I wasn't sure he would. Jack Bartlett doesn't exactly inspire trust in people—he's way too...shady? Is that the word I'm looking for? The fact that I never un-matched him on the LoveU app can only be chalked up to sheer laziness.

So when I gave him my number to pass along to Abe, I wasn't entirely sure he would actually give it to him.

But he did.

And here we are.

And for the first time in months, I'm wearing a skirt and a sexy blouse. I have my hair curled and a face full of makeup, compliments of Hannah and Bethany. Also, I'm wearing heels.

High. Heels.

What?!

Everything about this evening feels right.

Perfect.

I resist the urge to touch my hair and push it aside. I'm nervous, and the tension between us could be cut with a butter knife.

Sexual tension.

God, I want to sit in his lap.

Crawl right in it and kiss the side of his neck. Smell him. Run my nose along the smooth, freshly shaved skin there.

I shiver at the thought.

"Are you cold?"

"Me? Um, no." Quite the opposite, in fact.

"If you are, I have a sweatshirt in the back seat of my car."

The back seat of his car…

I haven't made out in one of those in ages. It used to be a favorite pastime of mine and Hannah's in high school, letting boys make out with us in their cars but never letting their hands stray above the belly button or below the equator.

God, what teases we were.

I smile into my wine glass, recalling the many hickeys I received summer before senior year.

If he plays his cards right, maybe I'll let Abe give me one later.

Oh who am I kidding? I'm definitely going to let him touch me in all the places later.

I smile again, directing it at him, blushing prettily to see what he does with it, how he reacts to my attention.

Abe lays his arm on the table, his large hand laying limply upon the white linen tablecloth, and I stare at that open palm. Is it an invitation to put my hand in his? Or is he just resting it there?

Shoot.

This one is hard to read.

Regardless, before I can think twice, my hand slowly finds its way to the tabletop, too, fingers gracefully drumming the wood. My other hand cups my chin as I lean forward, elbow resting on the edge.

Abe flips his hand over.

Our fingers are inches apart.

One inch.

Millimeters.

Brushing, touching as we smile stupidly at one another.

The pads of his fingers singe my skin and I flip my hand over so he can trace across my palm, my heart racing. The tip of his forefinger runs along my thumb—up, then down. Along my index finger. Middle. Pinky.

It tickles, but I hold still, not daring to move an inch.

His finger feels like heaven. It's just one, but the sensation is heated, and it warms me from the inside out. That one single touch.

Tingles zip through my body, one at a time. Slowly and lightning fast—it's hard to decide which it is because I can barely catch my breath.

I hope he can't hear it in my voice—I sound like I've just jogged a mile in these high heels.

"Thank you, but I'm fine."

"Let me know if you change your mind." His voice is raspy too.

Thank God I'm not the only one.

I want to leave here and go somewhere private, somewhere I can stroke his handsome face. Kiss his nose and each corner of his mouth. It's a gorgeous pout, the stuff dreams are made of, and I'm not likely to get it out of my mind any time soon.

My appetite is gone; I don't even want dessert.

Couldn't eat it if it was stuffed down my throat—too much nervous energy, anticipation thrumming through my veins.

My eyes connect with our hands; mine are shaking slightly. It's minimal, but I notice it with every stroke of his finger against the tender skin of my palm.

It's one of the sexiest sensations I've ever experienced.

"Do you have any brothers and sisters?" he asks.

"Yes. One of each. Younger sister, older brother."

His head bobs up and down. "Oh yeah, that's right."

Did we talk about this already? "Sorry?"

"I mean—you must have mentioned it when we had that double date."

I didn't think so, but I must have. "What about you?"

"I have one of each—brother and a sister, both younger."

"Awww. I bet they look up to you."

"My brother does, yeah. Hero worship. He wants to be a wrestler, too. It's a lot to live up to."

"That's cute. I don't remember ever worshiping my brother—he was such an ass when we were younger," I laugh, remembering some of the stupid shit Derek has pulled over the years. Pranks and jokes.

Dumbass.

"But you get along?"

"We do now. Sort of." Our fingers entwine as I speak. "During Christmas when we were both home, he put clear tape across my bathroom door, so in the middle of the night when I got up to pee, obviously I walked right into it and my hair got all tangled."

This makes Abe laugh. "How old is he?"

"Old enough not to pull crap like that!"

Abe is not on my side. "That's hilarious though."

"It wasn't hilarious at two in the morning."

"Did you get him back?"

I scoff, squeezing his fingers. "Of course."

He waits for the story.

"I'm patient, kind of like a viper waiting to strike." Abe's eyes widen at the metaphor. "Relax, I'm not going to murder you or anything, but I do have mad waiting skills." I play hide-and-seek like no one's business and win every time. "Anyway, the goal is always to scare the shit out of the other person—except my parents. They get really mad when we do it to them." Especially my mother, who rants about us giving her a stroke. "So my brother keeps a bunch of pillows on his bed. He has his own place, but during the holidays he sleeps in his old room at my parents' house. My mom kept it the same. Anyway, if I crawl in under the pillows and flatten out, you can't even tell I'm there."

"Oh Jesus, I can see where this is headed."

My grin is wide. "Exactly. I crawl in, and it's dark, and he's just getting in from being out with his idiot friends. I lie there quietly, for. ever. It takes him forever to come into his room because he lingers down in the kitchen stuffing his drunk face. Comes up, gets his pajamas on, goes to the bathroom. I'm lying there, listening to the whole thing, dying from heat stroke. I bet it took him a good twenty minutes of screwing around before he gets in bed. I'm still as a tomb, and his head is resting on me."

I remember it like it was yesterday.

"But then it gets to be too much, and the giggles start. I can't hold it in any longer, and I start to laugh. And he shoots off the bed yelling 'What the fuck Skylar!' and my parents bust in because we're being so loud." I'm laughing now as I recount the story. "Moral of the story: I made him wet the bed."

"He pissed the bed?" I've never seen a person's eyes go so round as I've told a story.

I've never been so proud of my prank. I preen like a peacock. "He did piss the bed."

"Speaking of which"—Abe pulls his hand back—"I should hit the bathroom real quick. Give me a second, I'll be right back."

I watch as he retreats, my eyes lingering on the straining muscles in his back as he walks. The wide, defined latissimus dorsi. His spine, visible through the thin fabric of his dressy polo.

His squatter's ass.

I think back to those images on the web, the photos of him in his wrestling singlet, which barely leaves anything

151

to the imagination. Every corded muscle. Every thick vein. His back, shoulders, and dense thighs all on display for my wandering, prying eyes, and I wonder what I'll do with them when I finally get the chance to put my hands on his skin in real life—not just in my imagination.

It's been forever since I've touched a guy, so who knows if I'll know what to do with myself.

Time will tell.

He's been gone a few minutes when his phone begins to buzz. It's facing upward so when it lights up, my eyes naturally wander to the screen...

...drawn to that familiar yellow icon in the corner of the display, the LoveU logo prominently glowing.

My face flushes, filled with surprise.

He's still swiping and chatting with girls on the app?

My heart sinks like a stone to the bottom of a deep pool, the excited nerves turning to dread. Impulsive, my first instinct is to get up and leave; common sense tells me to stay, says he and I are not committed enough that I have a say in this.

I have no right to tell him what to do.

We are on our first date.

Still, the shock of seeing the app light up his phone is a bit too much. It's the cold bucket of reality I needed dumped on my head; he's too good to be true.

Smart, handsome, funny. Kind and polite.

I thought he was one of the good guys. Thought maybe he was a one woman kind of guy.

Guess I was wrong.

The proof is lighting up his phone every few minutes, and I feel dumb sitting here waiting for him to return from the bathroom, not a clue what I'll say when he sits back down.

Another three minutes and he's back, all smiles, returning the napkin to his lap before giving me his undivided attention. Placing his hand back on the table so I'll take it.

My heart.

My hands remain in my lap, one clasping the other, fidgeting as I find my words, needing to speak my mind.

I'll regret it if I don't.

"What's wrong?"

Add insightful to his growing list of amazing qualities.

"I'm not sure. Maybe I'm overreacting."

"What happened while I was in the bathroom? Did something happen?" He sits up, ramrod straight, glancing around the restaurant. "Why is your face so pale?"

Is it?

My hands fly to my face and I press on my cheeks; they're hot, not cool. My heart inside my chest palpitates.

I hate confrontation.

I lick my lips, wishing I had lip balm. "Maybe this isn't a big deal. I don't know—I hate that I'm bringing it up, because this is our first date and we're having a really good time, but your phone keeps going off, and I couldn't help but notice…"

He waits, making no move to touch his cell.

"Just look at your phone, Abe. I promise I'm not a

snoop, but it kept lighting up while you were in the bathroom and I couldn't help but notice the app that was popping up."

His eyes bore into me before he picks the phone off the table, palms it, and taps it with his giant thumb.

Looks, sees the notifications.

Looks at me.

"Skylar."

Just one word—my name—and I know he's guilt-ridden. I can see it in his crestfallen expression.

"This isn't what it looks like."

"Really? Because it looks like you're on a date with me and still talking to other girls online."

"I'm not."

"Look, it's none of my business—I don't care what you do."

Lies, lies, lies.

Because if he's going to date me, it will be my business, and I expect him to be faithful without having to discuss it time and time again. It will be an expectation from day one.

This moment is our day one.

Or was.

He seems to be weighing his options, an internal debate flashing in his eyes about the explanation he's going to give me.

"Whatever excuse you're dreaming up in your head, just save it, okay? Tell me the truth."

He has nothing to lose...except me.

"I'm going to be brutally honest with you, okay? Can you hold off on commenting until you hear me out, let me say what I need to say, and promise not to get mad?"

Promise not to get mad? Is he serious? I'm already halfway there!

"Nope."

To add insult to injury, another notification from LoveU comes in, the glowing screen harsher than the crash of a cymbal, punctuating how awkward this situation has just become.

"Is that another girl?"

He doesn't check the phone, but we both know it is. "I'd be lying if I said it wasn't."

The silence between us isn't only awkward; it's deafening.

"Would you say something?"

Something, I think sarcastically.

"I'm not the one who's supposed to be explaining themselves. You are."

"You think this is easy? I feel like such an idiot."

That makes two of us.

Then, I do that thing girls do when they're pretending not to be pissed; I passively aggressively act like I'm fine. "I have nothing to say. Everything is great. Dinner is great. I'm just waiting for you to tell me what's going on, Abe."

"I'll tell you when you stop looking so pissed off."

"Do I look pissed? That's weird. What makes you say

that?"

Abe's big body reclines in his seat; arms crossed, he studies me from across the table. "For starters, your nostrils are flaring."

My fingers fly to my face, feeling around the skin of my nose.

Shit, he's right—my nostrils are flaring. That can't be attractive.

"Your skin is bright red."

"That's because I'm so pale. It's warm in here."

"And your leg is bouncing up and down under the table."

I rest the palm of my hand on my knee, applying pressure to make it stop. The water glasses and silverware immediately stop rattling.

"Anything else?" I can't keep the snark out of my voice.

"No." He's quiet now. "You look like your feelings are hurt."

How observant he is.

My feelings *are* hurt, but I'm not about to lay it all on the line for a guy I just met, on our first date. I don't have that right.

Do I? Or would I just sound crazy and controlling?

"Will you let me explain?"

"I thought you already did." I lower my voice to a deep baritone, mimicking a man's voice and doing an atrocious job of it. "Skylar, it's not what it looks like."

Wow. When did I become so snippy?

Abe is patient, waiting me out. Waits for my cheeks to return to their natural color, my leg to stop bouncing, my nostrils to stop flaring.

I think he's also waiting for me to stand up and walk out.

Instead, I tilt my chin up. "Okay, I'm listening."

"You were right when you assumed it was the LoveU app. I was on it, but it's not my account. I don't have one of my own."

"What does that mean?"

"I'm logged in under Jack's account."

That makes no sense, either. "So you're spying on him?" Or does he just want to look at girls without having his picture posted online?

"No. I'm..." He lets out a deep breath. Runs a hand over his short, cropped hair, fingers digging into the back of his neck. Rubbing. "It's not spying. It's more compli-cated than that."

It's complicated.

God I hate that term.

"Is this some kind of joke to the two of you? Do you sit around the locker room making fun of the girls he goes on dates with?"

"No, it's not like that, either."

He's doing a horrible job explaining the situation— whatever it is—but now I'm invested in the story and need more details. I need to know what's going on.

"Can you be more clear, Abe? All you're doing is confusing me."

"All right, but don't get mad."

He said that already. "You said that already."

"I know—I just don't want you to walk out on me."

What if I don't have a choice? What if this whole fantastic date was for nothing? What if I go home and cry the rest of the night because what he's about to tell me is going to crush me?

What if, what if, what if...

"Then let's hope what you're about to say isn't that terrible."

Another dreadful silence.

"Abe?"

"Skylar, I really like you."

That's never a good sign.

He shifts uncomfortably in his seat, and I focus on the three buttons of his polo shirt, the bright color complimenting his complexion and black hair.

"The thing with the app—it isn't a joke, but it's not about me. It's about JB."

I nod slowly. "Uh huh." I wish he'd just spit it out already.

"He might come off as a total..."

"Prick?"

"Right. We'll go with that." Abe laughs nervously. "He might come off as a total prick, but he's actually insecure. And when his girlfriend broke up with a him a few months ago, he was a complete fucking mess—pardon my language."

A total mess.

"Then another guy on the team told him the best way to get over a girl is to get under another one."

"Uh huh…" The pieces still aren't clicking together as he struggles to place them for me.

"Do you get what I'm trying to tell you?"

A laugh escapes my lips. "Um, no. Not even a little."

"Jack has no confidence. He's bad at grammar, hates making conversation, has no attention span."

"O-k*ay*…"

Abe is watching me, expecting an aha moment any second now, but I have news for him: there isn't one coming. He's gonna have to spell it out for me.

"Abe, just tell me wha—"

He's finally impatient enough to interrupt. "I go on the app and pretend to be him."

Ohhhhh. Oh!

"Oh."

I have no idea what else to say; everything finally makes sense—sort of. JB being emotionally distant on our dates (which I thought was normal, considering our age and his maturity level). JB not wanting to discuss anything personal because he knew nothing about me and probably never read back through the messages to find out what makes me tick. JB not being invested because it wasn't *him* putting in those long hours of conversation with me.

JB wasn't the one making me laugh.

JB wasn't the one giving me butterflies in my stomach.

JB wasn't the one giving me false hope.

JB wasn't the one causing me to daydream through my classes.

None of that was JB.

It was Abe.

Abe Davis is a liar.

#DOUCHEBAG

You know she's mad when she says Good-Night at 6pm and she texts it in "that tone."

Abe

Every heartbeat that passes is fucking torture. I wish Skylar would say something. Anything. I wouldn't even care if she called me an asshole. Or a sonofabitch, or a jerk—anything to put me out of my misery and break this miserable silence.

I have no idea what to do with my hands, so I take them off the table and rub my palms up and down my thighs, the denim soaking up the sweat accumulating on them with every passing moment.

She hates me; she must.

I can see it in her blue eyes.

They went from warm to cold in an instant, brows bent in that instinctive way.

She's hurt.

"Skylar, I didn't mean—"

"For any of this to happen? Could you be any more cliché right now?" She takes the napkin off her lap and sets it next to her fork and knife. "What happens next? Are you going to say you didn't mean for any of it to happen? Save it—I've heard those lines before, but they were better scripted in the movies."

Clearly this is not the time for me to point out that she's being a tad melodramatic.

"That's not what I was about to say." Okay—maybe

it *was*, but I'm not dumb enough to say it now. "JB and I have been doing this for months and you're the only one I swiped on who was ever worth his time."

Wrong. Thing. To. Say.

"Oh, you've been doing this for months, eh?" She laughs, head actually tipping back, the sound coming out of her throat an odd combination of ironic and sardonic. It's slightly maniacal, if I'm being honest. "And I'm the only one worth his time. I'm *so* flattered!"

You know those scenes in the movies where the guy finally realizes he's in deep shit because the woman sounds like she's lost her damn mind, repeating things back to him and saying irrational shit?

I never thought it would happen to me, but I'm living that classic moment, except this is my fucking reality, and I'm not sure what to do about it.

Molecular biology homework? That I can do. Swap out a car battery? Sure. Write a fake letter of recommendation for a friend? No problem.

This?

No clue.

"You're still on the app." She states it as a fact. "You're sitting here with me, and you're still swiping."

"But none of those dates are for me."

Skylar isn't impressed with my answer. "I've never met such a yes man."

Whoa.

Wow.

Okay. Not cool. "I'm not a yes man."

Skylar rolls her eyes. "Sure you're not."

"I'm not." Why am I arguing with her? She's clearly itching for a fight—and she couldn't be more wrong.

She yawns, feigning boredom. "It's one of two things: you're a yes man, or you sincerely enjoy doing it. Which one is it? Pick one." Her tone is hard; she expects me to answer.

"Neither."

Skylar makes a buzzer sound in the back of her throat. "Wrong. Try again."

What the fuck…

"Would you listen?"

"It's one or the other, Honest Abe. You either love swiping or you're Jack's bitch. What other explanation is there?" She looks satisfied with herself, like a dog that's just eaten a whole cake before its owner entered the room. Or a girl who's just backed a man into a corner knowing she's won the argument.

"I don't enjoy it."

She plucks the lemon out of her water and sucks the rind. "Sure." Her fingers plop it back in the glass.

"I'm not his bitch—I don't know why you'd assume I was."

"Okay. You're not his bitch." Another sarcastic roll of her blue eyes.

"Can we please stop calling me his bitch?"

"Yup. Whatever you say, Abe."

Now, I might not know jack shit about women or relationships, but I know this for a fact: it's never a good sign when a girl starts agreeing with everything you say.

Never.

Basically, I'm fucked.

The problem is, Skylar isn't my girlfriend, or my friend. The problem is I like her—but because we're not in a relationship yet, she's going to walk out that front door and never speak to me again, and she has no obligation to hear me out.

"I do nice shit for people, okay? Why is that an issue?" As the words leave my lips, I know they're a crock of shit for the simple fact that I've been lying to her for weeks. About who I am and who it was talking to her, and how I feel about her. How Jack feels about her.

Skylar's right eyebrow raises. "Do you seriously expect me to answer that question?"

"I'm a nice fucking guy, okay?" I wouldn't say I'm mad, but I'm getting there. She's not listening or hearing me out. "Since when is that a crime?"

"You are *such* a nice guy." She's patronizing me.

But I am. I'd give the shirt off my back to someone who needed it.

I do so much shit for people, it's borderline stupid. I do shit for people when I don't have the time, or the money, or the inclination—but I do it anyway. Last semester I spent every day for an entire week straight studying with Taylor Bronson for the LSAT. Two weeks ago, I drove thirty-six miles out of town to help Lyle Decker change his flat tire because he'd never done it himself before, and he doesn't have AAA. Yesterday I lent Peter Fletcher fifty bucks to buy a textbook. (I'll never see that money again.)

"Are you nice, or are you a pushover?"

Skylar is *savage* when she's pissed.

"What the—"

"Sorry, but that's what it sounds like to me. You might think you're being nice, but you're enabling people."

"I'm not enabling anyone—I'm being a good friend."

"And what 'nice' things are they doing for you in return?" She uses air quotes around the word nice. "Friendships go both ways."

"It's different for guys."

Why am I defending myself?

Because you know she's right. The guys on the team take advantage of me. But I'm from the Midwest, raised to be Christian and *give* without expecting anything in return—the true definition of selfless.

So the fact that she's giving me shit about helping people? It's beginning to chap my ass.

"Can we stick to the topic at hand here?"

"Oh good—let's keep talking about what a big liar you are."

Shit.

I walked right into that one.

Skylar is right, though. She's abso*fucking*lutely right. "Look, I'm sorry you got caught up in this whole thing—"

"You mean you're sorry you got caught."

I have no reply to that, and Skylar goes on.

"Abe, you and I both know I'm not dating you now that you've lied to me."

I do know that, but it's not going to stop me from trying.

I might be a damn liar, but I'm not a quitter.

She just doesn't realize that yet.

"Is there any way I can change your mind?" I stare straight at her, unflinching, until she's forced to break eye contact and look away. Her pretty, delicate fingers sweep a stray lock of hair away from her face, teeth biting down into her bottom lip as her head gives a little shake.

No.

"Do you want to keep talking about this?"

Another shake of the head.

No.

"Do you want to stay and eat or should I pay the bill?"

She pauses, thinking. "We'll split it."

Fuck.

Fuck, fuck, *fuck.*

I have no choice but to concede. "If that's the way you want it, Skylar."

"It is."

Nothing has ever felt so final, and nothing has ever felt so terrible.

I hate myself right now, hate what I've done—to her and for JB.

"For what it's worth, I…" It sounds like I'm choking

on my words, throat constricting. "I think you're pretty fucking perfect."

Her lips part.

"No one is perfect, Abe. I think you just proved that." Though barely audible, her words are blunt, and they hit me right in their intended target: my chest.

My heart.

"What do you mean?"

Her pink mouth curves, her body twisting in her seat so she can remove her purse from the chair.

She puts down some cash then stands, pulling the long leather strap over her shoulder. "I thought you were perfect, too, until about ten minutes ago. Too bad you went and ruined it with the truth."

Her exit is dramatic, punctuated when she flips a sheet of long brown hair over her shoulder and stomps out, purse swinging.

The perverted, male part of me has eyes that latch onto her tight ass, admiring it as it sashays away, one bold stride after the next, until she's out of my peripheral.

Seconds tick by.

Minutes pass, and I'm getting my change from the waitress when Skylar returns, chin up, shoulders pinned back, head held high.

Performance ruined.

"I need a ride."

Me: *Look. I know I'm the last person you want to hear from...*

Skylar: *That is correct.*

Skylar: *Save your apologies—I didn't want them in the car, and I don't want them now.*

Me: *I'm not texting to apologize; I'm texting you to ask if we can start over.*

Skylar: *haha.*

Skylar: *No*

Me: *Skylar, please. I told Jack to piss off, removed the app from my phone, and want nothing more to do with it.*

Skylar: *The app isn't the point here. The point here is that you lied. I know nothing about you, Abe. Everything you told me was about JB.*

Me: *Then let me get to know you—please.*

Skylar: *I said no. Don't make me block you from my phone, too.*

Me: *I'm sorry. I know I fucked up.*

Skylar: *Yup.*

Me: *There's no way I can make it up to you so we can start over...none at all?*

Skylar: *Hard pass.*

Me: *All right, then I guess...*

Me: *Goodbye?*

I stare at my phone, at the blue bubble from my last text, willing her to reply.

She doesn't.

I had the last word, and it was *Goodbye*, and she doesn't bother with the courtesy of a response back.

I feel sick.

And guilty. And like a complete, fucking douchebag.

How did I end up as the bad guy in all this?

I can't concentrate on my meet, where there are thousands of wrestling fans in the stands. The auditorium is loud, thrumming with energy, none of which is coming from me.

Instead of warming up like I'm supposed to, I'm staring off into the dark recesses of Iowa's stadium when a giant hand clamps down on my shoulder. It's mammoth, and it's attached to someone even larger. Someone larger than life.

"What the fuck are you doing just standing here?"

Zeke Daniels is an alum, a champion himself who comes back to help the coaching staff during meets at home every now and again—and he's glaring at me, disgusted.

"I'm distracted."

"Distracted enough to get your ass handed to you in thirty minutes by a guy who wants the pin more than you do?"

Yes. "No. No, I'm good. I'll shake it off. I just…"

Not one for beating around the bush, Zeke sighs impatiently, knowing instinctively I have a personal problem but not wanting to address it. He doesn't give a shit, but he has a job to do—and that job is to fix my head and get me in the game.

He's blunt. "What the fuck is the problem?"

"Nothing. We're good."

"You look like you're about to puke all over those pretty little shoes of yours." He runs a tan hand through his black hair. "Is this about some woman? Did some chick get into your fucking head? Spit it out, we're losing daylight."

Yes. "No."

He doesn't believe me. "Jesus Christ, don't lie to me. You're running out of time before they blow the whistle. If it's not a girl and your dick hasn't fallen off, why are you standing there looking like someone pissed in your bowl of Cheerios?"

This guy is brutal, no time wasted on peppering his speech with flowery sentiment. Zeke Daniels isn't into mollycoddling, and he certainly isn't going to start with me.

Fuck.

"It's a girl."

"No shit, Sherlock. What's the fucking problem?"

"I met her on LoveU, pretending to be JB, sent him on a date with her, she hated him, set her on a double date with me, we had chemistry, got her number, took her out this weekend, she found out I was lying, now she hates me."

I word vomit all that out in one breath then inhale sharply, sucking a healthy dose of air back into my lungs.

Zeke stares.

Blinks once.

Twice.

"So. You catfished her."

"No—that's not at all what I was doing!"

He looks bored already. "But basically that's what you were doing."

"Catfishing is when you use fake pictures and pretend to be someone you're not," I argue.

His dark, thick brows rise. "Isn't that what you were doing?"

"No, because JB is real, and they are his pictures and he is the one who went to meet these girls."

"So Skylar was talking to you, and went to meet with JB, while talking to you, then you continued pursuing her as *you*, but using JB's account. Did I get that right?"

"Yes."

Oh.

Oh fuck.

I was catfishing her. A little bit, sort of.

Wow. I'm not as smart as I thought I was.

Lips parted, Zeke shakes his head slowly. "Seriously. What the fuck is wrong with you guys?"

My shoulders drop, head bent. "I don't know."

"I take it she's not talking to you?"

"No. She hates me." I sound pathetic.

"That's a bit harsh—it's not like you can cheat on her if you're not actually dating." I wasn't expecting any words of solidarity from him. "Bet she called you a liar and all that garbage? Man, chicks are so full of drama."

"Violet isn't full of drama." His fiancé of one year is the softest-spoken woman I've ever met, and the only one who could tame a beast like Daniels.

"That's because Violet is a goddamn *saint*." His voice is gruff, filled with pride, eyes softening at the mention of her name. "I shit on her once or twice back when we started dating, and with a woman like that, it's hard to bounce back. Any girl who knows her worth is going to fucking stick it to you and stick it to you hard. You have to be smarter than they are." Zeke looks me up and down. "Which you are *not*."

"*Thanks.*"

"That wasn't a compliment."

I know that, fucker. I was being sarcastic.

I don't say that shit out loud though, because he'd kick my ass, and I'd have to let him.

"So what do I do?" I'm in serious need of help, sound like I'm desperate, and will take advice anywhere I can get it—even if it's from the biggest asshole this wrestling team has ever had on it.

"Let me think about it. I'll have to text Violet—she'll know what to do." He gives me a confident nod, pleased that he's on his way to solving my dilemma, then his hand returns to my shoulder, squeezing. He speaks slowly like he's talking to a child. "Kindly remove your head from your own ass so we don't have to do it surgically, take your fucking warm-up pants off, and pound out your goddamn stretches like you're supposed to be doing." He claps my back. "Got it?"

"Got it."

"I'll circle back around."

I watch him saunter away, head bent, tapping away at his phone. Wonder what he's telling his girlfriend about the situation and hope they can help me untangle this mess.

Bending at the waist, I push off the standard-issue black and yellow warm-up pants we wear before our matches and then I'm standing in nothing but my tight black singlet. I yank up the straps and adjust them, pulling the nylon fabric out of my ass crack.

I pop a squat on the mat, bending at the knees, then lower myself into a sitting position. Bend at the waist until I'm able to grip the balls of my feet in my fingers. Stretching my calves, kneading at the muscles of my hamstrings, the burn from the pull a painful reminder that I've been slacking lately.

My mind wanders.

What am I going to do?

Normally, I wouldn't care. I'd tune the issue with Skylar out like I do with everything else and move on. It was never my intention to date in the first place, so why this one? *Why this girl?*

By all accounts, she's more reserved. A bit anti-social. Beautiful in a subtle way, kind and funny and good. My mind wanders again, down the front of her blouse, mentally counting the buttons there—five—then mentally slipping them out of their fabric until her shirt is parted down the middle.

Skylar had smooth, gorgeous cleavage I tried not to gape at while we were at the table, and it took a heroic effort to keep my eyes up. Pale skin. Freckles between her breasts and across the bridge of her perfect nose.

Pink cheeks and even pinker lips.

There wasn't a moment she wasn't smiling.

At me.

Blue eyes lit up right up until the moment I returned from the bathroom and ruined the entire date by being a colossal idiot.

I unfurl myself from the floor, rise to my full height, and pull back on one leg, working my calves for a second time. Arms. Back. Move my head in slow circles to loosen my neck, all the while preoccupied with my thoughts of Skylar, her tits, her voice.

My lies.

Was I catfishing her?

That's not what I considered what JB and I were doing to be; in my mind, I was utilizing a skill he doesn't possess—making idle conversation with beautiful strangers to learn more about them.

I have it in spades.

JB sucks at it.

What JB lacks in social graces, he makes up for with his face, strength, and body. Deep voice, megawatt smile, dimple in his cheek.

Chicks love that shit. They lap it up, hardly caring that he's a dickhead. They only care that he's good-looking, good in bed, and goes down on them—a fact he constantly brags about and one I sometimes hear acted out from my bedroom in the middle of the night.

Oh JB...Oh...Oh, don't stop doing that...

There have been nights I've wanted to suffocate myself with a pillow to escape listening to his sexcapades.

It would be easy to have a few of my own, but I'm not that guy. I don't do casual, and never have—not even in high school, or as a freshman in college when everything was new and exciting and girls were throwing themselves at me because I was on the wrestling team.

At this school, wrestling is a pretty huge fucking deal, and I'm in the middle of it.

My eyes scan the auditorium, the bleachers and seats, searching for someone I know isn't there but looking anyway. Torturing myself like a fool.

Why would she come?

We're not dating and she hates me.

Still, a part of me—the sick, eternal optimist within—thinks she might be curious enough to show up, knowing I would never spot her in a crowd this size.

I scan it, back and forth, up and down, before finally giving up.

Zeke Daniels is standing with the rest of the coaches, head bent, listening intently to one of the assistants, nodding. I can hardly believe he offered to help me—Zeke, who gives zero fucks about anything and anyone.

Well. Except his blonde, petite fiancé.

I've seen them together a few times with some preteen kid they haul around, though it's not very often because

Zeke and Violet have both graduated and moved on, doing whatever it is they do when he's not here pitching in.

Giving back.

I hear his parents are loaded—have what some people call "fuck you" money—and he's working for his dad now, though I've never asked him outright; it's none of my business, and I would feel rude bringing it up.

As if he senses someone watching him, he looks up and our eyes meet, his head now tipping into a knowing nod.

You got this. Don't fuck it up.

I win my match by the skin of my teeth, despite almost getting my ass handed to me straight out of the gate because my head wasn't in it. An elbow to the teeth and a few faceplants to the mat brought me back to reality real quick.

I take a cold shower after Coach chews my ass out, shouting obscenities along with the countless mistakes I made that almost lost me the match, that lost the team points.

All because I was focused on a girl with eyes as blue as the sky.

"All right pissflap, here's what we got." Zeke stands next to my locker in the locker room, thumb scrolling along the screen as he looks down at his cell. "Violet said you're going to need the roommate's help to pull this off."

Hannah?

Skylar's pissed-off, combative roommate Hannah?

No doubt she's heard the entire saga and has my picture—along with JB's—on the back of her bedroom door with darts in both our foreheads. There is no fucking way *that* girl is going to help *me* win back her best friend. Hannah would rather stick a fork in her own eye before she'd deign to help me hook up with her precious roommate.

"Any other options?"

He checks his phone. "Violet says no."

"You didn't even ask!"

He shrugs. "She said what she said. I don't have to ask her twice."

A knot forms in my stomach that feels oddly like jealously. A relationship where there is no questioning the other person and their opinion is respected by default...

It's called trust.

The irony is not lost on me.

I don't know how, but Zeke produces a cell phone number, holding out his phone so I can save it into mine.

"What's this?"

"The roommate's number, you fuckwit."

"Did you pull that out of your ass?"

"No. Violet got it for me."

"How?"

"Are you going to question everything I say?"

"Yes?"

His sigh is long, and loud, and he tips his head back and gawks at the ceiling, Adam's apple bobbing. "Violet got it from Jameson—Oz Osborne's girlfriend—and Jameson got it from a friend who has a friend who works at the movie theater with Hannah."

"Are you being serious?"

"*No.* How the fuck would I know where Hannah works?" The perpetual dark cloud lingering over him darkens. "Violet went on Instagram and searched for Hannah then messaged her for her number. Jesus, it's not hard to find people these days."

Oh.

Right.

"Give the roommate a call, explain the situation, get her on your side. Easy." He socks me in the bicep. "Got it?"

"Got it."

He looks skeptical, side-eyeing me. "Do you though? I think you're going to screw this up."

"I said I've got it."

"Want me to help?"

"Hell no!" The last thing I need is Zeke Daniels hanging around like the plague. Because where he goes, his best friend Oz goes, and where Oz goes, that idiot Rex Gunderson shows up—then before I know it, the whole wrestling team will know how I fucked up my dating life.

Besides, I don't need JB knowing about any of this until I'm good and ready to tell him. No sense in pissing him off prematurely. There's a chance this entire scheme is going to blow up in my face and nothing will come of it, so why get his panties in a twist?

"You know what chicks love? Kids. If you found yourself a kid, you'd have this in the bag." He's deep in thought, rubbing the stubble on his chin.

"You have spare kids lying around, smartass?"

"As a matter of fact, I do."

Shit, that's right. He spent a few years volunteering with a mentor program. The lanky little boy he used to hate spending time with he now treats like a younger brother—one he totes around everywhere.

It's so bizarre.

But so is seeing him with his girlfriend, a girl you'd never match him with in a million years. If there was a photo next to the definition of opposites in the dictionary, theirs would be next to it.

"You know what's better than one kid?" He's really warming to this kid idea. "Two kids. Maybe even a puppy."

"No." I raise my arms and pull on a clean t-shirt, presenting him with my back.

"Aren't you taking a shower?"

I shoot him the stink-eye. "What are you now, my mother?"

"I'm just asking."

Not to be disrespectful, but, "Why are you still standing here?" He can go now. The looks he's shooting me and the fact that he's invading my personal space are making me cagey. Paranoid.

Twitchy, even.

"You're like a car wreck," the bastard is saying. "I can't peel my eyes away—I have to know what happens." He leans against the metal lockers, crossing his ankles and arms. Cocky. "I'm invested."

Invested? Jesus Christ with this guy. "I have it handled."

"*Ehhhh…*" Zeke isn't convinced.

I turn to face him, shucking the rest of my singlet, kicking it off and retrieving it from the ground. It will get tossed in the laundry in the corner of the locker room, cleaned, and returned for the next meet.

Digging through my duffle, I find gray boxer briefs. Pull those on, all the while ignoring the looming shadow beside me.

Why is he still here? Why does he care? This is a guy who doesn't give a flying fuck about anything; suddenly he has a vested interest in my dating life?

I'm in hell, that's what's happening—there can be no other explanation.

Resigned, I ask, "What the hell am I supposed to say to Hannah? You know how girls are—Skylar probably told her every last detail, probably cried all night and—"

"Ate all the ice cream?"

"No. I was going to say plotted revenge."

"Oh yeah, that makes more sense. A scorned girl is ruthless, but her friends are worse."

"I didn't scorn her." Why is he so dramatic?

"Right. You catfished her—that's even worse." When I go to argue, he holds his palm up to shush me. "Don't say it. We both know that's what you did, because you're a dumbfuck and you weren't thinking straight."

I've never been called a dumbfuck by anyone in my entire life. I've been called brainy, smart, too sharp for my own good… never a *dumb*fuck.

"Fine. Whatever." I root around for mesh shorts and step into them. "What am I supposed to say to Hannah?"

"The good news is, when you call—don't text her, because all she'll do is chew your ass out then block you—she won't know it's you, so she's going to answer her phone."

True.

"Maybe say some shit like, 'Wait! Before you hang up...' so she doesn't hang up."

I roll my eyes.

He's not impressed with my dismissal of his suggestion. "You should be writing this down."

"That *one* sentence?" I feel around my upper torso like I'm searching for a writing utensil. "Gee, looks like I don't have a pen."

"Don't be a smartass." First I'm a dumbfuck, now I'm a smartass.

"Hold up. Quick question: do you think I should tell JB about this?"

"Are you out of your mind? First of all, he's the one who got you into this mess. Secondly, all's fair in love and war, and he's a moron. He's going to cockblock you left and right and three ways from Sunday and still not want that Sky *whatever-her-name-is*. So forget it. This is no longer his fucking business—completely out of his jurisdiction." He's giving me a hard glare. "Any other stupid questions?"

"Nope." Just that one.

"Good. Now as I was saying—once you have Hannah's attention, play up the fact that you've never done anything this stupid before."

Which is true.

"And you're a smart dude who made a really stupid mistake."

Also true.

"And that if she helps you out, you swear you'll never do anything this fucking stupid again, and if you do, she's welcome to chop your nuts off with whatever dull object she can find."

"That's my only option? Her chopping my nuts off?"

His brows rise. "Stop talking. I'm on a roll here."

God he's an asshole.

He's also gone silent, brows furrowed, forehead creasing. "Fuck. I lost my train of thought." The glare he gives me could shrivel anyone's nuts by four sizes.

"I'm sorry!" I blurt out, slightly traumatized by the exchange to begin with. This is so weird, getting advice from him. Zeke has barely spoken ten words to me in the three years I've been on the team, and suddenly, he's playing matchmaker.

"I guess start with Hannah. If that doesn't work, give up, because dude—don't be a stalker." His favorite thing to do is look people up and down, and he does it to me, again. "If I find out you're creeping on her, I'll sock you in the balls."

I cup a hand over my scrotum. "I don't want you socking my balls."

He stares at me like I'm mental, lip curled on one end. "No one wants to be socked in the balls, dipshit."

Okay then.

Guys are like, "I'm cut from a different cloth."
First of all, you're a napkin...

Skylar

"Sky, can I talk to you for a minute?" Hannah scrapes her fingernails on my doorframe as a courtesy—the action makes my skin crawl—then enters without waiting for a reply.

It's late, and a Thursday, so we're both in our pajamas, but it's clear only one of us has been studying while the other has been lying on her bed, staring at the ceiling for the past thirty minutes.

That'd be me.

I roll toward the wall, giving her a wide berth to sit on the edge of my mattress, the weight of her body sinking down, her palm resting on the swell of my hip as she bounces up and down a few times.

She gives me a nudge, eyes soft behind her black framed computer glasses, which she pushes atop her head so she can see straight. "Hey."

"Hey. What's up?" It's nice that she popped in for a visit, but I'm not sure I'm done wallowing in my own misery yet.

"Have you been crying?"

"Pfft. Me? No." A little, but I won't admit it. Crying over a guy who lied, one I wasn't even officially dating, one I barely know?

Lame. *Pathetic.*

Hannah doesn't contradict me, just gives me a look

that says *When you're ready, we can talk about it*, and I'm grateful for that. Still, there is a part of me that *does* want her to push the Abe issue, because I *do* want to talk about it. About Abe, and this fucked-up situation. A part of me wants to give him another chance—wants to talk to him—but that part of me won't admit it.

I need permission. Affirmation that I'm not losing my mind.

"You know, I've been thinking," Hannah begins, crossing her legs and bobbing one idly. "Remember that time in high school when Kevin Rogers paid Lyle Stevens five bucks to write me love letters?"

"Who doesn't remember Kevin Rogers?" He was always trying to convince people he was related to country music legend *Kenny* Rogers, claimed his parents changed his first name to Kevin only so there would be no confusion. Sadly, *no one* confused Kevin Rogers with Kenny—not even when he'd bring his acoustic guitars to parties and sing "The Gambler".

Kevin simply could not carry a tune.

"Remember when we found out about the whole thing?"

"Yes. You were so mad you made your dad start a bonfire so we could roast those letters." They were written on spiral notebook paper, folded into triangles, and slipped into Hannah's locker every morning. She would pore over them, every single one, smitten.

Until Lyle spilled the beans, professing his own true love for Hannah, hanging Kevin out to dry. It was the biggest scandal Mount Pleasant High School had seen in years.

"Who were you more pissed off at? Kevin or Lyle?" I ask.

"Both, at first. But then I went back and reread some of those letters—I never told you this, but I saved a few from the fire pit of revenge—and they were so sweet. I still have them, you know." She tilts her head to the side in thought. "I should look Lyle up, see what he's doing these days…"

"Oh god. Do not look him up." Hannah is such a creeper sometimes.

"I forgave him you know."

"You did? How did I not know that?"

"Because I knew you were mad at him, too. Because I'd been so…not mad. I was embarrassed."

Embarrassed.

She goes on. "Is that part of the reason you're not talking to Abe? You're more humiliated than angry?"

I haven't spun it that way.

"Why are you bringing this up?" My best friend was right alongside me that night when I got home, rallying, raging, and incensed on my behalf. Swore she'd tear him a new asshole. I quote: *"I'm going to find that sorry SOB, and when I do, I'm gonna…I'm gonna… Well. I don't know what I'll do, but I'll think of something. He better watch out!"*

She was so loud, the neighbors called the apartment complex management to complain.

"The whole thing made me feel really ridiculous."

"Which part?"

My face scrunches. "The part where I caught him in a lie, Hannah! The part where his phone was buzzing and I sat there looking at the stupid LoveU app blowing up his phone! That part!"

"So...is that the only reason you're not talking to him?"

Okay—now I'm confused. I contort my body so I'm sitting, looking her straight in the eye. "What is this about? *Hannah*. What did you do?"

Shrug. "Nothing."

"Then what's with all the questions? Did you auction me off or something? Put my face up all over campus like those wrestlers did last year to get their buddy a pity date?" My bestie is loyal, but she also wants to see me happy. "Does your Kevin Rogers story have anything to do with me?"

"Yes. They're eerily similar, and I forgave Lyle. He thought he was doing his friend a favor—*and* he ended up being a really good kisser."

"Hannah! What the fuck?"

Another shrug. "What! He felt so guilty! He was so sweet."

"How long were you sneaking around?"

"I don't know—two or three months? Until Rick Roth asked me to the spring fling and lured me to go with his sweet, sweet ride."

She is unbelievable. "His Honda Civic?"

"No, his dad's Tahoe. We made out like crazy in the back seat. And other stuff."

"What kind of stuff?" Now she's got me wondering;

she would have told me if she banged Rick Roth in the back seat of his dad's SUV, wouldn't she?

"Not *butt* stuff, if that's what you're thinking."

Good lord. "Why would I think that! I never said anything about butt stuff."

Hannah pulls a face. "When someone says the word *stuff*, my brain immediately goes to *butt*." She doesn't even look embarrassed. "Butt stuff. Can't help it."

"Did you have sex with Rick and not tell me about it?"

"No, but I let him touch my lady business."

Yeah, that's right—I do remember her mentioning how terrible he was, all fingers and not enough tongue. Poor guy must not have studied up hard enough. It was so bad, she refused to go out with him again.

"I should have gone to the dance with Lyle. He went with Mindy Kissler and she said he gave her two orgasms."

"But he was in love with you!"

"You can't blame the guy for moving on after I gave him the green weenie, Skylar. The best way to get over someone is to get under someone else."

"Who told you that?"

"Um. No one?"

"Hannah."

"Ugh, fine—it was that loser JB. When we were at the restaurant, at the bar, he was hitting on me pretty hard. I wanted to clock him, but I fought the urge."

"Why didn't you tell me!"

"I didn't think I had to! We both hated the guy, and I

knew you weren't going to see him again, so why add salt to the wound?"

"There is no wound. The only hurt I feel is—" I stop myself from saying it, though we both know what was about to come out of my mouth. *The only hurt I feel is from Abe lying to me.*

Because I like him.

Liked. Past tense.

"But now that you mention it…" Hannah is all soft whispers and sweet talking.

"I wasn't mentioning it."

"Regardless. I just have one thing to say, one little nuggy of advice."

Nuggy? Instead of nugget? Great, now she's abbreviating everyday words to make them cute.

"Let's say Abe did fall for you—what then?"

"Hannah. He lied."

"Did he though?"

Is she for real? "Uh—yes."

"But the account wasn't his, and he never claimed it was."

"What's your point?"

"My point is, he would go in, swipe on people, have a quick chat with them, turn the chat over to JB, and bail until the date was done. You were the one and only person he actually had conversations with. The only one."

Wait. What? "How the hell do you know all this?"

There is no way Jack Bartlett told her this information;

on our date, he was still pretending we knew each other, albeit extremely poorly.

"*Hannah.* Did Abe contact you?"

She avoids my glare, picking at the cuticle on her right hand.

"Hannah! Look at me. Look me in the eye and tell me Abe didn't contact you!"

She won't turn her head.

"Oh my god, I'm going to kill you." This is beyond…I don't know what, but it is! It's beyond! "He got to you, didn't he? You're on his side now!"

Finally, she spins her body. "I am on the side of true love!"

Oh.

My. God.

I roll my eyes; it's the only possible response, really. "Abe Davis is hardly my true love."

"He could be! How do you know if you don't give him a chance?"

I don't believe this. "Oh my god, what did he say to you? Is he paying you? Blackmailing you?"

"Give me some credit here, would ya? I know sincerity when I hear it, and I heard it in that boy's voice."

Fine.

I might be a skosh curious. Just a smidge.

Like, *this* much.

"All right. What…" I clear my throat, determined not to sound eager. "Start from the beginning."

191

Hannah clears her throat too, winding up for a good storytelling. "It was a dark and stormy night…" She raises her arms and wiggles her fingers, like she's about to tell a good haunted house story.

Did I mention she drives me insane sometimes?

"I'm going to smother you with a pillow."

"Yeah, yeah, yeah, you say that all the time." My roommate gets comfortable on the bed, leaning back, pinning a more serious expression to her face. "Monday I get a call from an unknown number. Normally I'd never answer, but I was waiting for my doctor to call with some lab results, so I answered it." Dramatic pause. "It *wasn't* my doctor."

Lab results? She is so full of shit.

I flop to my back, knowing I'm in for the long haul. She's going to drag this story out and torture me with it.

"The first thing Abe said to me was '*Don't hang up*,' real hurried like, which was a weird thing to say because I had no idea who was calling at that point." Hannah rolls her eyes. "And obviously the first thing I wanted to do was hang up. Haha. But…I *didn't*."

Confession: I am hanging on her every word and she damn well knows it.

"The second thing he said after I agreed to hear him out was, 'The second I saw Skylar, it was like a punch to the gut. I knew I wasn't going to make it out the other side without some collateral damage.'"

I hold in a bated breath.

Exhale. "What's the third thing he said?"

Hannah pretends to think on it. "The third thing was-

192

sss...the third thing...hmmm." That index finger with the bright blue nail taps the end of her chin.

What. A. Freaking. Brat. "Hannah. I'm *going* to kill you."

"All right, all right. Calm down. I'm thinking." She pauses a few moments. *"Oh, now I remember. The third thing he said was something like, 'I know you both probably hate me, and I'm not expecting you to help me—but I'm hoping you will. All I want is to talk to her. In person would be great, but I'll settle for anything at this point.'" I get another cursory glance. "He's desperate."*

I bet he is.

"He's desperate for *you*."

"Now you're just trying to butter me up."

"I don't know, Sky—this one might be worth a little headache over. He sounded miserable."

"He doesn't even know me."

"Maybe not yet, but he wants to. And any guy who fights for a little bit of your time? They don't come around often—not in this lifetime, and not on a college campus."

She's right. How many men in their twenties, in this day and age, care about someone other than themselves? On a college campus, where Abe Davis could date anyone? Sleep with a different girl every night of the week?

And he wants me.

He even put himself at the mercy of Hannah Stark, the biggest female sasshole in Iowa, and lived to tell the tale.

"What does he want?"

"He wants to see you."

193

"When?"

"Tomorrow at eight o'clock."

Friday? "Where?"

"Aisle four at the used bookstore downtown."

"He wants to meet me at the used bookstore?"

Hannah nods. "I think it's cute! And quiet. And it's Friday, so you're hardly likely to bump into anyone you know."

"Right. 'Cause no one goes to the bookstore on a Friday!"

"Skylar, you need a place where you can talk. It's perfect—don't be a brat."

As I'm quietly debating my options, Hannah's voice breaks in, low but firm. A tone meant to push me out of my comfort zone for my own good. "I think he's one of the good ones, Sky."

I trust Hannah. She looks out for me; always has, always will. I'm putting my faith in her and trusting her now.

I can't get my heart broken by Abe Davis twice.

I won't allow it.

But I know she won't allow it, either.

"Okay. Tell him I'll go."

"Perfect. Meet him in aisle four."

I haven't had sex in so long I
forgot how to moan.
What if I fuck it up and start
barking?

Skylar

Aisle four, aisle four… where on earth is aisle four?

I walk slowly through Nebbles Secondhand Book Bazaar, counting steps much like I would if I was walking to my death. Or to a date I was dreading because I was looking forward to it so much.

I took special pains to get ready, Hannah doing my hair and makeup so it looks as if no one did my hair and makeup, the jeans and blouse casual but pretty. Flat shoes. Two bracelets. Hoop earrings.

The bracelets jingle, clanking together as I walk, peering my head around each corner, knowing when I finally reach aisle four and spot Abe, I'll be taken aback—just like a jack-in-the-box. You know it's coming, but you're never quite prepared.

I pass the self-help section, then architecture. Books are piled on the floor at every end cap, some as high as the low ceiling.

The place is mostly empty, except for two guys thumbing through records near the entrance and an older gentleman in the history section.

Non-fiction.

Fiction.

Aisle four.

Romance.

He has his back to me, fingers pushing in a thick paperback novel so it's lined up with the rest, and I watch as he levels out a few more with the side of his palm so they're even.

Anal much?

"Hey." I don't know what else to say, or how to greet him.

Abe spins around, surprised.

I'm fifteen minutes early, but then again—so is he.

"*Hi.*" He's shocked I actually showed up; it's there, written on his face. His hungry eyes are drinking me in, head to toe, expression schooled but communicative.

He's relieved. Excited.

Blushing.

"You look gorgeous." I'm not sure if he meant to blurt that out, but the words warm my insides a little, and I immediately thaw.

Dammit, that's not good. I am a fortress of steel! Here to hear him out and nothing more.

Lies, lies, everyone tells them…

"I know." I sound so bratty, but I'm glad he thinks I look gorgeous. I wanted him to—I want him to know what he'll miss out on if he ever lies to me again.

If I'm being honest, I might be missing out, too. Abe gets a perusal of his own as I skim over his jeans and the blue plaid, flannel shirt he has tucked into them. Tan leather belt. Sleeves rolled to the elbows.

Shit.

Shit, shit, shit, I'm a sucker for arm porn, and Abe does it well—too well. Those forearms of his are tan and toned and making my mouth water, just a lil bit.

I can smell him from here; the aftershave and shampoo are fresh and masculine, his hair finger-combed and slightly damp. Dark. Thick.

"Want to sit?"

"Where? The floor?"

Abe looks chagrined, but it passes quickly. "I know it's the floor, but…it's clean."

"No, this is fine. The floor works."

I lower myself to sit, legs stretched out across the aisle, and we're facing one another—my back to one shelf of paperback romance novels, his back to the one directly across from me.

Abe grabs a paper bag that is lying nearby, folding over its top, setting it aside so it's almost behind his back.

"What's that?"

"Apple slices and crackers. And…two protein bars."

I can feel my brows shoot up. "You brought *snacks*?"

"I know it's eight, and we both probably ate, but I thought, what the hell. Just in case."

It's almost like a picnic, on a much smaller scale. Thoughtful. Definitely something a sweet boyfriend would do if I had a boyfriend who did sweet things.

Which I don't.

"Thanks for showing up."

I hesitate, pondering the level of brutal honesty I want

to dish out then deciding he can take it. He deserves it. "I wasn't going to come. I wanted to stand you up."

"Why didn't you?" His question is measured, tone careful.

I roll my eyes. "Hannah insisted on driving me."

Abe nods with a smile. "She knew you were a flight risk."

"She did. She knows me all too well, I'm afraid." I can barely look him in the eyes; he's so handsome and my heart is beating so fast right now. My lashes flutter as I force my gaze to his face. "What did you say to her? One second she wants to gouge your eyes out with a dull spork then the next she's bouncing on my bed singing your praises. It was vomit-inducing."

He laughs again, white teeth a little crooked on the bottom.

Adorable.

"I don't know…I just told her the truth."

"Hmm. Well, it worked, because here I am."

I didn't even put up a fight, not really; my heart was never in it.

Glancing at him again, my stomach flutters, ripples floating to the base of my throat—who could stay mad at that face? Abe Davis is a teenage dream, and now he's mine, too.

"You already know what I'm going to say about what happened," he begins. "Do you want to talk about it again?"

Not really.

Yes.

"I'm tempted to say yes, but…I don't suppose it would serve any purpose." I give myself a mental pat on the back for sounding so adultlike and rational. I'm impressed with myself, and I hope he's impressed with me, too.

"Skylar, I…" Abe lifts his ass off the ground, repositioning himself on the concrete floor. "It's been a really long time since I've been on a date. Years."

"Are you trying to tell me you have no idea what you're doing?"

"Yes."

Good. That makes two of us. It'll be like the blind leading the blind—which could be a train wreck, but oh well.

"I'm not sure I know what I'm doing either, but I know I'm not interested in dating around. I know myself well enough to say I don't do casual very well." I take a peek to see how he responds to this news; in not so many words, I just told him I'm the kind of girl who wants to be exclusive, expects loyalty, and wants a commitment.

Especially when it comes to sex.

I don't sleep around. I don't freely give blowjobs, participate in make-out sessions, or let anyone touch my body unless they're committed to me.

That's the deal, take it or leave it.

His nod is slow. "When I do something, I'm all in."

Stupidly, we grin at each other, all the bullshit from the prior week fading away as his brown eyes crinkle at the corners and those white teeth bite down into his bottom lip. Abe breaks the contact first to look down at his shoes—dark gray suede boots. Kind of dressy, kind of not.

Hip.

Is that a thing? Do people say that?

My face tips up toward the dim lights until my eyes are scanning the wooden bookshelves, hundreds upon hundreds of books shoved precariously on each row. Dusty, this store is full of shadows, yellow pages, and worlds waiting to be discovered.

"How did you find this place?"

"My mom is a librarian, and she found it parents' weekend. It's kind of her thing, finding bookshops in whatever town she's passing through or visiting. She's a book nerd."

"Are *you*?" Clearly he knows his way around this place if he knows where the *romance* section is.

"Yeah, I read a lot."

Ugh, my heart can't take it! "Do you come here often?"

He only seems slightly embarrassed. "It's a great place to come clear your mind, sitting here among the stacks."

"Do you always sit on the floor?" I mean—it's concrete and not even remotely comfortable.

"No. There's one table in the back, but the chairs aren't great. I do homework here sometimes."

A hidden gem.

I love it.

"Abe?"

"Hmm?"

"If you liked me so much, how could you let your roommate take me out?"

It's the million-dollar question I didn't realize was in

the back of my mind, one that takes him a few minutes to reply to. I'm patient, waiting while he sits quietly across from me, thinking.

"I don't know."

I can see that there's more coming, so I wait some more.

His lips part. "All I know is that I prayed like hell that first date was going to suck."

"It did." I laugh. "He's pretty awful. Not in a mean way, just...he's selfish. It's not necessarily a bad thing—I'm sure there are girls out there who are into assholes, but I'm not one of those girls." Jack Bartlett will never be my type, not even with his handsome face and fantastic body. "Plus, he wasn't as tall as it says in his profile." My eyes roll, but I'm grinning.

"Am I tall enough for you?"

I squint sideways at him. "I don't know. I can't remember."

"Maybe we should stand up and measure."

"All right."

Abe crosses his legs and rises in one fluid motion, extending his hand down to me; his palm is warm but rough. Calloused and hardworking. Sends shivers down the back of my spine.

We're face to face but not eye to eye, and I stand ramrod straight in front of him so we can measure our height difference, my hand on the top of my head aiming straight at his chest, resting there.

Landing just at his collarbone.

One whole head taller than I am with flat shoes on.

I don't dare glance up, but my hand stays put, on his chest, flattening against it all on its own. Palm on the fabric of his soft flannel shirt, the heat from his body—and the beating of his heart—warming my skin.

Abe doesn't move.

To anyone coming across us...I can't imagine what we look like, standing here in the aisle, bodies practically touching. Innocently at first.

Always innocently at first...

Then.

Abe pulls back, creating space, his arms reaching behind my head. I can't see what he's doing until he produces three thick hardcover books from a top shelf and bends to set them on the floor.

He takes my hand.

Guides me up so I'm standing on top of the makeshift step stool, several inches taller than I was before.

Well. This is innovative.

My chin tips up, directed once again by his fingers, and I swear, my bottom lip trembles a little. Just a bit from both nerves and excitement.

I haven't been kissed in ages—years, it feels like, though it's probably only been months. Some drunk guy at the bar hardly counts; it was sloppy and wet and unmemorable.

Okay, maybe not so unmemorable since I'm remembering it now.

Focus on his mouth, Skylar!

His pouty, full mouth.

Abe doesn't cup my face or run his fingers through my hair—but he doesn't have to. The energy between us is static. Supercharged.

The chemistry is like nothing I've ever felt with anyone.

And to think I almost threw it away.

One heartbeat at a time, our lips slowly touch. It couldn't be any slower, but it buys me time to memorize this moment to replace any old ones. To lock it away for tonight, when I'm in bed, lying in the dark underneath my covers.

Alone.

When our warm breaths finally mingle, beneath the soft lighting of the secondhand bookshop, Abe slips his other hand around my waist, pulling me in. Soft lips. Gentle. Pressing against mine.

First one corner of my mouth then the other, kissing those tiny divots on either side of my lips.

I want to touch him more, but I'm not sure how. It sucks being twenty-one and this inexperienced and awkward, but that's my reality and I have to live with it.

No shame in my lack of game.

We're not making out. We're kissing and it's so sweet. His lips taste like coconut lip balm and I could stand like this forever, on this small stack of books, letting him kiss me like this, in this place.

So. Romantic.

We pull back at the same time we hear voices, my

hands returning to my sides, but still, only an inch or two separates us.

His grin is lopsided. "See? The perfect height."

A figure rounds the corner; a wide-eyed woman with a wire basket pauses, unsure how to proceed. Her eyes dart to the floor—to the books beneath my feet—then our flushed faces. The hands dangling at our sides.

The sheepish look on my date's face.

We've been busted.

The woman doesn't say a word, but it's obvious we're in her way—and that she isn't going to budge from the end of the aisle until we've moved.

The woman wants romance novels? We'll let her get to the romance novels.

I run a hand through my hair, flustered, smoothing down the strands that got mussed when Abe ran his hands over my shoulders. Clear my throat. "Should we find your table? Go sit maybe?"

He helps me down off the stack, offering me his hand even though it's not at all high. Picks up the books and returns them to their proper places.

Grabs my hand again, tugging gently toward the back of the store.

"Yeah, let's see if it's open."

It's not. Another couple sits in the chairs, reading, and Abe slips his arm around my waist. "Let's get out of here, then."

"Where are we going?"

He shrugs. "Any suggestions?"

Not really. The university might have a huge enrollment, but the city it's in? It's small, run entirely on the student population. When summer break arrives and the co-eds return home, it's virtually a ghost town. So, as far as things to do on a weekend besides hitting the bars? The options are few.

"Park. Roller rink. Coffee shop. Um…sit down by the lake?"

"We could."

But it's a bit too cold for that. I would freeze my ass off in this top.

He can hear the hesitation in my voice. "Inside then."

Hmm. What's quiet, private, and intimate?

"I say we just get in my truck and drive."

"Perfect."

Abe's truck is bigger than I was expecting, and clean, and when I hop into the passenger side, he twists his torso to watch me buckle my seatbelt.

"What are you looking at?" I'm blushing already and I wish it would stop.

"You. In my truck."

What a weird thing to say.

"It's nice."

Aww. Never mind what I said about it being weird. I'm not used to guys complimenting me, or being sweet, or…

Now it's my turn to watch Abe as he starts the engine, lets it idle a few seconds before putting the truck into reverse and pulling out of the parking spot in front of the bookstore. It's such a quaint little place. Quiet. And now etched in my brain bank as the perfect location for a first kiss.

The night grows dark, darker still when we make our way to a remote overlook point on campus. It's a bluff, famous for its hiking trails overlooking the entire city, the university, and the river running along the edge of town. From it, you can see clear to the next county, and at night, the streetlamps below twinkle and shine, lending the most romantic glow to a pitch-black sky.

Stars. The moon.

The shadows of all the trees.

We stay in the car when he parks, surrounded by a few other vehicles, one overhead lamp fifty feet or so away the sole light in the near vicinity. It flickers wanly, weak and dim, needing a bulb replacement but casting enough light so I can see Abe's face when he cuts the engine.

"It's so quiet up here," I muse to fill the empty airspace between us.

A center console separates us, and I wonder if it's the kind that can be folded up to create bench seating. A furtive glance in the back seat tells me there's plenty of room there, too.

My body gets warm.

Girl parts prematurely tingle—he hasn't spoken, or touched me, and here I am, getting turned on by the sight of him in the near dark.

Get a grip, Skylar. Get. A. *Grip*.

"You know so much about me already, and I know almost nothing about you," I start. "We have to play catch-up."

"Good idea." Abe gets comfortable, reclining his seat back a few inches from the steering wheel. "I love it here. I used to hike up here when I was a freshman but haven't really been back since."

"Why?"

"No time."

"Do you not have a lot of free time?"

"I do, plenty. I just use it kind of…stupidly, I guess."

"Doing what?"

He thinks. "Doing shit for other people, mostly—if I'm being honest."

"That's not a bad thing."

He thinks on that, too. "Is it when you're taken advantage of?"

I want to touch him then, reach my hand across the space and lay it on his big, brawny forearm—but Abe doesn't need my comforting. He's not looking for pity, he's just stating facts and making conversation.

"It's still really nice that you do good for other people, and you should never feel guilty about that. It says more about you than it does about them."

I can see his smile in the dark and bask in the fact that I put it there, that I said something that made him happy.

"True." His arms stretch, hands gripping the wheel to stay busy. Fingers tap the leather.

"Who bought you this truck?" I blurt out then wish I

could retract it. It's none of my business who bought it for him. It's just…we're so young, and it's so nice and new. Still smells like the showroom floor. "I'm sorry, that was rude."

"Promise you won't tell?"

"Promise."

"I use the money the athletic department grants me as an allowance to make my car payments, and my parents pay my rent because they don't know about the allowance."

"Resourceful."

"Some would call it that. Some would call it shady as fuck."

"I was gonna say that but didn't want to insult you." I laugh.

"Let's make a deal: I want to be the one you're always honest with, no matter what. Eventually I want to be the one person you tell everything." He steals a worried glance at me. "Is it too soon to say that?"

Yes.

Kind of?

But I love that he said it and completely agree, so I nod like a bobble head. "All right. We have a deal."

It takes me no time to forget why we're up here, where we were before, and what happened last week, because all I want is for Abe to touch me. So, I summon my courage to test our new pact.

"Abe?"

"Skylar?"

"Since we're being *hon*est…"

His interest is fully piqued, mostly by my hushed tone. Even to my own ears it sounds rather sexy. *"Yeah?"*

"I've kinda been wondering if this center console folds up."

His eyes stray to the middle partition with its empty cup holders. "As a matter of fact, it does."

"May I see?" *Whoa, Skylar, where did that voice come from?* I sound like I'm asking to see something else entirely.

"As a matter of fact, you may."

Unbuckled, Abe's hands dig under the hard plastic between us, pushing it up, nestling it like a puzzle piece, creating a bench in the front of the truck.

"There's so much more room for activities," I joke.

"And stuff."

Stuff. I'm reminded of the ridiculous chat I had with Hannah and her saying butt stuff, and I stifle a laugh—no one wants to explain that conversation on a first date. Abe does not need to know how perverted girls can be.

"What's so funny?"

"Nothing." Then I remember we promised to be honest. "Actually, that's not true. You said *stuff*, and it made me think of Hannah saying…*uhhh*, butt stuff the other afternoon. Long story."

I leave it at that, and he doesn't prod, and now we're back to staring at one another in the dark, wanting so badly to close the gap between us. The air practically crackles from the energy.

"I…have no idea how to respond to that."

"Please don't. I'm begging you," I say, and we both laugh nervously. Laugh until we're both acutely aware of how alone we are, surrounded by strangers in a secluded parking lot, overlooking the city below.

Nothing but space between us, begging to be filled.

Surprisingly, it's me who moves first, resting my hand where the console used to be, trailing a finger across the dark, gray seat. I lay my palm upside down.

Leave it there.

As bait.

Not surprisingly, Abe takes it, sliding his own palm against my skin, back and forth—not lacing our fingers, but it's almost more erotic. Back and forth, the tip of his middle finger lagging behind, nail tickling the delicate skin of my hand.

I shiver.

Bite down on my bottom lip, glancing out the window at the cars parked beside us.

A sea of tinted windows.

"Maybe instead of talking we should…" I don't know how to put this, so I just throw it out there. "I want to get to know you and everything, I really do, it's just—I want to kiss you even more right now."

"Same."

We move at the same time, meeting in the middle, mouths fusing, instantly combustible.

Open mouths. Wet tongues.

I ache for him.

Ache for his *hands*. They're swiftly in my hair, holding it back, his mouth releasing mine to nip at the side of my neck. Gently sniffing, nose rubbing below my ear.

"You smell so fucking good."

"God that feels good." I sigh, tilting so he can kiss the column of my slender neck. I'm insatiable for his mouth on my skin, lips, and body after three hot seconds.

This doesn't bode well for my chastity later, not when I've been so chaste for so long.

"What turns you on?" I ask on an exhalation, head tipped back, allowing him free rein.

"About you? Everything."

"Oh Abe, I *like* that answer."

"I like *you*."

"I like your hands, too. They're huge." Mmm, his hands…

"I like your *mouth*."

I'm sitting at an awkward angle, still in the same spot, body twisted in his direction but not close enough to really touch him. With only one solution available, I shift, back to the door, ass scooting down, removing both my shoes before setting my feet in his lap.

My head hits the seat and I'm flat on my back, legs spread, the invitation impossible to misinterpret: *Come here.*

Abe doesn't hesitate, his giant body looming over mine, moving between my legs. Kissing me while he runs a hand up my denim-clad thigh, fingers finding the hem of my shirt, pushing it up as his hand slips underneath.

Keep going, keep going, keep going, my brain chants, wanting—no, needing him to touch my boobs.

He keeps going, dragging his palm along my ribcage, up over my stomach, forefinger tracing the underwire of my black satin bra. Runs it along the full curve of my breast, sliding it under the strap and pulling it down.

My shirt gets pushed aside. Up. Bra along with it. That rough, calloused hand cups me, thumb stroking my hard nipple.

Mouth sucks it.

This is what I want, this is what I want…

I grasp at his hair. Tug. Run my fingers through it while he sucks me, lapping with his tongue. Blowing cool air across the hardened tip.

"Oh…"

I feel between our bodies for his erection, knowing full well I'm going to find it straining in his pants. And I do.

We're both panting hard as I go for his zipper, wanting to touch it, wanting to stro—

"Fuck. Stop," he rasps. "Skylar, I…don't know any other way to say this. It's going to sound fucking terrible." Abe's fingers gently roll my nipples and I could die from how good it feels.

Die.

"Just say it." What could it be? *Oh god.* Self-doubt takes over like a wave crashing onto a calm shore. *What if he hates my boobs? He hates my body, thinks I'm too—*

"Dry-humping you is neat and all, and I want you to

stroke my cock, but what I *really* want is to fuck you. So bad."

He wants to fuck me? That's great news! It's none of those things I just mentioned; forget I said all that.

"You want to have sex with me?"

"Duh. Can't you feel my cock?"

Cock.

When it's not gloriously rubbing the denim seam in my jeans, it's digging into my thigh. Big and thick and—*hard*.

So yes. I can feel his cock.

Do I want it inside me? That's the big question I have to answer. And honestly…

I gather my wits, and my common sense. "Abe, I want you too—so bad—but I'm not having sex in the front seat of a truck, no matter how bad I want you inside me." There. I said it.

"What are we going to do? We can't go back to my place—JB is home, and if he sees you, he'll get fighting mad."

My teeth chew at my bottom lip. "We can't go back to mine—Hannah is there, and she won't leave us alone if she sees us walking in the door."

Or hears us having sex in the other room. I'd never live it down. Not in a million years.

"That's better than being at my place. JB comes into my room unannounced all the goddamn time. I have no privacy."

Pfft. "You think that's bad? Even if I lock my door, Hannah can pick it open with a bobby pin. She's worse than a petty thief."

Abe is quiet for a few seconds, solving our problem. "Would you mind climbing in through my window instead of using the front door? At least JB doesn't pick locks."

"What's the worst thing that will happen if he finds me at your place?"

"Uh. He might punch me, but I doubt it. But he might."

"Can you live with that?"

"Um, *yeah*. I can live with him decking me in the face for a chance to fuck you in my actual bed."

Oh Jesus, that's kind of romantic. "How high up is your window?"

"First floor. I'll give you a boost."

Sounds reasonable enough. "Okay. Let's do it."

"I thought you said you were
done with him?"
First of all, that was five minutes
ago. He's a different person now,
stop judging me.

Abe

"**D**o I need to call the cops?" Skylar and I both pause at the interruption coming from the house next door. The sound of another window being cracked open stops me from giving her a final boost into my bedroom, hands splayed firmly on her backside.

I slowly lower her back to the ground. Pivot.

It's one of the neighbor girls, now hanging out their bathroom window. "Did you hear me?" she says, leaning further.

"I live here. Don't call the cops."

"Prove it."

I feel around for my wallet, knowing that even if I pull out my driver's license it will be useless since my school address isn't listed on it. "Um…"

"What's your name?" the girl asks, holding out a can of something I can't make out in the dark. Raid? Hairspray? Bear spray? It's hard to tell in the dim light.

"Abe Davis."

The can lowers and she sets it on a hidden countertop. "You passed."

"Thanks?" …for not spraying us both in the eyes with mace?

"What the hell are you doing climbing in through the window? Lose your key?" the voice wants to know, and

217

rightfully so. If I saw some strange dude hanging from her window, I'd try to stop him, too.

"Uh, nope. Didn't lose my key."

"Front door busted?"

"Er...no."

"What then?" She's impatient, wanting details. "You have ten seconds to explain yourself before I call the cop shop."

Two seconds ago she acknowledged she knew who I was!

My hands give Skylar a gentle nudge forward. "This is a girl my roommate met on LoveU. He isn't into her—"

"Gee, thanks," Skylar murmurs begrudgingly, giving me a bump with her elbow.

"—but I am, and if he sees her inside, he's going to get pissed, so we have to sneak in through the window."

The girl—whose face I still can't see because of the backlighting—holds up her palm to stop me. "Say no more. I totally get it." There's a quick pause. "How many roommates do you have?"

"Just the one."

"So it's the guy with the sandy blond hair?"

"Uh, yeah..." What's her point?

"My roommate Sybil has the hots for him, but she's a big wuss." Even though I can't see it, I know an idea is forming in her head. "I could do you a favor and invite him over if that would help you out—but then you'd owe me."

"You'd do that?"

"Sure. You'd be helping me help you and helping my roommate grow a pair of lady balls and maybe hit on the guy once and for all." The girl rests her elbows on the encasement, chin in her hand. "She leaves the house when he leaves every day, even when she doesn't have classes, but she refuses to talk to him. It's getting pathetic. Maybe if he's in our actual living room and we give her a few shots of vodka, she'll say hi."

"That would be fucking awesome."

"But then you owe *me* a favor," she clarifies.

"Deal."

She stands, fishing a phone out of her back pocket. The light illuminates her face, and I can finally see it clearly in the dark. "Give me his number and I'll text him."

I grab my cell, too. Pull up JB's contact and tap for his number. "Ready?"

"Go."

"555-1254. His name is JB."

The girl chuckles. "Oh, I know what his name is. We know allll about this kid, down to his weight and shoe size." *Okay, that's just weird.* "Sybil has the entire 411 on him; memorized his bio on the wrestling website." Pause. "She's not a stalker or anything."

"Hey, even if she was," I joke, "I'd still be giving you his number right now."

This gets me a laugh from Skylar, and...

"What's your name?" I ask, walking toward her and offering my hand through her bathroom window. "Sorry we haven't met. I'm Abe, and this is Skylar."

"Rachel. Nice to finally meet you. We watch you a lot. Did you know we can see straight into your bedroom?"

No. I. Did. Not.

I knew *I* could see *them,* but it hadn't occurred to me for one second that they could see me. Or that they would watch me.

"You can?"

Rachel laughs. "*Ohhh* yeah, we sure can. We *surrre* can."

Translation: we can, and we do.

Next to me, Skylar lets out an, "Oh jeez."

Rachel goes on. "You should probably think about getting drapes. We can't see your bed—"

Thank God.

"—although Felicity has tried, but we can see pretty much everything else you do. Rebecca loves watching you do push-ups, and sometimes Fel will sit on the toilet to watch you sit at your desk. She totally digs your nerdy glasses. So yeah, none of us is complaining about the view."

Christ, that's a little creepy. Isn't it? Am I wrong to be a bit skeeved out?

My mind reels, trying to remember what kind of other shit I do while I'm in my room alone besides sleep, eat, and *jerk off*—which I usually only ever do in bed…I think?

Shit. There was that *one* time I masturbated in the rocking chair, but that was during the day between classes and practice.

I think?

Fuck.

"We don't mind the show."

Skylar does *not* need to hear this so I steer her back toward my window, praying that when I shove her through it, she doesn't fall onto my desk and break my laptop. Or make a shit ton of noise. "Okay, well, it was great chatting with you Rachel. Buh-bye now."

"So good meeting you in person, Abe." She spares Skylar a glance. "You too, new girlfriend. Don't worry, we won't watch you."

Oh my god, I do not even believe her.

I have to get Skylar the hell out of here before this girl embarrasses me any further.

"Hey Abe? Love those red Valentine's Day boxers," Rachel teases. "Oh, come on! Don't look so tense about it. Relax, I'm just giving you a hard time."

But I *do* have red Valentine's Day boxers—don't ask me why my mom sent them last year for the holiday, along with a pack of red boxer briefs—and the fact that Rachel has seen them without me knowing it makes my watching their silhouettes through their sheer curtains child's play.

Wait. Did they know I was watching them? They had to know.

Fuck my life.

"No worries, wipe that look off your face," Rachel goes on, phone in hand, face lit up by its glowing screen. She's tapping away. "I'll shoot JB a text right meow and make it convincing, and he'll be out of your place in a few minutes. Guaranteed."

221

I don't know what she's going to say to him; I can only imagine.

"Remind me to get blinds first thing in the morning," I mutter to Skylar.

"Uh, in the morning? How about right *now*?" she quips, chagrined, foot already hovering above my cupped hands as I squat down, forming a step. "The stores are still open. We can run to Walmart."

"Not the worst idea." I boost her easily and wait as she gets her bearings, straddling the window ledge, one leg feeling around in my dark room for footing.

She has great calves.

"Stop doing that—you're distracting me! You want me to faceplant into your floor?" She laughs as she removes her leg from my wandering hands. "Okay. Let me go hit the light."

"No don't!" I'm practically shouting, hissing into the pitch-black space between the houses. "Leave it off, he might see the light under the door."

Loud sigh. "Calm down, I will."

"Do you hear anything?" I ask. "Anything at all?"

"Like what?" Her voice comes out of the dark shadows of my bedroom. I can hear her feeling around, bumping into things.

"Like, oh—I don't know, the front door opening? Jack *leaving*?"

"Hold on, let me check."

Silence.

More silence.

Then, Skylar reappears, staring down at me from my window, hair hanging in sheets around her beautiful face. "Yup, I think I hear something. It sounds like someone by the front door may be putting boots on?" She extends a hand to hoist me up, but I got this covered. "Why don't you wait for him to leave and come in the front door?"

"How is that any fun?"

Skylar pulls a face. "Good point."

"Push the desk out of the way if you can," I tell her, backing up a bit, about to take a small, running start. "Then move out of the way."

Getting into my room is easy, takes me no time at all. I don't mention this to anyone—ever—but back in the day, my mom used to make me take gymnastics. At first it was because my sister Monica was afraid to take the class alone and Mom wasn't allowed to sit through the class with her.

So she signed me up, too, and well—let's just say I excel at the pommel horse.

I make it in the first attempt and don't tear my guts out in the process.

"Holy crap!" Skylar is impressed.

Perfect dismount.

I call that a win.

My shoes come off first, and I kick them toward the closet door; Skylar's are already resting there, neatly arranged. My eyes adjust to the dark and I can make out her figure seated at the foot of my bed, resting against her hands, back arched as she watches the shadow of me moving about the space.

I've lived in this room for three years, so my movements are automatic, fluid. Two steps to the desk, two more to the closet. Six to the door. Seven to the bed.

Down the hall, the sound of the front door opening and closing as JB heads next door.

I now owe Rachel a favor and don't even care.

My shirt comes off as I go, one button at a time until it gets tossed to the hardwood floor.

When I reach her, I bend, grabbing beneath her knees, arm sliding under, the other at the small of her back. Lift.

She gasps as I carry her to the spot where I sleep and deposit her there, as gently as I can. Walk my way back around to the foot of the bed and crawl—in just my jeans— toward her, hands running up her legs, thighs, and waist. Shoulders and neck dipping, nose nuzzling between the apex of her thighs. Give her a long whiff just to hear her gasp again. Bite down on the denim and burrow.

A few seconds is all I need; I'm totally turned on. Rock hard.

Blood coursing through every single vein at a breakneck pace, knowing how this little party is going to end.

Cool it, Abe.

Idly—some would say lazily—Skylar watches but doesn't participate as I run my palms along the hemline of her pretty shirt, intent on its removal.

She moves a tiny bit, shifting her hips so I can push up her shirt. Gaze trailing me in the dark. Lips softly parted.

They shine when she licks them.

I harden when she licks them.

Within moments, her top is gone, discarded, tossed somewhere with mine and I bend my torso, mouth on a course for her skin.

"Take my pants off, too," she requests, still just lying there, hands now raised above her head, head resting on the pillow. Hair fanned out, black against the stark white.

"Yes, ma'am." Her wish is my command, my fingers plucking at her button-fly jeans. One. Two. Three.

Done.

"You're going to call me tomorrow, right?" Her voice is timid.

"I won't have to, because I'll be looking at you when we wake up," I tell her, tongue flicking her pussy over the thin fabric of her panties. I suck, heating the patch between her legs.

Her back arches, head coming off the pillow. "Oh my *god*, Abe."

"Shhh, babe, you have to be quiet. Just in case." I suck her through her underwear again, hooking the silk out of my way, tongue pressing into the slit.

Skylar's head hits the pillow and she cranes her neck, teeth biting down on the cotton casing. "You have to stop, I'll never…ohhhh…"

I stop licking, rising on my haunches to unbutton my pants, the zipper whirring mingling with the sound of Skylar's heavy breathing—and mine—as I shove my jeans and briefs down, over my lean hips. Work them off and throw them both to the floor. Spread Skylar's legs, leisurely dragging my calloused palms over the smooth, perfect skin of her inner thighs. I kiss along them, starting at her knees—

225

they're shaking—hips already working in slow circles above my head.

Wanton. Sexy.

She wants it; I could taste it on her and now I can see and smell it.

My plan isn't to make her come.

It's to make her crazy.

Briefly my thoughts stray to protection; I haven't had to buy condoms in ages, but I think there's at least one that's unexpired in my desk drawer. Somewhere.

Unless she's on the pill; I wouldn't mind going in bareback, and she has nothing to worry about from me—I'm STD-free and get tested regularly. Plus, I haven't had sex in fucking forever. We haven't discussed it, but I'm pretty sure she hasn't either.

Especially judging by how tight she is when I slide a finger inside.

Her head thrashes, fingers white-knuckling the pillowcase like she's on a thrill ride, which she kind of is.

My face.

I haven't even seen half of her body, having spent most of my time with my mouth between her legs, so I give her one last lick, flicking the tip of my tongue up and down a few times just to hear a gasp escape her throat.

Kiss her pussy. Her lower abs when I work my way up, the tip of my forefinger tracing her belly button, nestled in her pale flesh. Skylar isn't skinny, or thin, and her stomach isn't flat—she's soft. Curvy like a woman should be.

I kiss her sternum, right under the satin of her burgundy bra. I can see in the sliver of light that it's clasped in the front—a tiny golden V, shining in the moonlight, and I free it. Spread the cups and let them fall.

My body lowers itself beside her, dick throbbing against her outer thigh so she's flush against me when my hand roams over the swell of one breast, then the other. Palm it, loving its weight, thumb rolling over her nipple.

Breathy sigh.

Languid moan.

A gasp when I tweak it gently.

This isn't about me; this is about *her*.

"You want me to lick it?" I ask her, whispering near her ear, breathing on her skin, my nose running along the column of her neck. "Should I lick your pretty nipple, Skylar?"

"*Yes.*"

"Yes, what?" I torment her a little longer.

She shoots me an irritated look, eyes narrowed, arms still laced above her head, making her tits lie full and round.

Lips pursed, she doesn't respond.

Point taken—she's not submissive.

Got it.

"Sorry." Not wanting to piss her off, I apologize, already whipped.

When I dip my head to suckle, Skylar's fingers plow through my hair, digging lightly into my scalp, massaging as I drag my tongue over her nipple. Round and round and round…

Suck.

Lick.

Blow so it puckers.

Kiss her everywhere: breasts, collarbone, the base of her neck. She tips her head back, giving me freedom to explore; I move, my body hovering over hers, dragging my hard cock over her hot, wet…

Pussy.

Up. Down. Up. Down along her slit, the head of my erection teasing her just enough that we're both about to start begging for some relief.

I know she wants me to push inside by the way she's moving her hips and grabbing at mine. Pulling me closer. Impatient.

But I'm not wearing a condom yet, and we haven't had the talk. Besides, foreplay is underrated and we're in no rush, so I plan to take it nice and slow.

She doesn't. "Abe…"

"Not yet." It's *killing* me, but the pain feels better. I want us to both really want it. Hard and good.

"You're doing this on purpose."

I am.

I'm driving us both mad.

"Just stick it in."

"Stick it in? I'm insulted, kind of," I manage to say. Barely. Skylar is wet, slick, and freshly shaven downtown, and my dick is gliding over her slit effortlessly, just as desperate to be inside as I am.

Her head gives a frustrated thrash on the pillow as she tries to raise her lower half. "Slide it in, whatever you want to call it—I'm not a poet."

"Patience is a virtue," I soothe, lips caressing her hair.

"I'm trying to give you my virtue." Another wiggle beneath me.

"Wait." I stop moving. "Are you a virgin?" Shit, why didn't she tell me? This changes *everything*.

"No, I'm not a virgin. It was a figure of speech." Skylar exhales. "But it has been a long time and I've only done it a few times so it's probably still going to hurt."

Up. Down.

Up.

I kiss her on the mouth, our tongues deliciously entwining—I'm getting off on knowing she can taste herself on my tongue since I was eating her out not five minutes ago. "I'll go slow."

A little nod. More tongue. "Mmm, okay."

"My lazy little love muffin," I croon into her hair, still dry-fucking her without putting my dick inside, loving the endearment.

Love muffin is cute and so is she.

Jesus, sex has addled my brain, turning me into a pussy.

"Who are you calling lazy?" Once again, Skylar draws her arms over the top of her head, interlacing her fingers while I get her good and worked up. Doing nothing but still sexy as fuck.

"You, just lying here while I do all the work."

"I'm sorry I'm being selfish. Also not sorry because this feels so good I could go right to sleep."

"Uh, that's not a compliment."

This is one of the strangest conversations I've ever had, and certainly the strangest conversation I've ever had when I'm about to have sex.

In fact, I don't remember talking while I was banging someone. Ever.

It's the best kind of strange I can think of, and a good sign that Skylar and I are meant to be.

Meant to be? Wow, I sound like a girl. Next I'll be writing her love poems and throwing rocks at her bedroom window and holding her purse.

All of which I would one hundred percent do.

Skylar finds the pulse in my neck and kisses me there, lips lingering on my throat, tongue darting out to moisten my skin. "You smell so, so good."

My dick gets harder.

"Fuck, Skylar, if you keep doing that…" I'll probably come before we get to the good parts.

"Do you like it when I do that?" She kisses me again then nips at my earlobe, voice husky with sex. "Do you like kisses, baby?"

I die a little at *baby*.

"Yes," I hiss through my teeth, liking it a whole fucking lot, so much so that even my brain is spewing out curse words like a drunken sailor. "Yes I like kisses."

"How much?"

"A lot." I'm an idiot who is incapable of forming complete sentences. "I like them a lot."

Her warm mouth is on my shoulder, dragging along the toned muscles. Hands soon join her mouth, her palms exploring the hard tendons of my biceps.

"God Abe, your body—I *love* it."

"Yeah? Tell me all about it."

"First put it inside me."

"Skylar," I croak. I sound like a prepubescent teenager whose balls haven't dropped.

"Please, Abe," she begs.

"We don't…I'm not wearing a condom."

"Well go *get* one then," she snaps.

I stop moving entirely, balls throbbing. "Okay, but I'm pretty sure it's a hundred years old." *Shut the fuck up, idiot! What are you doing? Trying to talk her out of safe sex?*

Skylar sighs, loud and heavy enough to wake the dead. Rolls her eyes. "Get the one in my purse."

"You have condoms in your purse?"

"I have *uh* condom—as in one. I wasn't sure how all this would go and wanted to be sure."

Miserably, I heave myself off, buck-ass naked, and feel my way through the pitch-black recesses of my room. "Where's your purse?"

"I think I threw it by the desk chair. Hurry, I'm cold!"

This is what we get for waiting to have the condom talk; I could have had it sitting next to the damn bed.

"Where?" I can't find her fucking purse, have no idea

231

what it looks like; plus, it's impossible to see with my desk shoved from its original spot.

"Check by my shoes by the closet."

It's by the closet, set on top of her shoes—bingo, we have a condom and now we're back in business.

Except…

"Where inside your purse?"

A sigh. "I don't *know*, I just tossed it in. Root around—there's not a ton of stuff in there."

Right. Root around. "Gotcha."

It takes me thirty more seconds to find the fucking thing and throw her purse back to the floor then I scramble, trying not to kill myself on the way back to my bed. Tear the wrapper open, throw it to the ground, and roll on the rubber before I hit the mattress.

It's a bit tight, but I'm not about to complain right now.

Dick hanging between my legs, I begin the crawl back over her beautiful body.

"Do you want me on top?"

"I want whatever you want."

We're both breathing heavier now; this wait is about to make me go insane. I want to bury myself—thrust, pump, and come.

"I think I want to be on top," she tells me.

One last kiss on the mouth and I'm rolling to the empty side of the bed, lowering my knees and legs so she can climb on board.

I skim my hands over her backside when she settles

down, her smooth ass cheeks filling my hands. Leaning forward, she kisses me, tits hanging in the perfect position for me to cup them with my giant hands.

"Mmm, you feel good," she croons, leaning down to nip at the skin of my collarbone. "Taste good, too."

She hasn't sunk down on me yet.

I try to say, *I aim to please*, but the words won't come out, because it's the same moment Skylar lines herself up and lowers her body.

"Holy *fucking…*" sh-shit.

A tiny gasp of air fills both our lungs. She's taking her time, each second measured, killing us both in the unbearably slow process.

She *is* going to kill us. I'm going to fucking die if I can't bury myself deep.

My hips want to thrust up, cock filled with so much blood my brain gets lightheaded. No way could I walk out of this room and operate a motor vehicle, or take a sobriety test, or add two numbers together.

Skylar sinks lower, taking the last of my brain cells with her.

Two plus two is eleventy hundred.

Her breath is shaky. Labored. Hands pressing against my makeshift headboard—a giant Iowa wrestling flag I have pinned to the wall.

I hope she doesn't accidentally tear it down while we're screwing; it's only hanging on by a thread—well, by four tiny brass push-pins, one in each corner and—

"Fuck, Skylar." I'm the one gasping when she swivels

233

her hips, rocking back and forth on top of me, kind of like a rodeo queen fucking a bucking bronco.

Bad analogy.

"God you feel good," she whispers into the darkness, and all I can hear are the short breaths she's taking as she rides me.

"Does it hurt?"

Because she is really fucking tight, gloriously so. Snug. Warm. Wet. Tight.

A motherfucking dream come true.

"It kind of does but in a good way. I...it burns just a little, but I don't care—you feel so...mmm, Abe, stay just like that, don't move." Her hips continue their steady, rhythmic rotation, languid and unhurried, hands still pressed against the back wall.

When she angles her neck, I catch a glimpse of her reflection in the light; her eyes are closed, teeth bearing down on her bottom lip. She's concentrating.

"Mmm...oooo..." Her sex noises aren't loud, but they're sexy. A bit porno-worthy, but that's just my opinion. "Put your hands on my ass please."

So polite.

I comply readily. "Here?"

"Can you move your fingers so they're..." Her ass squirms, trying to direct me.

I move my fingers, assuming she wants them closer to her crack, and I must have flipped a magic switch because Skylar moans. Fucking moans loud. The fucks get harder. Deeper.

Tossing her head to the side, Skylar's hair hangs in my face.

I spit out a few strands that land in my mouth, mindful to keep my fingers near her asshole.

Skylar is a bit dirty, a bit naïve—a powerful combination.

"Just like that, yeah baby…"

She's sexy as hell. So goddamn sexy.

She's also talking to herself, lost in the moment, caught up in whatever shocks are overtaking that sweet pussy of hers, head lolling from side to side every few moments.

Lost. She's lost in herself, and I'm lost in her and it's freaking gorgeous.

I fucking love her.

One swipe.

One date.

Sweet. Salty. Bratty. Kind—and all mine.

I get lost in her, basking as she rides my hips, pressing down, pelvises rubbing together, the connection deep. She lowers a hand from the wall and lets it glide over the firm pecs of my chest, thumb flicking my nipple. Reaches behind and places it over mine, pushing—so I push harder.

Pushing deeper still.

Grind. Swivel.

Gasp.

Groan.

As I watch her lips part in ecstasy, I can't help wondering if they'll ever be wrapped around my dick, sucking it.

Which is the worst possible thing to wonder when you're trying not to come in under three minutes.

Too. Fucking. Late.

"Shit, Skylar, I'm gonna come."

"No." She's barely paying me any attention, lost in the sensations of her own impending orgasm. "Not yet."

Goddamn she's a greedy little asshole.

"No?" I think my brows must go up, but I can't tell for sure. My entire fucking body is one tingling nerve. "You want me to pull out? I'll last longer."

"You pull out and you die," she whines.

Fuck, what does she want me to do! I'm three seconds from blowing my load.

"Skylar," I warn. "Cats. Mom." *Fuck, do not think about your mother right now.* "Uh. Horror movies. Cats again. Dead deer on the side of the road…"

"What are you talking about?"

"I'm trying not to come."

"Oh my god, Abe, do not say that shit out loud."

"Sorry."

"Mmm, good boy…"

Annnd she's back to sounding like a porn star.

That.

Does.

Not.

Help.

I buck harder, thrusting up. Pulling her down, going as

deep as I possibly can. Dig my fingers into her ass cheeks without digging them into her asshole—I'm not into butt stuff. Bend my knees, raise my hips so we're elevated off the bed, working my core muscles and fucking her hard, as best I can from the bottom while she fucks me from the top.

"Yes...oh god, yes, keep doing that *don't stop.*"

I'm going to die anyway from exhaustion; I'm in great shape, but this might kill me in the end. Goddamn my abs are already aching, but if it makes her happy...

"Abe, god...ooo shit...oh baby, yes. Fuck, fuck, *fuck...*"

I'm single. But if you see me out with someone, mind your business. I'm doing interviews.

Skylar

"**G**ive me all the details."

"There aren't many. I met him at the bookstore—it's so cute, by the way—and we sat there for a few minutes chatting, no big deal. Then I made a joke about his height and he said, 'Let's compare,' so we stood up, measured, and that's when he kissed me."

"He kissed you right there in the middle of the bookstore?" Her voice is wistful.

"Yeah—it was pretty romantic."

"Did you stand there all night making out? I would have."

"No, Hannah, we did not stand there all night making out, because we were in public. I have *some* class you know." I rub my thighs together; they're almost as sore as my crotch, the consequences of last night's sexcapades pulsing between my legs. Ouch. "Actually, we were only at the bookstore a grand total of probably twenty minutes. Some lady interrupted us, so we left."

Hannah stares, unblinking.

It's so odd the way she tries to manipulate me into telling her stuff; she should be an interrogator.

"Then we went to the overlook."

"And made out?"

"Er. Yeah, for about a minute."

"Did he touch all your lady parts?"

"Yes. No. I mean—he touched my boobs."

"Did he make you come?"

"Hannah!"

She leans back, satisfied. "I'll take that enthusiastic response as a yes."

"Fine. Yes. He made me come, but it wasn't at the overlook."

"Did you let him bang you?"

"Hannah!"

"You know what, Skylar?" She throws down her blanket in an indignant huff. "If you didn't freak out every time I asked you a personal question, it wouldn't be this much fun. Did you or did you NOT let the kid bang you last night? Just answer the damn question and stop acting like a prude!"

"*Yes*, I let him bang me!" I pause, putting a cocky grin on my face. "Or did I bang him—that's the real question."

"Skylar!" Now she's the one yelling. "Stop it you did not! Were you on top? Is that what you're telling me?"

"Yes." I laugh. "I read somewhere you increase your chances of having an orgasm being on top, and I finally wanted to have one…or five…so I made him be on the bottom."

"I bet he was fighting you off with a stick. Does he have a big…you know. Wiener?"

I shoot her a peeved glance. "That's private."

"Come on! I'd tell you."

Yeah, she would tell me, whether I asked to know or

not, and she described it in great detail. "Not my problem."

"It is your problem because you're stuck with me, and you know I won't shut up until you tell me."

"Ain't that the truth."

She ignores my sarcasm and dives into the specifics. "So he *doesn't* have a big wiener. Is it tiny? Like this big?" She holds her fingers apart a few inches.

I roll my eyes. We are not having this conversation.

"So it's small? Yikes." She's giving me shit—I know this. But her persistence is making me stabby. "You poor thing, banging a teeny weenie."

"Shut up. It's not that small."

"So you admit that it's smallish."

I am not walking into her trap, I am not walking into her trap.

"I didn't say it was small. Stop saying that."

Okay, I'm kind of walking into her trap. It's a pretty trap, with bows and bells and glitter.

"How big is it? Just point to an object in the room that it resembles." Hannah holds up the TV remote. "This big?"

Oh my god. "No." I swat at her. "Get that thing out of my face."

She grabs a water bottle off the coffee table. "This big?"

"Gross."

"Did he put it in your face?"

Yeah, he did—and I loved it.

"You dirty little hooker." My best friend giggles like a moron. Like a twelve-year-old boy who just saw a boob for the first time in his life. "Was it in your mouth?"

Because I don't know how to respond, I laugh.

"Holy shit. You gave him a blowie."

"I didn't blow him." I can't stop rolling my eyes at Hannah. "But you don't have to make it sound like I've never given a blowjob before." I sound cocky—like I know what I'm doing. Which I don't, and she knows it.

"That *one* time doesn't count—you were both drunk, and he came in under two minutes. It was the easiest blowjob known to man. Those take no skill. You just put the dick in the mouth, blow, and boom—come all over you."

True.

"Your jaw didn't even hurt the next day," she kindly reminds me, smirking. "That's not a blowjob."

I reach for my chin, my thumb and forefinger bracing my jawline as I shift my mouth back and forth, grinding my teeth.

"So you had sex last night. This is outstanding. I'm so proud of you, roomie."

Whatever.

"Okay, back to his dick." Hannah is persistent, I'll give her that, and a master at bringing conversations full circle. She leans back on the couch, hugging her knees. "Would you say it fit inside your boner garage, or did it have plenty of room for another car? You know—room for two?"

"There definitely wasn't room for two."

"Nice. And you didn't back the car onto the garage, did

you?" Her brows go up and down salaciously.

"Are you talking about anal? Or doing it doggy style?"

"Either one. I'll take what I can get."

My mouth drops open. "Why are you like this?"

"Humor me—I haven't been on a date in weeks. It's dry as the Sahara in my desert down south."

"Somehow I doubt that. You masturbate daily."

I hear her—and her vibrator—almost every morning and every night. Sometimes during the day if we're both home at the same time between classes.

"It's not the same thing and you damn well know it. A vibrator cannot replace actual cock and balls." She stretches out on the couch, impinging on my space and laying her legs over my lap. "Actually, I can live without seeing a guy's balls. They're so ugly." Hannah shudders melodramatically. "Worst part of the dick pic."

I wouldn't know.

"But," she goes on with authority, "I can't live without the D, and that's what they're attached to. Unfortunately."

"A guy can have sex without his testicles, Hannah—haven't you taken biology?"

"Can we stop talking about balls? Gross. Stop."

"Oh, *that's* the topic that makes you uncomfortable? Balls?" She is unbelievable.

"Yes. Let's move on—tell me more about the sex with the hot wrestler."

"You think Abe is hot?"

"Uh, yeah—duh. I can't believe he's still on the market

243

with those eyes and those shoulders. Rawr." She sees the blank expression on my face and stops. "Sorry."

"Know what you should do, Hannah?"

"No, but I bet you're going to tell me."

"Take some of your own advice. Download the stupid LoveU app and find someone to..." I search for a metaphor. "Fill your tank."

Her lip curls. "Seriously, Skylar? My *tank*? There's a visual I could have done without."

Pfft. "This is a conversation I could have done without, but you left me no choice."

"Oh god, you knew damn well I was going to pounce on you the minute you walked through the door, so don't act surprised. You're my best friend—it's my job." Hannah spreads her arms wide. "I don't see Jessica or Bethany lining up to hear the gritty details." I push her legs off me and stand. "Thank God for that. They can't keep secrets."

"Don't you walk away from me, young lady! We're not done here. Come fill my tank! With stories! Come fill my love tank with stories. Pleeeeeeease..."

I laugh all the way to the kitchen, setting my bowl on the counter next to the sink. "Keep it down in there. You want Nathan and Misty to call the office on us?" *Again.* "One of these days, your loud screeching is going to get us evicted."

"We can live with JB and Abe—that dude has the hots for me so bad."

"JB?"

"Uh, *yeah.*"

I can see that. Hannah seems more like his type: flashy, outgoing, with light blonde hair and fire on her tongue and in her brown eyes. She's beautiful, lively, and sexy.

And hard up.

"Why don't you hit him up to fill your love tank?"

"I don't want or need a hump and dump from some random dude, okay? My ego couldn't take it. I want to screw someone who's going to at least call me the next day so I can block his number."

I return to the couch, sitting cross-legged in the corner. "Here's a thought: maybe you should try getting to know someone first."

"Stop." Her palm is raised, halting my speech. "Now you sound like me. Plus, you know I'm not looking for a boyfriend."

"I know you're not *looking*, but what if one finds you?"

"Not into it." Her tone is dismissive, and now she's actively ignoring me. Or pretending to. "No longer listening," she sing-songs, focused on a magazine.

"Giant penis."

The magazine gets tossed to the carpet as Hannah flies off the couch. "I knew it! I knew he had a huge penis!"

"All I said was giant penis. You need to calm down and rein in the vocal stylings."

I'm laughing, she's laughing—we're so loud there is no doubt we'll be getting a phone call from the property management to give us yet another noise warning. We simply cannot contain ourselves.

Hannah is hilarious.

"If I didn't know any better," I say after I can breathe again, "I'd think all you're doing is trying to use different words for a dick in one evening."

"I have a list. It's very much coming in handy right now, I must say."

"Why the hell do you have a list of alternatives for the word dick?"

She fluffs her hair. "I'm going to write a romance novel one of these days. It's on my bucket list, and you can't keep using the same name over and over for peen. It has to be different. And you can't call it a man sword, or a shaft. That's gross—readers would hate that."

I'm at a loss for words myself here. "*Uhhh…*"

"I have other lists, too. Like for sex, and your downtown lady business. And a *huge* list of curse words." Hannah sighs, content. "I love the internet. Did you know there are entire videos online listing profanity? You can spend hours doing that."

"And you've spent hours doing that?"

"Just once, when it was raining." Rain. As if that's a valid reason for blowing an entire day watching YouTube videos. "Anyway, I have a folder filled with words. You can borrow it whenever."

We have gotten so off topic, my head is spinning. "I'm going to bed."

"Fine. But I'm not letting you off the hook—we're going to finish this conversation later."

My back hits my bedroom door and I lean on it, biting back a smile. Hannah might be nosey, outspoken, and inappropriate, but she's also the best best friend anyone could ask for. So, when she brings Abe up again, I'll give her all the dirty details she wants.

But for now, they're mine.

All mine.

━━━━━━━━━━━━━

Abe: *Thinkin bout you. What are you up to?*

Me: *I just climbed in bed. Hannah and I were talking.*

Abe: *About us? Haha.*

Me: *Yes, actually.*

Abe: *So she knows?*

Me: *Yeah, she knows. She won't say anything to anyone though. I trust her. What about JB?*

Abe: *No, he didn't come home this morning until we had to leave for practice.*

Me: *He spent the night next door?! Whoa. Rachel really pulled through. I wonder what favor she'll call in.*

Abe: *I don't even want to think about it. You girls scare me.*

Me: *Do I scare you?*

Abe: *Uh, yeah—you're kind of dirty and mean in bed.*

Me: *MEAN?! How am I MEAN?*

Abe: *Not letting me come?*

Abe: *Cum, I mean.*

Me: *No need to be grammatically correct; I knew what you meant.*

Me: *And I'm sorry about making you wait, but I feel that since it had been so long since I had an orgasm, I deserved it. LOL I know that sounds so awful.*

Abe: *It's been a long time for me, too.*

Me: *And JB has no idea?*

Abe: *Nope.*

Me: *Well...there's going to be a point where he finds out. What then?*

Abe: *No idea. I'll figure something out.*

Me: *Can you do it soon? If I have to spend the rest of my life climbing in and out of your bedroom window, I'm out. Sorry. It's fun the first few times but the novelty will wear off, trust me.*

Abe: *I know—I'll tell him.*

Me: *Should we do it together?*

Abe: *No. I was thinking I should wait until he starts seeing someone? Maybe then he won't care.*

Me: *I don't see why he cares NOW. He does not like me.*

Abe: *It's a guy thing. He'd get jealous. Territorial. Like he peed on you already.*

Me: *That's so stupid.*

Abe: ****shrugs****

Me: *What are you up to this weekend?*

Abe: *I have a meet tomorrow.*

Me: *Where?*

Abe: *Here.*

Abe: *Hello?*

Abe: *Are you there?*

Me: *I'm here. I'm waiting for you to invite me.*

Abe: *Really? You'd want to come?*

Me: *What kind of a question is that?*

Abe: *Wow. Okay, this is awesome. It's on Saturday.*

Me: *When does it start?*

Abe: *Eleven.*

Me: *I will see you there.*

Abe: *There are going to be tons of people because we're wrestling Penn State. It's a big deal.*

Me: *Are you telling me to get there early, or are you telling me you're not going to see me?*

Abe: *Both.*

Abe: *But I'll find you.*

Abe: *There's a student section, but sit on the north side* *when you come in, with the parents. It'll be easier to spot you.*

Me: *Uh...which side is the north side? Help a girl out with directions.*

Abe: *When you come in the main doors, hang a right, wrap all the way around, and go in through the north entrance. There's a big sign above those doors.*

Me: *Gotcha. Will your parents be there?*

Abe: *No, you're off the hook.*

Me: *Thank God—we've only been on one date.*

Abe: *I'd still introduce you if they were coming.*

Me: *As what?*

Abe: *As my girlfriend?*

Me: **blushes**

Abe: *Cool?*

Me: *Yes.*

I don't care if she goes through
my cell phone. If she wants to
ruin her day, that's all on her.

Abe

I was right when I told Skylar the stadium would be packed. Penn State always draws a massive crowd every year, but this is insane. It's loud and chaotic as fans find their seats, the student section at capacity and the parent section filling up fast.

I stand in my warm-ups, eyes scanning that part of the auditorium for Skylar's familiar brown hair and cute little ass.

"What the fuck are you doing?"

"Nothing."

"Don't lie to me, dipshit. Do we need another pep talk? Is this about that girl again?" Zeke Daniels gets in my face, all up in my personal space, lips drawn tight. "We went over this—did you not follow directions?"

"Yeah, I followed directions." I don't elaborate, bending to re-tie my shoe so I'm not forced to stare back at him.

He taps his sneaker. "And?"

"And it worked out, just like Violet said."

"So I was right."

Jesus. "Violet was."

"But also *me*."

"Whatever." I huff. "Fine, yes, you were right."

"And?"

"And...what?"

"Why are you staring off into the goddamn crowd?"

I'm silent, working on the laces of my other shoe.

"Ohhh, I get it," Daniels sing-songs. "She's coming to-day, isn't she?" I don't reply, so he keeps talking. "Are you ready to throw up? Is it making you nervous?"

"Would you shut up?"

"I can't. I'm basically your matchmaker now."

"No you're not."

"Yes I am. Without me, she wouldn't have gone out with you again."

That's probably true, but he's annoying and I'll never admit it to him. I just want him to walk away and leave me in peace so I can warm up and watch for Skylar.

"Does dickweed know yet?"

"Who?"

"Jack," Zeke grits out impatiently. "JB, whatever the fuck you guys call him. Bartlett. Does he know you're boning his online girlfriend?"

"No."

"Well now you have another host of problems, don't ya?" He looks smug and arrogant and oddly pleased at this new development in the saga. "You need my help."

It's not a question, but he's looking way too hopeful for my taste.

"No!" I shake my head vigorously, the entire match I have ahead of me forgotten by the pair of us. "No. *Fuck no.* No way."

Zeke examines his fingernails. "False. I think you do need my help."

"Can we not do this now?" I'm worse off than I was five minutes ago, preparing to face off against our biggest rival in the conference. "This isn't helping."

"Your head is lodged so far up your ass anyway—I was sent over to remove it, by the way. Now that we know you're still having lady problems, let's fix it together. I'm into it."

"We're not in this together."

His mouth says, "*Ehhh*," but his body says, *Oh but we are.*

He needs to stop doing this to me; it's giving me anxiety.

My eyes dart up to the stands, and as luck would have it, at that exact moment I find Skylar shimmying her way across the fourth or fifth row up, that sassy roommate of hers trailing behind. Poking Skylar in the ass then laughing. Toting a big red and white striped popcorn container then bending when it spills.

Jesus.

I observe it all from where I stand. Skylar's hair is down, falling around her shoulders. Black t-shirt with the school's yellow logo. Jeans. Sunglasses perched on top of her head. Black purse hanging from her shoulder, its gold chain shining under the bright lights.

Unfortunately, Zeke notices me noticing and snickers beside me. "You are in such deep shit."

I glower as menacingly as I can, mimicking the glares

I've seen him give more times than I can count on two hands.

He laughs—fucking laughs—head tipping back, Adam's apple bobbing. "Oh you whipped little puppy. You should see your face right now—it's priceless. Which one is she?"

"I'm not telling you which one she is."

"Just point to her. I won't make a scene."

"No."

"What color is her shirt?"

Idiot. "Yellow and black." Just like the ten thousand other people in the stadium, most of which are wearing school colors, either Penn State blue or Iowa black and gold.

He stares off, dark obsidian eyes scanning the crowd. Then,

"The one with long brown hair? Blonde chick next to her?"

The fuckkkkk... What is he, some kind of Houdini?

"I'm right, aren't I? She's got brown hair, and she's in the parent section—right where I'd stick my new girlfriend—and her sidekick is a hot mess, am I right?"

"Shut up."

He prattles on, "Oh! They see us!" Zeke's arm goes up to wave. "How nice, the little blonde one is pointing over here and your girlfriend keeps slapping at her hand like you're doing to me." He grabs my limp arm by the wrist, creating a floppy salute. "Wave and say hello, shithead."

"Put your goddamn hand down!"

255

"Relaxi taxi, bro." I've never seen him this jovial, and it's seriously wigging me the fuck out. "God, this shit is hilarious! Your girlfriend is freaking out at her friend, you're freaking out at me—everyone is freaking out!" He makes a *blahhhhh* sound and I want to sock him in the nuts so bad to make this end.

"And JB—or BJ as I'm going to start calling him—doesn't have a damn clue." He claps a hand on my back. "This is going to be such a fun day. I can't wait to see how it ends."

I swear to fucking God…

Zeke starts walking away. Stops. Pivots back around. Snaps his fingers, remembering something. "Oh, by the way—your dick looks super small in that singlet. Has anyone ever told you that?"

What.

A.

Douchebag.

Skylar

"Can't you just walk in a straight line like everyone else? Do you have to talk to everyone on the way to our seats?"

"Yes I must. That was my old chemistry professor back there—it would have been rude not to say hello."

Hannah gets too close and knocks me in the back—yet again—with the box of popcorn she insisted on getting.

"He had no idea who you were."

"Professor Lewis? Are you kidding? He was thrilled

to see me!"

"That was Professor Langley. He's an English professor."

"It was?"

"Yes."

"Well no wonder he looked so confused!" She laughs, bumping into me.

No sooner do I say, "If you don't freaking be careful you're going to spill that," than she spills half her popcorn, making a huge mess before we've even sat down. "Can we just sit? Please?" I plop down, patting the seat next to me.

"Yeah, yeah, yeah, I'm coming," she gripes, as if I'm the one causing the commotion. Settles in. Eats. Stares down at the floor, where blue mats are set up and coaches and coaching staff loiter with clipboards, headsets, and serious expressions. "Your secret boyfriend sure looks mad. Who is that guy he's arguing with?"

"I have no idea." But Abe sure does seem angry about something.

"He looks like a giant asshole."

"Who?"

"The guy with the black hair. Duh."

Phew. I thought for a second she meant Abe and was about to get defensive. "I'm sure he is—he looks like a giant prick."

"Whoa, Abe's getting kind of feisty," Hannah is saying between bites of popcorn. She's shoveling it in with one hand like a bad meme. "Oh look, he's waving!"

Before I can react—or grab the back of her shirt collar—Hannah pops back out of her seat, arm flapping in the breeze, waving down to the wrestling floor.

At the pissed-off-looking asshole, and at Abe, who looks like he wants to punch him.

I slap Hannah's hand down. "Would you sit down! Oh my god, *sit.*"

"*Rawr.*" She meows like a feral alley cat, a sound she knows I hate. "You're so salty."

"I just don't need you waving your arms all over the place. People are trying to see."

"Literally nothing is happening. Why are we here so early?"

"Abe said to get here early, that's why."

"Oh Abe said, Abbbbe said," she teases, popcorn crunching. "*Blah blah blah, I'm Skylar. I have a boyfriend now.*"

She's the worst.

But.

Regardless, I preen, the words making me all warm and fuzzy inside.

"Shut up, I do not sound like that."

"*Blah blah blah I'm Skylar and I'm getting laid.*"

"It was *one* time." We did it once and I'm still sore between my legs; I've had to roll out of bed the past few nights to waddle into the bathroom. "And I still can't walk straight."

"That's the sign of a good fucking."

"No, that's the sign of a girl who hasn't been sexed in

an age."

"Those first few times hardly counted. Neither of you knew what you were doing."

Hannah thinks she's so wise.

"That's the same thing you said about the blowjob situation."

She points a finger up toward the ceiling to punctuate her point. "Also true."

"Whatever."

"Don't pout. You're getting the D, which is more than I can say for myself."

"Now who's pouting?"

My best friend ignores me, cocking her head and gazing down toward the court. "Don't you think Abe looks pissed?"

It's hard to say from here, but once the big brooding guy stalks away, Abe begins to pace back and forth along the edge of the blue wrestling mats, hands behind his head.

Then the lunges begin, his thigh muscles flexing, thick and hard and tight…all words that describe his penis and my vagina and dear God I've got sex on the brain.

I shift in my seat uncomfortably.

"What's the matter, little mama? Does the sight of your man in spandex get you all hot and bothered?"

"Shut up."

"Look at JB over there, strutting around in his singlet. Shit, I wish I had boy-noculars so I could check out his package." She squints in his general direction. "It's so hard to see it from here. I hope they put it on the jumbotron."

"They're not going to put his dick on the big screen."

"They might."

"They won't."

She nudges me. "You're the one who made me come—can you at least be optimistic? Stop being a Debbie Downer and let me have some fun."

I'm trying. "Sorry, I'm so nervous."

"Why? It's not like he's going to come charging over here at you through the stands. I doubt you'll get the chance to even talk to him afterward. There are a billion people here."

More like a few thousand.

"I am surprised he spotted you, though," Hannah admits through the ridiculous amount of popcorn in her mouth. "He must have been looking pretty damn hard."

"I'm surprised too, but he did tell me where to sit so he kind of knew where to look."

"True. He must have an eagle eye, because what are the odds he'd actually see you? Everyone looks the same—except those assholes in blue."

The players—I mean, wrestlers—all shuck their warm-up attire, an assistant coming around to collect the discarded pants and jackets as the guys continue to stretch in place when the lights in the stadium dim. Above us, the jumbotron comes to life, the arena filling with loud music as an announcer's voice booms through the speakers. Video clips of previous wrestling meets play on the massively large screens, the winningest wrestlers from each team flashing overhead one by one with their statistics.

My heart stalls when the headshot of Abraham Davis' handsome face stops front and center. Name. Age. Year. Weight. Height. Wins. Pins; I have no idea what the terminology is because I haven't googled a thing about the sport.

Does that make me a bad girlfriend? A terrible sports fan with no school spirit?

Or just lazy?

Either way, I vow to do a bit of research at some point so I don't sound completely naïve if Abe brings it up. Or asks a question, because how embarrassing would it be if he did, and I had no idea what a Macho Man Randy Savage is or who sings "Let's Get Ready to Rumble".

Wait. Is that even the same sort of wrestling?

Hannah bumps me with her free arm. "This is so exciting. Now I do wish I'd boned JB—he's hot."

"It's the dim lights. Makes him look like less of a douche."

"Yeah, you're probably right." She gives me a side glance, offering me her bucket of popcorn. "Want some?"

"No thanks."

"You sure? You didn't eat before we left."

Is she keeping tabs on me now? "I would choke and die."

Hannah rolls her eyes. "I haven't been to any sporting events in forever. I feel like a failure. Look." She points. "Just look at all those skanks over there, hoping to get laid by one of these guys later."

261

"I think they're called jock chasers."

"Jersey chasers," she adds knowingly. "Yup. Wantin' that M-R-S degree."

"I don't think these guys can go pro. It's not like football—I mean, what is there after this?"

"The Olympics," Hannah says with authority, and I wonder how the hell she knows all this.

Music plays. Lights flash. Little by little, the house lights come back on, a spotlight on the center mat, signaling the first match of the day.

It's not Abe. It's not JB. It's some kid named Bryan Vanderwahl and I can barely watch as he flips and flops like a fish out water, gasping for breath and losing the good fight. Poor guy, and in front of all these people, too.

"No girl is going to want to bang that one later," Hannah announces, loud enough for anyone to hear.

"Would you shut up? What if that lady over there is his mother?"

She clamps a hand over her loose lips. "Shit, sorry."

One more guy.

Then another, and another, and another until...

Abe.

Tall, strong, beautiful Abe.

I can't watch. What if he loses? I'll die. What if he's the kind of athlete who's inconsolable after a loss? What if he's angry and wants to be left alone? Do guys cry when they don't win?

What will I say?

"Uncover your eyes, you chicken. You're missing it." Hannah removes the arm I'm using as a shield to block out the match now in progress down on the mats and forces my hand back into my lap. "You're the worst girlfriend ever."

But Abe isn't losing.

He's…got the Penn State kid hoisted in his arms, about to lay him out on his back, and the crowd is going wild—so loud I wish they'd all just shut the fuck up so I can concentrate harder, because *whoa*.

"He could totally lift me up if he wanted to," I say breathlessly, spellbound.

An affirmative nod from my roommate. "Damn right he could."

"Like, he could lift me over his head. As if I weighed nothing."

"You're not in the circus—calm down with the acrobatics, Greatest Showman."

Irritated, I give her a poke. "Whatever. I'm going to ask him to lift me above his head. I have to know what it's like."

"Blah blah blah, I'm Skylar and my boyfriend is stronger than Hercules."

Abe

I win my match, thank Christ, because Skylar is watching and I'd feel like a pussy if I lost. Overall, our team won, though just barely and by the skin of our thin, nylon singlets.

263

It felt good.

I feel great.

I loiter on the mats once the meet is officially over, shooting the shit with a few dudes from Penn, one eye on the stands and Skylar's black t-shirt clad body. I want to catch her before she leaves, but it doesn't look like she's going to hang back, as much as it appears Hannah is trying to make it happen.

The pair stand, waiting patiently as parents and fans file out, making their way toward the stairs leading to the lobby of the stadium.

Casually, I glance over my shoulder, counting members of my team who're also straggling and give a shout-out to the big man upstairs that JB has gone to the locker room.

I war with myself; wait until I can text Skylar or walk over and say hello in person?

"Don't be such a pussy," a voice calls out from behind me.

I will not turn around and acknowledge Zeke Daniels.

"The coast is clear. Get over there before my nut sac shrivels up, which it does every time I watch you romance a woman."

I will not turn around and acknowledge Zeke Daniels.

"If you don't go over there, I will."

This time I do turn, because he's loud and projecting, and, "Would you shut the fuck up already? I'm going!"

"You didn't say please."

I fucking hate this guy.

Still.

My feet propel me forward, hands jammed into the lining of my black and yellow warm-up jacket, pasting a smile on my face when all I want to do is vomit on my black shoes.

Fifty feet from Skylar—too far for her to hear me when I call out her name.

Thirty feet and I try again.

Twenty.

Ten.

It's Hannah who hears me, giving her best friend a shove and tripping her up in the process. Skylar whips around, agitation etched on her face until Hannah points down.

Skylar follows her finger.

To me.

I raise a hand in greeting. *Hey.*

"Hold on one second," she mouths while she waits on the swarm of people in front of her, waiting so she can use the stairs to go against the tide—toward me.

I meet her against the cold metal railing, resting my hands on the bar, leaning in to kiss her mouth.

"You taste salty."

"It's sweat, sorry."

"I don't mind." She blushes. "I like it—it's sexy."

My sweat is sexy.

"What'd you think?"

"Abe, you're amazing." She's out of breath, chest heaving like she's the one who just held Blake Cartwright down for three seconds. It doesn't sound like much, but when the dude is two hundred pounds, fifteen percent body fat, and fighting like hell to get out of the hold, it's a sonofabitch to accomplish.

"You think so?"

"*Yes.* I've never seen a wrestling game in person before."

I could kiss her face. "It's called a wrestling meet." But I forgive her.

"Gosh, I knew that—I'm just nervous, sorry."

Out of habit, I shoot a glance over my shoulder at the mats and the dwindling numbers. If I don't get into the locker room soon, someone is going to notice.

"JB is going to a party tonight—want to come over?"

"Are the girls next door having a party?"

"No, this one is at a frat house. His cousin or something is a Lambda."

"What did you have in mind?"

"We could hang out and watch a movie? Or go out— but I figured since I have the place to myself for a change, you might want to come over?"

"I'd love to come over."

I get close enough to kiss her again. "I'm going to shower then I'll be home in about an hour. We have meetings and shit afterward then I can take off."

"Am I crawling in through the window?"

I laugh. "Use the front door."

"Are you sure? That was kind of fun, you know?"

"I'm not making you climb in through the window, Skylar."

She squints one eye at me. "Isn't it a little early for a frat party? Don't those usually start at like, ten o'clock?"

"Yeah, but it's his cousin and it's their annual whateverthefuckit'scalled mixer so they need all hands on deck early. I think JB wanted to rush but his grades suck and they wouldn't give him a bid. Every once in a while he likes to go and pretend to be a brother."

"That's kind of nice of him."

"I mean, he's there to get drunk and laid, so it's not like he's in it for the charity."

My girlfriend laughs.

Girlfriend.

I toss the word around in my head, loving the way it sounds.

Now she's the one kissing me. Booping me on the tip of my nose before shooing me off. "All right. See you at your front door in an hour."

267

Him: How is it possible your single?

Me: *you're

Skylar

"Why am I so nervous?" I pull at my sleeve, hating the way this shirt looks on my body. It's pink and blousy and totally inappropriate for a Saturday night at some guy's house, hanging out in his bedroom.

My boyfriend's house.

Hannah hands me a different shirt. "Because you know you're getting fucked."

"Must you say it like that?"

"I speak the truth."

As much as I protest, she is a hundred percent correct. I rub my thighs together, testing their sensitivity.

Not horrible. Not great.

I feel like I've done a million squats and thigh abductors at the gym and forgot to cool down and stretch afterward. Little bit tender, little bit achy.

Definitely throbbing.

I debate the wisdom of having sex tonight while I swap out shirts, tossing the pink blouse to my bed and pulling on the white t-shirt Hannah's chosen. It's basic, except for the sleeves, which are pretty badass—like ribbons at the shoulders, crisscrossing every which way.

I tuck the tee into my jeans, step into a pair of wedges, and let my hands fall to my sides. "How do I look?"

"Great, actually. Real cute."

Hmm. A suspiciously sweet thing for her to say. I raise my brows. That's it? That's all she's got?

"I'd bang you."

There it is.

It's weird approaching Abe's door.

I fidget, pulling at the hem of my jacket, darting looks to the side yard and house next door, paranoid JB will come walking around the corner at any second. I rack my brain for an excuse.

"Would you like to buy some Wilderness Girl cookies?" I laugh to myself, saying the words out loud, sounding like a fool. "I was just passing by and remembered you lived here, and I happen to have a microeconomics question if you have a free minute?" Shift on the balls of my feet. "Join my cult? I have pamphlets in the car."

Abe saves me from myself, pulling open the blue front door before I have the chance to knock, then the screen, making room for me to pass and bending to kiss me when our bodies brush against the other.

This just might be my favorite part of being a couple.

The hello kiss.

The goodbye kisses aren't too shabby, either, but we've really only had one of those.

"Hello to you, too." I ease past, removing my jacket as I stand in the little entry, which is basically just a patch of stained linoleum flooring surrounded by carpet at the door.

It's evident no women live here. It's tidy but boring

and brown, decorated in secondhand chic. No offense to Abe or his roommate, but the whole living room is kind of depressing. Brown couch. One chair—a recliner. The television and some gaming equipment.

That's it.

No pictures, no clock, no pillows or throw blankets.

Not that it's necessarily a bad thing; it's just different than what Hannah and I have going on at our place. Area rugs. Framed art. Pictures of us on every wall. Plants. Wallpaper in the kitchen.

Every nook of our apartment is bedecked. We move in three weeks before the semester starts every year, just to decorate. And the holidays? Ridiculous.

Abe's place definitely needs some touches, and I'm just the girl to do it.

Maybe just his bedroom once we get to know each other better and he won't consider it meddling. Listen to me, already wanting to make his room cozy without asking him—my mother would be appalled.

"Are you hungry?" he wants to know when I'm standing in the center of his living room, still surveying the area.

"No, I ate before I left." Yeah, I ate: a cut-up apple on a plate with a heap of peanut butter and chocolate chips. Not what you'd call a well-balanced meal, but I couldn't stomach anything else—nerves wouldn't allow it.

"Want to watch a movie?"

I glance at the giant flat-screen television anchored to the wall.

"Do you have a TV in your room?" I didn't notice one

in the dark the other night when we were fooling around.

"Yeah, but it's not as big."

"Honestly, I'd be more comfortable hanging out in your room tonight, just in case JB comes home." Not that I want to hide from the guy, but I kind of want to hide from the guy.

If Abe doesn't want to tell him about us, there has to be a reason why. Short temper? Jealousy issues? I'd rather not poke the hornet's nest prematurely without a well-thought-out plan.

"We can hang out in my room." *We're going to end up there eventually anyway*, I hear him thinking.

"Lead the way."

I follow him down a short hallway, sticking my head into the bathroom, letting my eyes roam as if seeing every-thing for the first time. Single sink. Medicine cabinet for a mirror. Toilet with the seat up. Bathtub with a basic, navy blue shower curtain. It's drawn back and there are only three bottles on the lined insert: one giant bottle of sham-poo, another of conditioner, and a colossal body wash.

No window.

JB's room is directly across from Abe's and his door is ajar, so I give that a looksee, too. His bed is a simple mat-tress on a steel frame, and it's unmade. In fact, the covers are mostly on the ground, the fitted sheet loose from one side of the bed, exposing the mattress beneath it.

His clothes are everywhere, piled haphazardly on the floor. Wooden dresser covered in cologne bottles, trophies, spare change, wrappers, papers, and a bunch of other un-identifiable...things.

A condom box sits on the bedside table.

Nice.

Actually...

I tap Abe on the back. "Maybe you should grab one of those?"

"One of what?"

He's not as enthralled by his roommate's room as I am.

"Condom."

"You want to steal my roommate's condoms?"

"I wouldn't call it *stealing.*"

"Technically it *is* stealing because we wouldn't be giving it back. And besides, I took care of it already—ran to the store after class yesterday."

Oh my god, he bought condoms? That's weirdly sweet and I'm glad for it, glad he made the effort to keep us both not pregnant.

I hug him from behind. "I have the best boyfriend."

He pats my hands at his waist. "You're only saying that because I haven't done anything to piss you off."

Yet, I silently add with a grin. He hasn't done anything to piss me off *yet*. I can't imagine him doing anything to upset me—well, other than the small detail of him lying to me at the beginning, but I was just collateral damage from his dysfunctional relationship with his roommate.

That is not a topic I'll be touching any time soon.

I plop down on his bed as he closes and locks the door then joins me in the middle of it. I sit cross-legged and he mirrors my pose.

We're facing each other, smiling, the only two people in the world.

"Hi," I say foolishly, at a loss for words.

"Hi."

"Are you tired?" His wrestling match looked exhausting, a well-fought and drawn-out victory.

"Not really."

"Sore?"

"Not yet." He laughs. "But I'm sure I will be. I always am."

"Want me to rub your back?" I offer it up selfishly; I'm dying to get my hands on his bare skin and hard muscles.

His grin is answer enough. "Only an idiot would turn down a back rub."

Abe is already reaching for the hem of his hoodie, dragging it and the t-shirt underneath over his torso. His abs are rock solid, flexing with the motion as he lifts his arms to remove his clothes.

Thank God he can't see my face—or the hard swallow.

"Um...I'm a novice masseuse, so you should lower your expectations of this massage. It won't be deep tissue or anything."

He bends forward, kissing my lips. "It's going to feel amazing."

"It'll probably feel more like butterfly wings," I caution.

"I love butterflies."

"Uh. Okay." I crack my knuckles, posturing. "Here I

come!"

The massage starts off okay. I'm next to him on the bed, kneeling and kneading, my hands lacking the proper oil or lotion to make them glide.

Still. I use the tools the good Lord gave me—my palms—pressing as deep into his back as I can without hurting him. Pressing with the tips of three fingers like I'm kneading a loaf of dough, which looks idiotic.

And I'm only doing it because if I don't, I'll end up sliding my hands into the elastic waistband of his athletic pants and groping his beautiful squatter's ass when I'm supposed to be rubbing his back.

"Maybe you should sit on me."

Say what now?

"Sit on you?"

"Yeah, you know—climb on."

"Your back?"

"Yes. It might be easier to get my shoulders." He cranes his thick neck to glance up at me. "You won't hurt me—you barely weigh anything."

Okay, now I *know* he's lying. I weigh *plenty*, and it's hardly nothing. But I clamp my lips shut since he's clearly delusional and thinks I'm a delicate flower.

I'm not, but whatever.

"Did you know seventy percent of all massages lead to sex?" I ask him, fingers gliding down his ribcage in a very unmassagey way.

He shivers. "Is that a fact or did you just make it up?"

"It's a fact." I think. "I feel like I read it somewhere."

"Sounds legit." Abe laughs, his whole gorgeous, toned body shaking gently.

"Does it?"

His neck cranes again. "Did you make it up?"

"No!" I laugh. "I mean—I can't quote the source, but…"

"Do not tell me the source is Hannah."

Okay, so maybe the source *was* Hannah. "It could have been, I don't know."

I release my hands from his body when he rolls over, grabbing the palms that were just on his lower back and placing them on his abs for me.

My fingers splay, thumb beginning a slow motion over his belly button.

"I think you made that statistic up so you could get frisky." His deep voice is husky, eyes intent.

"Not true."

"Prove it."

"I think *you* just proved it all on your own." My eyes slowly travel to the tent in his pants, Abe's erection jutting out.

He follows the line of my gaze before reconnecting with mine. Scowls.

"I think your dick is protesting a little too loudly against your burden for proof. It wants the statistic to stand as fact."

"He's not the boss of me."

"Oh, it's a he?"

"I mean. I'm a guy—dicks can't be a female."

"Just...*please* do not tell me you have a name for it."

He does not hesitate. "Little Abe."

I wrinkle my nose at him. "Seriously? That's the most creative thing you could come up with?"

"It's not like I sit around thinking about shit like that."

"Good point. Because if you did, we'd have bigger problems than the one wanting my attention right now."

I slide a fingernail over the fabric covering the length of him and he groans, head flopping back onto the mattress.

"Does Little Abe want to play?" I baby-talk to his penis, giving it a stroke through his pants. "Widdle Abey Wabey."

"Stop talking like that. *Fuck.*" Abe's big head immediately pops back up so he can properly glower at me. "When you say it out loud, it sounds really fucking dumb."

"No shit, Sherlock," I tease. "Can we just call it 'your dick' like normal people and move on with our lives?"

"Yes. You're the one who asked if I named it."

I roll my eyes at him. "You should have just said no."

"You set a trap and I walked into it."

"I was not setting a trap. It was an innocent question I didn't think you'd have an answer to."

"You still outsmarted me. You're a mind ninja—and coupled with the power of massage, I had no control over my answer."

Such a ridiculous, sweet thing to say. I stroke him again, loving the firm muscle gliding through my fingers. Loving the fact that I make him hard. Loving the fact that he wants me.

That he thinks I'm smart and funny and sexy.

I think he's brilliant and smart and so, so sexy.

We're well-matched.

"You know what else little ninjas have control over?" I drag my palm slowly along his inner thigh, his warm skin heating my hand.

"What?" he whispers—as if he doesn't already know.

I work my way up past his thick thighs, over his lean hips, my fingers deftly working the waistband of his pants.

"Really little little ninjas."

"So I can't call my dick Little Abe but you can call it Little Ninja?"

"Little *Little* Ninja."

"Can we not insult my dick?"

It's far from little—quite literally *just* manageable enough to…do what I'm about to do with it.

Which is put it in my mouth.

And suck.

And try to *blow his mind*. It's a sex act I've never considered myself good at, one I've never been anxious to perform (the one time I performed it) and therefore haven't repeated since.

I attempt to tug his waistband down over his erection, try to be casual and sexy about it, but the stupid pants get caught on his penis, sending a furious blush creeping up my chest, up my neck, to my face.

The second attempt is successful, and I have them down over his hips in a flash, marveling at the taut power in his hips and thighs, which flex from the contact of my fingers.

I remove the pants completely—Abe isn't wearing boxers, or briefs, or anything remotely resembling under-wear—and debate my next move.

He watches silently, arms going behind his head, fin-gers laced together. He's got a front row seat to the action, and he's a keen observer.

I wish he wouldn't watch; this could end horribly.

His body is chiseled perfection—ridiculously so—made of stone and steel and heat. Perfect abs. Gorgeous arms. Mouthwatering thighs. Beautiful, hardworking hands; I marvel that they've been on my flesh.

Abe moans, eyes closing (thank God) when, finally, I lay my palms on his skin, trailing them along the cords in his legs. Inwardly, I moan, too, just from touching him. From anticipation, really, the saliva in my mouth an indi-cation that I want this almost as much as he does.

Perhaps I'm lustier than I give myself credit for.

Hannah will be glad to hear it.

What would she do right now? She's more adept at sex play than I am, and why am I even calling it that? Sex play? What am I, eighty?

Hannah would go right at it—put that dick in her mouth and go to town. But I'm more hesitant, gauging how deep it will go once it's in my throat, not wanting to choke and die.

Death by blowjob.

"Yes officer, she suffocated swallowing my cock."

When I laugh, one of Abe's eyes opens. "What's so funny?"

Shit. Way to ruin the mood, Skylar.

"Nothing."

His eye slides closed again. Lips parted, breath hitching when I grip his hard-on in my hands, testing its weight. Give it a few practice strokes up and down, tentatively, not wanting to squeeze too hard.

Is there such a thing? Don't guys like a stiff tug? Is there such a thing as a bad blowjob?

I really should start watching porn to score some pro tips.

Before I lower my head, I remove my top, my bra, and—get naked. I'm tempted to rub up against him but fight the urge, aligning my body into position so I can get comfortable when I lower my torso. Dip my shoulders, hovering over his shaft.

Shaft.

Yeah, that's what I said.

It fits in my mouth snugly, the tip hot and salty, too. Begin a steady bob with my head, synchronizing the sucking and bobbing and adding my hand to the party.

Pleased I've managed to do three things at once, I relish the sounds coming from Abe's throat. The moans and groans. Occasional thrust from his hips when I hit the sweet spot, sucking harder. Sinking onto it farther with my mouth until it hits the back of my throat, something I thought would make me choke.

It doesn't.

High fives all around.

I don't know how long I blow Abe; he hasn't come yet. Hasn't tugged on my hair or given the *I'm gonna come* signal. So I suck. And stroke and,

"Baby, I want to fuck you."

I shake my head no. I want to finish him off.

"Skylar, please," he begs.

Nope.

I'm going to blow him then he's going down on me, and we can both fall asleep satisfied.

I'm so excited I can't stand it.

My girl parts tingle. Get wet. I can feel it even as I go down on Abe, am conscious of the hormones building inside my body, making me crazy horny and sex-starved.

Foreplay. Is. The. Shitttt.

"Are you sure?" He interrupts me again, his big hands stroking the back of my head, fingers giving my loose strands a tug. Gentle. Still, I can feel the tension in his hands; he wants to bear down and direct but is resisting the urge.

I make a mental note to tell him he doesn't have to be such a damn gentleman all the time. It's okay to be dirty with me. I like it. I want it. Maybe not all the time, but occasionally would be sexy.

Then I feel it.

I feel his balls tighten in my hand, a small pulsing in the base of his cock and his murmured, "Shit, Skylar, I'm gonna…I'm gonna…" He taps on my shoulder, the universal sign for *Stop blowing me, I'm gonna come.*

But I don't stop because I'm going to swallow that semen if it's the last thing I do. I'm not a spitter; I *refuse* to be a quitter.

Damn, I should put that on a t-shirt and sell it—bet I'd make a fortune.

"Fuck, Skylar, fuck…"

Abe's abs constrict, his lower half jerking when he comes inside my mouth, the moan emanating from his chest a bit guttural.

"Oh fuck…"

I'm surprised to discover I don't taste it when he comes inside my mouth; it goes straight down my throat and never touches my tongue.

Huh. Who knew?

Lifting my head, I brush away the strands of hair that fell into my face when my head was bent and reach over to kiss his mouth. Our lips lock, his hand at the back of my neck, pulling me in, deepening the kiss.

Our tongues entwine. Wet. Hot. Kisses.

"Your turn," he tells me. "Lie down."

"Are you sure…" I feign protest.

His hands wrestle with my waist, taking me to the mattress. Give me a yank to position me, my head up near the headboard. Slowly, he eases his way down my body, arms braced on either side of me, raining kisses on my skin along the way.

Column of my neck. *Kiss.*

Collarbone. *Kiss.*

The valley between my breasts. *Kiss.*

My stomach. *Kiss.*

Belly button. *Kiss.*

His warm breath kisses my skin, too. Mouth opening when he's down between my legs, the tingling I felt earlier intensifying to a satisfying burn. *God, I want his mouth there so bad it aches.*

Throbbing. Aching. Need.

If there was ever such a thing...

I gasp loudly—a half moan, half gasp—when his tongue dips into my slit.

"Your pussy tastes so fucking good."

It does?

Thank God. I mean, how the hell does a girl even know what it tastes like? I did make sure not to eat anything gross today, like tuna fish salad or seafood or whatever, haha. Just loads of fresh fruit. In the event Abe decided to go down on me.

His tongue goes deeper. His lips suck harder. He uses a bit of teeth and I moan, unable to stop the loud sound from filling the bedroom.

I'm unable to keep my hips from gyrating, wanting it deeper and harder but unable to control him.

Abe spreads my legs, pushing them wider with his big,

gorgeous, sexy hands. Keeping them spread with wide shoulders. The thumb on his right hand finding my clit and pressing down like it's a hot button.

It feels incredible.

It feels like I never want it to stop, but I want to come so fucking bad. I don't, though.

But I do, "Oh god Abe *don't stop.*"

Don't stop, don't stop, don't ever, ever stop.

Abe growls like a caveman, bearing down and finishing me off as if his goddamn life depends on it. Leaving me lying there, lower half shuddering.

All is right with the world.

———

The first knock on Abe's bedroom door comes around twelve-thirty in the morning, an unobtrusive rap that wakes us from a sex-dazed nap. Abe is sprawled out, flat on his back in the middle of his bed, and I lie sated, snuggled up next to him.

The second knock isn't as tolerant. Full knuckled.

The third? Slightly aggressive.

Banging fist.

"What the hell?"

Abe and I both stir, stopping short when the doorknob rattles and his roommate's voice booms through the wood.

"Dude. Why is your door locked? Are you cranking one out?" JB rattles the knob again, trying to jiggle it free.

I roll my eyes at his crude terminology for masturbating but otherwise lie perfectly still.

Waiting.

"What's up?" Abe calls out, pulling the blanket over our naked bodies. What's the point of getting dressed when you're only going to have sex again?

"Fucker, open the door so I can tell you."

"I'm naked." It's not a lie, and I snake my hand beneath the covers to gently grip his dick. *Mmm, mine.*

"So?" Jack's voice is impatient on the other side of the door; I can almost hear him sigh. "I've seen your hairy balls before."

Abe does not have hairy balls.

"What do you want, Jack?"

"I want you to open the fucking door. Duh."

"Whatever it is, I'm sure it can wait."

"Why aren't you opening the goddamn door?"

Abe's patience frays. "What the fuck, JB. Lay off—I said we could talk in the morning." He shoots me a frustrated nod. "I don't know what his problem is."

"Uh—he's drunk. That's what his problem is." And according to my boyfriend, if he finds us in post-coital bliss, he's likely to have a coronary.

JB continues to bang like a petulant child who's been locked out of the bathroom while his mother tries to take a pee in private.

"I have to open the door."

"Uh. No you don't," Abe replies. He's already half off the bed, pulling on his pants. To me he says, "You have to

285

hide."

"Oh my god, I am not hiding. This is ridiculous. If you wait patiently, he'll go away."

"No he won't—it's going to drive him crazy that I'm not unlocking my door."

"It's not like he's going to come in the window."

"The window! Great idea." He starts gathering my clothes and tossing them at me, article by article until I'm frowning, bra hitting my chest. "Put that on."

Instead, I throw it back down to the floor. "What the hell, Abe? I am *not* going out the window!"

"What about the closet?"

"Stop freaking out. Why don't you just tell him?"

The pounding stops. "Dude, do you have a girl in there with you?"

We hold our breath, and I wait patiently for Abe to confirm it. "No."

My shoulders sag—this would have been the perfect opportunity to tell JB we're dating. What's the worst thing that could happen? They fight for a bit? Surely this isn't that big a deal. JB didn't even like me.

"This has gone on long enough. You said you were going to tell him. I knew we were going to hide out in here tonight, but you should see yourself."

"It's not my fault he's an asshole."

"It kind of is."

"What's that supposed to mean?"

"You do his dirty work for him—of course he's going

to act like an asshole. He thinks he controls you."

"That's a low blow."

This time, I get out of the bed and gather my clothes, pulling on my pants, bra, and shirt. "I'm not fighting about this."

"I don't want to fight about it either."

"That's why I'm leaving." I walk to the window and unlatch it. "I refuse to argue about this."

"I'm sorry about the window, babe. Let me get my sneakers and I'll come with you." He makes quick work of dressing, but when I turn, I hold my hand up in rebuke.

"Forget it. I'm going home—alone."

"Why?"

"Because. Until you grow a pair of balls and tell JB you have a girlfriend, you don't have a girlfriend."

"Skylar, come on."

"No."

"You're overreacting."

I toss my purse out into the dark, one leg half out the window, my hand gripping the encasement to steady myself. "And I think you're *under*reacting."

"It's dark outside," he futilely argues.

I couldn't care less if it's dark out. I. Am. Leaving.

"Yes. I can see that."

"You shouldn't walk home alone—it's not safe."

"Good thing I drove."

I drop to the ground, hen-pecking in the semi-darkness

for my purse, the glow spilling from Abe's bedroom window my only guiding light.

"Skylar, don't leave."

His attempt to reel me back in is a fickle, weak one that makes my lips purse. I whip around to face his window, seeking out his silhouetted figure in the dark.

"If you think I'm hiding in your closet from that asshole, you're out of your damn mind, and the fact that you would ask me to says more about you than it does about me." I pull my purse strap over my shoulder. "Don't call me until you care more about me than about what your roommate thinks."

It kills me to walk away from that house to my car, but I do it, one step in front of the other, legs moving faster the closer I get to my vehicle.

I'm parked in front of the house so it's not a long distance, but my heart is racing from adrenaline as I sit behind the wheel.

Abe

Don't call me until you care more about me than about what your roommate thinks.

Shit, Skylar sounded pissed.

I glance out the window at her retreating figure then back at my door, JB's fist connecting with the wood once more. Jesus, what's his damn problem?

I stalk across the room and give the door a good yank.

"There better be a goddamn emergency."

Actually I hope there isn't, because I'd probably have to be the one to deal with it.

"What took you so long to open this fuckin' thing?" He shoves his way through, glancing around the room. "I thought I heard two voices—you hiding someone in here?"

"No."

"I swear I heard a chick."

"Nope." I cross my arms over my chest and glare. "What the hell do you want? It's almost one in the morning."

JB flops down on the edge of my bed then reclines the rest of the way until his head hits my mattress. "I was bored."

He smells like stale beer, marijuana, and a few bad decisions.

"You were pounding on my door because you were bored? Seriously dude, what the fuck." Not cool. He caused a fight between me and Skylar, and she probably won't see me until I've told JB to piss off.

I really wish I could.

It would save me a lot of trouble in the long run, even if it causes fucking drama today.

"Where were you tonight? I thought maybe you'd come out."

"Nope."

He rolls to his stomach, feet hanging off my bed. Stinking up my clean comforter and fresh sheets. Well…they were fresh before I screwed my girlfriend in them.

"You're turning into a fucking pill."

"Get off my bed."

"I can't move my legs."

I nudge him with my knee. "I used that excuse when I was five."

"Can you get me some food?" He raises his head, propping his chin up with two hands. "Why are there two indents on the pillows?"

He's drunk and high and talking stupid, and he's going to notice that shit?

"You're drunk."

"You said you didn't have a girl here."

"I didn't."

He's back on his back, raising himself into a sitting position. "I've fucked enough chicks to know a head dent when I see one, bro. Why are you lying?"

I have no rational reply for that. "You're drunk."

"Not that drunk."

"Whatever." I bend at the waist, retrieving my shirt from the ground and pulling it on over my bare chest. A gray thong drops from its folds and lands back on the floor.

JB homes in on it.

"Is that underwear?"

I feign ignorance. "Is what underwear?"

"That thong on the floor."

I scoop it up and shove it in my pocket.

"You fucking liar." He stands. "Let me see."

I wave him off. "I'm not showing you the underwear."

"I don't even believe this—you were banging some chick in here and won't tell me. Was she a barker? Is that why you're hiding her?" He walks to the closet, pulling the doors open. "Where is she hiding?"

Out the window, in her car, and back to her apartment—*that's* where she's hiding.

I don't know who to blame for this fuck-up, myself or JB.

I watch as he checks out the closet, feeling around for a body. Dips to peer under the bed.

"Why would I be hiding a girl in my room? We're not in high school anymore and this isn't my mom's house."

"I don't know why you'd be hiding a girl, but you are. Where the fuck is she?"

My lips tighten as my brain mentally weighs the pros and cons of being honest. "Gone."

"Gone? How?"

Simultaneously, our eyes stray to the window.

"Shut the hell up, she did not go out the window."

I shrug.

"Dude, what is she, MacGyver? What'd you fucking do to her?"

"I didn't do anything. She didn't want you to see her here."

JB pauses, wheels spinning. "Why? Have I already put my giant purple eggplant inside her?"

Jesus he's drunk. "No."

"Then why did she leave? Who the fuck cares if I see

the two of you in bed—this is college, not a fucking convent."

"I tried to convince her to stay," I lie. "But she bolted."

Shit. Now I'm throwing Skylar under the bus, and if she heard me she'd be totally disgusted.

"So she's a psycho."

"Would you please leave so I can go back to sleep? It's one o'clock in the morning." I stand next to my bedroom door, holding it open with my hand on the doorknob.

Jack doesn't budge. "Not until you tell me who it is."

"Why do you even care?"

"I'm curious—humor me."

I'm silent.

"So it's someone I know."

Silence.

"Is it Tasha?"

"What? What the hell—no, it's not your ex-girlfriend."

He's quiet, thinking. "Is it someone I've dated?"

More silence.

"Shit. You just boned a chick I've dated? The fuck—who was it? That Miranda girl?"

He's never dated a girl named Miranda. He's never dated a Mindy, Michelle, or Mary, and it would be great if he could fucking remember their names without me having to remind him half the goddamn time.

"There is no Miranda."

"Dude, you're pissing me off. Just say it."

I stalk out of my bedroom and head to the bathroom, directly across the hall. "Oh—I'm pissing *you* off? Ask me if I give a shit."

He follows, unable to let the subject die. "What the hell is wrong with you?"

I run the water in the sink, stab toothpaste onto my toothbrush, and start scrubbing. Watch him behind me in the mirror, leaning against the doorjamb.

Suddenly, I want to smack his arrogant face.

I scrub my teeth harder.

"What's her damn name?"

"Go to hell," I mumble around my toothbrush, foam dripping from my mouth, frothy like a rabid dog.

"You want me to find out myself?" he booms, stepping into the room.

I roll my eyes. "Please. You can't do jack shit without me."

"What's that supposed to fucking mean?"

I face him in the mirror, raising a brow at his reflection. "If I didn't hold your fucking hand, you wouldn't even be able to jerk off at night."

"Fuck you, Abe."

I spit in the sink, rinsing my toothbrush with water.

"No—fuck *you*, Jack. Find a new errand boy. I'm done."

"You're so full of yourself, Davis, do you know that? You think you're so much smarter than everybody else. Well I've got news for you—you're not."

"Boohoo, big deal." I laugh, practically in his face. "Like I give a shit what you think of me."

"What is your damn problem?"

"You're my problem." My voice rises a few octaves and I finally turn to face him. "You're my fucking problem. You are."

"Oh, I'm the fucking problem? How about this? You're the fucking problem." He stabs a finger in my chest.

We sling the words *fucking* and *problem* and *fucking problem* around a few more times—sounding like absolute idiots—so many times I'm actually starting to get confused by the lack of control I have over the situation, and the argument.

"I'm fucking Skylar, okay? Are you happy now? We're dating and there's not a damn thing you can do about it."

There.

Let the drunk, high asshole choke on that bit of information.

I wait for it to sink in, really let it marinate to achieve the full effect before dropping another bomb.

"We've been dating since the two of you went out."

Damn the truth feels good.

Not as good as her mouth felt around my cock, but it's a close second.

"*What?*"

"Skylar is my girlfriend. She's the one who went out the window."

"Dude." Pause. "*What?*"

"Are you deaf? Do you want me to spell it out for you?"

It's a dig and he knows it.

"Screw you, Davis."

"Hard pass—your dick is too small. I'd rather be screwing Skylar."

"Right. Your 'girlfriend'." He uses air quotes. "What are you, in kindergarten? You haven't even been going out a month. How is she your girlfriend?"

"It's none of your business."

"What if I make it my business?"

"Oh, okay, Jack. What are you going to do about it, tell your mommy? Have your dad fix it?"

Spoiled, pampered Jack Bartlett, unable to fight his own battles.

"Screw you."

"I take out the garbage. I clean your shit up. I've changed your tires, written papers, made excuses for you with the coaching staff." Once I start listing off his offenses, I cannot seem to quit. "Lied to girls. Pretended to be you. Paid your half of the rent. Bought groceries. Lent you money. Cleaned up your puke."

"That's what friends do, asshole," he shoots back.

"Oh yeah? And what have you done for me, JB? Huh? Name one thing." I lean against the counter, waiting. "Go ahead. Tell me."

"You're a dick."

"That's it? I'm a dick? Whoa, way to hit below the belt."

Fucker can't even come up with one decent thing he's ever done to help me out or make my life easier when I have a life full of chaos myself.

Selfish prick.

"I know one thing I don't do—steal girls from you."

"Give me a damn break." I roll my eyes at him for the second time tonight. "Don't act like you care—you didn't even like her."

"So? That's not the point."

"What is the point then, huh? Get to it."

"I want to beat your ass so hard right now," he mutters, more to himself than to me.

"Go right ahead, big shot." I spread my arms wide, inviting him over. "Take a swing at me."

"Don't tempt me."

"For real, Jack—what are you waiting for? If I'm such a jerk for stealing your girlfriend, go ahead and punch me." I poke at my jawline with the tip of my finger. "Right here. Go ahead. Hit me."

I'm egging him on, the idea of being walloped in the face a welcome feeling in comparison to the one churning inside my gut.

Guilt.

Guilt.

Guilt.

"You don't have the guts to do it, you puss—"

JB fucking hits me.

Draws back and, with a closed fist, decks me right in

the fucking face before I have a chance to react, or duck, or move out of the goddamn way.

I rear back, shocked.

I know I was provoking him, but Jesus Christ, I didn't think he'd actually have the balls to do it.

Stunned, it takes me a few seconds to move. Then I lunge forward, hands gripping him by the shirt collar. He's unsteady on his feet, so I shove him against the wall with all the force of a man who has finally hit his breaking point. One who's had enough bullshit to last a lifetime.

JB's drunk ass recovers, managing another swing, this time catching me in the eye—which is bound to leave a mark—and I shove him again, locking his arms down with my entire body.

"Enough."

"You're not the boss of me," he retorts.

"Yeah, I am." He does nothing around here, and he can't tell me what to do; it's just taken me this long to realize it.

"I don't want you seeing that LoveU hoe again," he slurs.

"What did you just call her?"

"I said," he repeats slowly, "I. Don't. Want. You. Seeing. That. LoveU. *Hoe.*"

That's what I thought he said. "If you don't like it, pack up your shit and get out of my house."

His bloodshot eyes roll. "You don't own this place."

"No, but my name is the only one on the leasing agreement. You technically don't exist."

"What?" Why does he look so surprised? Did he not know this?

"I'm letting you live here because I'm a nice fucking guy, and you needed a nice fucking place to live, so I let you stay in my nice fucking house." I give him a jostle so I have his full attention. "Piss me off by hitting me again, and I'll call the landlord and have you kicked out."

"You wouldn't do that. You don't have the guts." He's a bit too cocky in my opinion, so I knock him down a peg.

"Try me."

His smug smile falters as he tries to readjust himself, attempting to wriggle out of my firm grip.

"Whatever. Let me go."

"Not until you're cool with me dating Skylar. And when she comes over, I don't want you to say a damn thing to her about any of this. Got it?"

His mouth thins into a straight line, refusing to concede.

"Got it?"

"And if I don't?"

"I *just* told you what I'll do—I'll kick you out." It's going to be awkward enough as it is after this. We've never been in a fight (mostly because I always bite my tongue), let alone a physical altercation. "And you're going to be a goddamn gentleman when you see her so she doesn't feel unwelcome."

His nostrils flare.

He hates being told what to do, and now I'm the one making the rules.

The long overdue ground rules.

"You're hurting me," JB whines.

I relax my hold on him so he can sag a little. "Oh chill out. I am not hurting you, you big baby."

"Yes you are. You're bigger than I am, cocksucker."

It's about time he recognized that fact.

It's about time he looked at me with some respect.

JB steps out of my hold, back into the hallway where he should have stayed to begin with.

"Fine," he says. "I won't be a dick."

"Fine. You can stay."

"Fine."

"*Fine.*"

Me: *I told him.*

Skylar: *New phone, who dis.*

Me: *Knock it off.*

Skylar: *Sorry. I've always wanted to do that.*

Me: *You're responding to me, so I'll take that as a good sign.*

Skylar: *You started the conversation with "I told him" so now I'm curious about what that means. It sounds kind of ominous.*

Me: *I told JB about us.*

Skylar*: Okayyyy...*

Me*: Will you let me explain myself?*

Skylar: *Yes.*

Me*: Really? I thought for sure you'd tell me to go fuck myself.*

Me*: Can I come over?*

Skylar: *Yes.*

Me: *When?*

Skylar: *Tomorrow night. 5:00.*

Me: *See you then.*

16

#DOUCHEBAG

The next guy that breaks my heart is getting pepper sprayed. Look, now we're both crying!

Skylar

"**A**be is coming over. Can you make yourself scarce? We have shit to talk about and I don't need you eavesdropping." I hunt my roommate down and find her in the bathroom, plucking her eyebrows, face inches from the big mirror hanging over the sink.

She shoots me a look through the reflection but continues gingerly grasping hairs with the tweezers and yanking.

"Eavesdrop? Who, *me*?"

"Yeah you."

"I guess I could lock myself in my bedroom and resist the urge to bang on the wall."

"Thanks. I'd appreciate it."

"What if you start having sex?"

I shouldn't deny the possibility of that happening but do it anyway. "I'm not going to have sex with you in the apartment."

This time Hannah does turn to look at me, tweezers poised in her hands. "Why?"

"Because you'll hear it and you'll never let me live it down."

"True, but you've heard me having sex a million times."

Not quite a million, but about five too many.

"I'd really prefer you did not hear me screwing Abe."

She sets the tweezers on the counter with a clang. "I cannot believe you just called it that. You strike me as the 'lovemaking' type."

"That sounds awful. I'm not in love."

"You're not?"

"No. It's been two weeks. One. I don't know—I'm not keeping track."

"You wouldn't be letting him come over to beg for mercy so soon if you didn't care about him. I know you well enough to know that."

That's true; I was tempted to make him sweat it out longer.

Hannah walks to the toilet, backs her ass up over it, pushes down her leggings, and sits.

Begins to pee while I'm standing there.

It doesn't faze me; I do it to her, too.

"When is he going to be here?"

I look at my wrist. "Soon."

"All right. I'll grab food and prepare to camp out." She finishes, poking at the toilet paper, letting it fall from the dispenser, then wipes. "But don't not have make-up sex on my account—and if it gets uncomfortable for me, I'll just pack up my shit and go to Jessica's."

"Thanks."

She washes her hands. "Do we have potato chips?"

I'm not the one who buys the junk food. "I don't think so?"

"Ugh, dammit. Those are the perfect food for camping out."

I scrunch up my face, confused. "Why?"

"They make noise when you crunch them. Drowns out the noise."

"There won't be any noise."

"Wanna bet?"

"No."

While Hannah adjourns to the kitchen to gather rations, I use the bathroom, too, peeing before fixing my hair. Even out my complexion with foundation, add blush, clean up my mascara. Add gloss.

Give myself a little grimace. "This will have to do."

Another voice cuts in. "You are not talking to yourself."

"You're supposed to pretend you're not here."

"Your boy isn't here yet so I still have time to butt into your conversations…with yourself."

Fair enough.

I meander into the kitchen so she can check me out. She's in the process of unscrewing the lid of a giant jar of peanut butter.

"How is this outfit?"

Hannah gives me a once-over. "Good. It says, 'effortlessly sexy without trying too hard.'"

"Good, because I didn't try too hard." I'm just wearing jeans and a gray t-shirt. Bare feet. The rest is pretty cute, though.

She dips a piece of celery in the peanut butter and bites down on it. It's loud and crunchy and obnoxious.

"Are you only planning to eat loud food?"

"Yes. Noise barrier." There is a knock on our front door, and Hannah scoops up an armload of snacks. "That's my cue to make like a tampon and get out of this hole."

Why is she like this? Seriously. Why? "Hannah, could you not?"

She sticks her tongue out, nudging her bedroom door open with her hip. Dumps the contents of her arms on her desk then winks at me, closing the door.

I hear it lock, as though I'm the one who needs corralling.

Nervously, I pat down my hair. Wipe my sweaty palms down the denim covering my thighs, take a deep breath, and open the door.

Hands shoved in his pockets, Abe stands bashfully. Almost shyly, he eyes the ground when I greet him, and it's obvious he's embarrassed.

"Come in." I give way so he can enter. He follows me to my room, walking to my bed and sitting on the edge of it. Stands.

Sits.

Stands.

I'd laugh if he didn't look like he was going to throw up.

"Skylar, I'm so fucking sorry."

I know he is, but, "For which part?"

He finally raises his head, lifting his chin to look me in the eyes. There is a dark crescent beneath his right one, purple and blue and yellow at the edges.

"Abe, what happened to you?"

"I had a date with JB's right hook."

"What does that mean?"

"It means he punched me in the face."

"What? Stop it—he did not!"

"Twice." Abe's giant hand rises, finger tapping a line along his jawline. That, too, is bruised.

I go to him, lifting my hand, the tips of my fingers hovering just over his skin. "Does it hurt?"

"Like a sonofabitch, but not as bad as I thought it would."

"Why would he hit you?" JB might be pompous and arrogant, but he doesn't strike me as the fighting type. Then again, I've been wrong about people before.

"He was pissed when I told him about us then he made a wisecrack, and we started arguing, and...he slugged me."

That is madness. "Are you being serious right now? Has he lost his damn *mind*? We went on one lousy date." And it sucked.

Abe's smile is wry, and when his mouth curves, he cringes. "It was two lousy dates, but who's counting?"

He is.

Adorable.

"That first date didn't count—it lasted less than ten minutes and he acted super weird."

"Okay. If you don't want to count that first date, we won't count it."

I don't want to count it; it was shorter than my ninth grade homecoming date.

"So tell me more about this fight you had. I've never actually seen a guy with a black eye." I desperately want to touch it but don't want to hurt him.

Dropping my hand, I also lower myself to the bed and sit, watching him do a short pace back and forth beside me.

"Does he feel bad?"

"I don't think so. He was drunk when he did it, and he's still sleeping so he hasn't actually seen it yet."

"How can he still be sleeping? It's like five p.m."

"I know, but he's really fucking hung over. Sorry. I mean *super* hung over."

It's sweet that he filters himself with me, though he doesn't have to. I don't need him to change; I just need him to show me some respect.

Which is why we're here.

"I also think he might have been a little high, but don't tell anyone I said that."

I won't. I would never.

"I thought athletes were given random drug tests."

"We are. Apparently he just doesn't give a flying fuck."

"What happens if they test him and he fails?"

"It's not likely, but if he did fail, he'd get suspended from the team and his parents would have one hell of a time trying to get him out of that mess."

I bite down on my lower lip, chewing in concentration. "He was seriously high? Dang."

Abe nods, still standing in the middle of my bedroom, taking up most of the space and looking foreign and big—but like he belongs here. With me.

"I think so. I guess he could have just *smelled* like pot, but I doubt it. I think he was smoking it. He wouldn't have hit me if he'd just been drunk. Or sober."

I rest back on my elbows. "Have you ever smoked pot?"

"Me? No. Never been tempted. Since we get tested for wrestling, I don't know what the fuck JB is doing. Pardon my French, didn't mean to cuss."

I wave him off. "I've never tried it either. I have a heart murmur, and it would freak me out not knowing how my body would react." I pause. "It's on my dad's bucket list though." Laugh. "He wants to smoke it."

"That's...an interesting thing to have on your bucket list."

I shrug. We're not here to talk about my father; we're here to talk about Abe asking me to climb out a window to avoid confrontation.

I cross my legs and dangle a foot. "So."

Abe stops pacing, faces me, rooted to the carpet. I almost expect him to drop to his knees to beg for forgiveness. Instead he raises his arms and hooks his hands behind his head.

"I don't know what I was thinking asking you to..." He waves a hand around. "You know."

I want him to say it, so I raise an eyebrow.

Just one.

He gets the hint. "I'm sorry I asked you to hide when JB came home. It was wrong and insensitive and really fucking stupid." He sucks in a breath. "I'm an idiot."

"Okay, let's not go down a shame spiral—we're both human and we both make mistakes." I think for a second, gathering my thoughts. "You just need to know that it wasn't okay. It made me feel used. I know you're not ashamed of me, Abe, and I know you weren't ready to tell him, but I don't want to be hidden away, either. That's not what I signed up for."

He blows out a puff of air. Rakes his fingers through his beautiful, thick hair. "I know. The thing is, when I was lying to these girls—to *you*—I didn't consider it lying. The LoveU account is Jack's, and Jack was going on the dates and had the final say in who he went out with. So I didn't really think I was doing anything wrong."

That kind of makes sense in a really messed-up way.

"It's really freaking hard to be honest with him. Everyone babies the kid—our coaches, his parents, me. He doesn't do shit around our place, puts in just enough work not to get his ass kicked during every match. I have no idea how he's even still on the team." Abe squats in the center of my room then lowers himself to the carpet, sitting with his legs out in front of him in the middle of my floor. "How did you know something wasn't right?"

"You mean how did I know you were lying? I didn't. The whole situation just seemed weird. JB was so attentive and fun on the app—well, you were. Then in real life, he

309

was just so blah, as boring and uninterested as a human could possibly be. It made zero sense." I poke his calf with the toe of my foot. "I wonder how many girls thought he was a weirdo but didn't say anything."

"He wouldn't have told me. His ego is…" Abe's head shakes. "Massive."

"He seems spoiled." My gaze softens. "Abe?"

"Yeah?"

"If you ever lie to me again, we're done." I fold my hands in my lap and give my thumbs a little twiddle. "Seriously done. No third chances—this one was a whopper. Then the whole window thing, and not telling Jack. And him punching you—I mean, come on." I stand and move over him, legs spread, one foot on either side. Lean in. "Am I nuts for taking you back? Is this crazy?"

His head slowly shakes. "No."

"It kind of is. No self-respecting gir—"

"Oh my god, it's not crazy! It was two times! We all make mistakes, some of us more than once. Get over it!" Hannah shouts through the wall, her exasperation palpable.

I lean in closer, our lips inches apart. "How you turned her to the dark side is beyond me."

"Am I the dark side?"

"Duh!" Hannah shouts again.

I'm seriously going to kill her. She's certifiable. Supposed to be minding her own freaking business—how can she even hear me? I'm barely speaking above a whisper.

I look Abe square in the eye, place my hands on his

face, palms cradling his firm jawline. "You know if we screw around she's going to hear everything."

Kiss him on the lips.

I'll never get tired of feeling these lips.

Abe's baseball-mitt-sized hands slide up my thighs, thumbs digging. Fingers migrating toward the fly of my jeans, deftly unbuttoning. Unzipping. Hook inside the waistband and tug them down around my hips. Down past my knees and shins. Helps me step out of them.

I'm standing over him, bracketing his body, crotch near his face.

Baby blue lace panties now the center of his attention.

My knees get weak watching him watch me, his hands back in position, unhurriedly creeping around the back to my ass. Abe squeezes my butt cheeks, sitting a little straighter from his position on the ground.

Arches forward until his nose is pressed into my stomach. Runs the tip slowly down to my center.

Legs unsteady, I have nothing to grab but the back of his head. I twirl a lock of his hair around my index finger, nails digging into his scalp. Of their own accord, my legs spread the barest fraction of an inch. Then a bit more when Abe's mouth heats the lace of my underwear, followed by his tongue. Teeth.

My eyes slide closed, head tips back. Sigh escapes my throat when those large hands wander again, left thumb hooking a bit of baby blue so his tongue can sink into me.

The other thumb joins the party, parting me.

I've never had anyone go down on me while I was

standing up; Abe is full of firsts for me. First orgasm.

First boyfriend.

First love.

I can't even handle the sensation of what's happening to me right now, cannot focus on what it feels like *because there is a guy giving me oral while I'm standing over him.*

I'm standing up. Receiving oral.

How do I...

What do I....

"Oh god, Abe, I think I might tip over." I haven't yet. But I might.

But I can't because then he'll stop and it won't feel good.

"You're not going to tip over, baby. I've got you." His hands are back on my ass, fingers precariously close to my crack.

I tug at his hair when he sucks harder, teeth giving my clit another nip, urging him on. Gyrate my hips like a porn star as he...as he...shakes his head a bit, going deeper.

"Mmm," I moan, head tipping toward the ceiling. Lashes fluttering so fast I can hardly focus.

Thumbs. Fingers. Tongue. Teeth.

Wet, wet.

"Fuck Skylar, I could dine on your pussy every night for dinner it tastes so fucking good."

My pussy tastes good, my pussy tastes good...yes it fucking does.

Shit. Now I'm swearing to myself.

It takes Abe a few more minutes to finish me off and have me trembling—and when he does, he pulls me on top of him.

Rolls me to my back and straddles me, bending for a kiss.

I can taste myself, the sex on his mouth and tongue, and I don't hate it. It's musky and hot.

Okay, fine. So it's a bit gross—but I'm not about to go telling him that; he's getting off on it. I can feel his erection through his pants, rock hard against my leg.

Together we push the elastic waistband down.

He's not wearing any underwear, and I'm soaking wet.

Easy in…

Easy out…

I gasp when he slides inside, still swollen and sensitive from my orgasm.

"You're so wet," he groans into my neck, arms braced above my head, caging me in. Cradling me. Rocking back and forth, back and forth…deeper and deeper…every muscle tight. Every nerve alive.

Our pelvises touching he's so deep inside…

"Holy fuck, oh fuck, I think I'm gonna come."

Huh?

Glassy-eyed, I'm on the verge of coming a second time and want desperately to know what that feels like.

He cannot be serious.

It hasn't even been two minutes.

"I'm sorry," he grunts, still pumping, skin damp.

A few more thrusts and the hot heat of him is inside me; I can feel it filling me and I marvel at the sensation.

A few more seconds and his hips jerk. Body twitches.

He pulls out, rolls over.

Pulls his arm out from under me and lays it over his eyes, dick blowing in the breeze, having spent itself prematurely.

"I can't even look at you right now," he mumbles.

"Why?" I laugh, planting a kiss on the side of his neck. I take a whiff of him; he smells so, so good and tastes salty.

"Because he came in one minute and forty-seven seconds!" Hannah shouts from her bedroom. "I timed it. Sorry folks—I am what I am!"

"Jesus Christ, why is she like that?" Abe moans, mouth grimacing.

"I don't know, babe. She just is." As I trail a finger down his sternum, he shivers. "But. The good news is, she'd shank someone for me. And now that she's on Team Abe, she'll shank them for you, too."

"She's right! I will cut a bitch!"

"I think you need an apartment with thicker walls." He blindly feels around for his pants. Locating them near my bed, he tugs them into place. "You're moving in with me. JB is out, Skylar is in."

He's joking—of course he is—but it still sends butterflies soaring within my stomach.

"That sounds nice."

"Get a room!" Hannah gives the wall a tap with what sounds like a spoon.

"We have a room!" Abe and I both yell back, laughing when we lock eyes.

Hannah huffs. I can literally hear it through the paper-thin walls. "Well go in the living room then!"

So we do.

Hannah

Three months later...

Skylar and Abe make me ill.

Oh, relax. Not in a sick, vomit enducing, *I'm going to puke kind of way*. Just…the kind of ill that makes me want the same thing for myself. A jealous, *I want that,* kind of feeling in the pit of my stomach when they're around the apartment.

I want what they have.

It's too damn bad I act like such an asshole half of the time.

Guys hate that.

They want sweet. Bidable. Sexy.

I am none of those things.

Fiddling with my phone, I tap open the LoveU app. Smile when I see a new match; grin when I open his profile and read:

Rex Gunderson. 24.

Yo yo yo ladies, I'm an alum, back in town for the next few semesters pitching in at the athletic building and wouldn't mind your company. A few things about me: funcle to a baby girl (she's not actually my neice but who cares). Hilarious. Big boy job. Has my own place. Loves fancy shit but prefer to do them in my sweats or j's. You: are legal and over the age of 18.

That's it? That's the entire thing? All he's looking for is someone over the age of eighteen? Have some standards, dude, even if you're just looking for a hook-up.

Still.

He is kind of attractive, in a skinny guy kind of way.

I bite down on my bottom lip and swipe, knowing I'll probably regret it later. Shoot him a message because there is nothing worse than waiting for a guy to make the first move.

Me: *What kind of fancy shit are you talking about here…? Inquiring minds want to know.*

RexG: *You know, the usual. Dinner, bars. Play a round of golf or two.*

Me: *In your sweat pants?*

RexG: *No, I wear real pants for that.*

Me: *Khakis?*

RexG: *No one wears Khakis anymore.*

Me: *Sure they do, I saw some yesterday.*

RexG: *Who was wearing them?*

Me: *My Lit professor.*

RexG: *I rest my case.*

Me: *So, I'm just going to come out and ask or it's going to drive me insane.*

RexG: *Go for it.*

Me: *What are you doing on this app, it says you're 24.*

RexG: *So? I just turned 24. That's not ancient.*

Me: *Aren't you a little old to be fishing in the school kiddie pond?*

RexG: *I barely just graduated. Why you gotta be like that?*

Me: *I had to get it off my chest.*

RexG: *I was checking out your chest earlier. Very impressive.*

Me: *Uh, gross. Stop, don't even go there.*

RexG: *Uh, why?*

Me: *You can't just say things like that. It's douchey.*

RexG: *Funny you should mention that; I never said I was a gentleman.*

Me: *You look like one. Kind of?*

Me: *Actually you look like a huge dork.*

RexG: *How about you just kick me in the nuts and get it over with?*

RexG: *And FOR THE RECORD I'm not photogenic and am WAY BETTER LOOKING IN PERSON.*

Me: *Says who?*

RexG: *MY FUCKING MOTHER, Jesus lady.*

Me: *Shit, I'm sorry. I have no filter—I wasn't trying to* *be a bitch.*

RexG: *Whatever, it's fine.*

Me: *I suppose you're going to unmatch me now?*

RexG: *Why would I do that?*

Me: *Because I'm being an asshole—WHY WOULDN'T YOU UNMATCH WITH ME?*

RexG: *Why are you yelling?*

Me: *Have some standards. All you have in your profile is that you're looking for someone over the age of 18. WTH?*

RexG: *Age ain't nothin' but a numba.*

Me: *So…what are you actually doing here if you're not a student? Are you a TA?*

RexG: *No, I'm helping out with the athletics. Mostly with the wrestling team, I used to be their manager.*

Me: *My roommate's boyfriend is a wrestler. Maybe you know him?*

RexG: *What's his name?*

Me: *Abe Davis.*

RexG: *He was a freshman I think the year I left the team; don't know him that well. He decent?*

Me: *He's awesome.*

RexG: *Cool.*

Me: *So you're on campus for how long?*

RexG*: Rest of this semester, summer, first term of fall.*

Me: *And you're looking to hook-up with someone?*

RexG*: Sure. If that's what you want.*

Me: *It's not.*

RexG: *Okay.*

Me: *That's it? Okay? You're not going to try and change my mind?*

RexG*: Do you want me to?*

Me: *Uh, NO.*

RexG*: LOL then I won't.*

Me: *It's really shitty that you're just here looking to get laid. Some of us are looking for the real deal.*

RexG*: I never said all I wanted was an easy lay. You did.*

Me: *Well, COME ON. Let's get real here. You won't even be here the entire year.*

RexG*: Says you're a junior. 22. You won't be there long either.*

Me: *But I'm here NOW.*

RexG*: So am I.*

Me: *Is this an athlete thing? Are you all just douchebags who sleep around?*

RexG: *I don't know, is that how Abe Davis acts?*

Me: No.

RexG: *Wanna throw some sweats on tomorrow and meet me for coffee?*

Me: *How early?*

RexG: *Whatever works for you.*

Me: *How tired do you want me to look?*

RexG: *How will you look at 9?*

Me: Horrible.

RexG: *LOL*

Me: *Why the hell are we even talking about this, I DON'T WANT TO MEET YOU.*

RexG: *That's fine.*

Me: *Stop doing that.*

RexG: *What am I doing, I'm agreeing with you.*

Me: *I REFUSE to fall for your jedi-mind tricks.*

RexG: *Listen, I don't know what I did or what I said, but you're kind of scary.*

Me: *WHY DOES EVERY GUY KEEP SAYING THAT?*

RexG: *Because you yell a lot. Guys don't like that.*

RexG: *And you keep putting words in my mouth, and making assumptions.*

Me: *Thanks, I got it.*

RexG: *And that part in your profile about "no shave November" and always being hangry? Also scary and confusing.*

Me: *I am who I am.*

RexG: *Hairy, hungry, and scary?*

Me: Yes?

RexG: *I don't know what to tell you, Bianca.*

Me: *Um, about that...Bianca isn't my name.*

RexG: *Okayyyyy... What is it then?*

Me: Hannah

RexG: *That's pretty, why did you use a different name? Didn't want any creepers messaging you?*

Me: *I just like the name. It sounds sexy.*

RexG: *Little liar, aren't you.*

Me: *NO! Just about that one thing...The rest is all me. I'm just—I can't help it if I'm awkward, and I say stupid shit, and I make inappropriate comments at inappropriate times.*

RexG: *You know—I could help you with that.*

Me: *Help me with what?*

RexG: *Help you date. While I'm here. I can teach you some shit, like how to talk to dudes and shit.*

Me: *This isn't a trick to try and sleep with me?*

RexG: *Nope. Twenty-six chicks have swiped on me in the time we've been talking. I'll be fine.*

RexG: *Do you want my help or not?*

RexG: *Hello? You still there?*

Me: *I'm thinking...*

RexG: *Don't think too long, I might change my mind.*

Me: *Fine.*

RexG: *Great.*

Me: Okay.

RexG: *LOL here's my number. Message me when you get the courage.*

It takes me two days.

The Teaching Hours

A HOW TO DATE A DOUCHEBAG novella.

August, 2019

OTHER TITLES BY SARA NEY

The Kiss and Make Up Series
Kissing in Cars
He Kissed Me First
A Kiss Like This

#ThreeLittleLies Series
Things Liars Say
Things Liars Hide
Things Liars Fake

How to Date a Douchebag Series
The Studying Hours
The Failing Hours
The Learning Hours
The Coaching Hours
The Lying Hours

Jock Hard Series
Switch Hitter
Jock Row

For a complete updated list visit:

https://authorsaraney.com/books/

ABOUT SARA

Sara Ney is the USA Today Bestselling Author of the How to Date a Douchebag series, and is best known for her sexy, laugh-out-loud New Adult romances. Among her favorite vices, she includes: iced latte's, historical architecture and well-placed sarcasm. She lives colorfully, collects vintage books, art, loves flea markets, and fancies herself British.

For more information about Sara Ney and her books, visit:

Facebook
www.facebook.com/saraneyauthor
Twitter
www.twitter.com/saraney
Website
www.authorsaraney.com
Instagram
www.instagram.com/saraneyauthor
Books + Main
bookandmainbites.com/users/38
Subscribe to Sara's Newsletter
www.subscribepage.com/saraney
Facebook Reader Group: Ney's Little Liars
www.facebook.com/groups/1065756456778840/